WOMAN OF THE WOODS

A *Meji* Novel by
Milton Davis

MV Media

A *Meji* Novel by
Milton Davis

Copyright © 2013
MVmedia, LLC
Published 2013
All Rights Reserved

ISBN 13: 978-0-9800842-6-9
ISBN 10: 0-9800842-6-1

Cover Art by Chase Conley
Interior Art and Maps by Christopher Miller
Cover Design by Uraeus
Layout/Design by Uraeus

Manufactured in the United States of America

First Edition

Map of
ADAMUSOLA

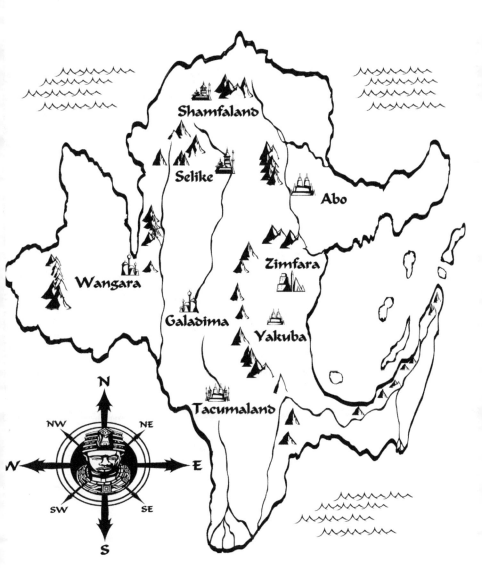

Map of
UHURU

Sadatina ba Hazeeta watched the Obana procession amble down the highway to the mountains, relief warm in her chest. The negotiations had exceeded her expectations. Peace was now the rule between Adamusola and Obana, a peace that would last as long as Obadoro, the Meji monarch, sat on Obana's royal stool. She had not expected him to accompany his diplomats, but he'd come to personally handle the negotiations. The two of them sat alone in her throne room sharing secrets that no one would know until both were long dead.

"How much longer must we stand here?"

The mansa looked to her left at the irritated face of her balogun and daughter, Kiden. The young woman shivered, and then pulled her cloak tight about her athletic form.

"Until I say otherwise," Sadatina replied with a smirk. "You have always been meek against the cold."

Kiden grunted, a response only the daughter of the mansa could express.

"You should be more respectful. This is a historic moment."

Godana Adus, gesere and historian of Adamusola, strummed his kora after his words.

"Peace now reigns over Uhuru now that her greatest mansas have shared good words. It is a great day indeed."

"A day that would be better celebrated before a warm fire," Kiden groused.

A brisk wind rustled Sadatina's robes.

"Kiden is right. It's time we go inside."

She turned to the tower doors and her servants opened them wide. She sauntered into the upper throne room, the elders, diplomats and other dignitaries covering their faces as she walked past. Her grandchildren waited at the end of the line, their exuberance lifting the weight of fatigue on her shoulders.

"Nana! Nana!

Sadatina knelt before them and they crowded about her, each trying to hug her.

"Don't smother your Nana!" Kiden said. Her daughter lifted Tewelde, the youngest, into her arms and he hugged her fiercely. Heewan and Hiwat, twin sisters, grabbed Sadatina's hands while Ghe'le, the oldest, stepped away with a frown on his face.

"Who can I hug?" he complained.

"You can hug me!" Abadi, Kiden's husband, lifted Ghe'le into his thick arms.

Sadatina looked at them with humble pride. Together they went to her private chambers. Sadatina slumped into her favorite chair; no sooner had she done so did her servants swarm around her.

"Leave us," Kiden ordered.

The servants hurried from the room. Kiden went to Sadatina and began unwrapping her turban.

"I'll do your hair tonight," she said.

Sadatina closed her eyes and smiled.

"Thank you, daughter."

Her grandchildren gathered about her feet, their bright eyes focused on her. "Tell us a story!"

"Leave your nana be!" Kiden scolded. "Can't you see she's tired? Ask Godana."

"No, no," Sadatina said. "I'll tell them a story, one it is time they heard."

Kiden stopped. "Are you sure?"

Sadatina nodded. "Yes, I'm sure."

She straightened in her chair and closed her eyes.

"Cha blesses us all in different ways, writing our paths in the stars. For some his blessings come early, but for others his blessings take time to appear. Such it was for a certain girl long ago."

"What was her name?" Hiwat asked.

Sadatina grinned. "Some called her the Woman of the

Woods."

"That's not a name!" Tewelde exclaimed. Sadatina chuckled. "It will be her name tonight. But before I tell you her story, I must tell you the story of another because it is his story that sparks hers."

"What was his name?" Ghe'le asked.

"His name was Ihecha."

Book I

The Warrior Priest

-1-

Ihecha Sama stood on the balcony of his temple wrapped in a heavy woolen cloak. The cold winds from the distant mountains blew his braids about like straw, the beads rattling as they struck each other in irregular rhythm. He'd ended his evening prayers moments ago and climbed the winding staircase to the iron-railed perch, attempting to decipher the message drifting in his head like a summer fog. For weeks he'd prayed almost incessantly, stopping only to relieve himself and take a scant meal. Cha was trying to speak to him, but somehow he was not receiving the divine word. In his twenty years as High Priest of Djenna, this had never occurred.

He continued to stare at the mountains. The distant peaks seemed the only clarity in his prayers, the only lucidity rising over the muddled meaning.

"Help me understand, Cha," he said out loud. "Show me your word."

He descended the stairs back to the main level of the temple. Young acolytes and students moved about the main hall, halting before him to bow slightly as they covered their faces with their hands in respect. The students wore white tunics that fell just below their knees. Braided leather cords wrapped about their waists and red cotton caps rested on their heads. The acolytes wore tunics as well with colored sashes signifying their rank. Ihecha's garb resembled the students, the only exception robe and cap woven of golden thread.

"We are blind in his light," they said in unison.

Ihecha did not reply, which was uncharacteristic of him. He was still distracted by the mystery of the message. He was wandering the atrium when a gentle tug on his sleeve broke his musing. He looked into the curious brown eyes of a young acolyte he knew well. Tisha Aboko was an inquisitive and fearless girl well known to all the temple instructors for her burning curiosity and amazing intelligence. She was also known for her total disregard for rank and respect.

"What is wrong with you?" she asked.

Ihecha fought not to smile as he gave her a scolding stare. She challenged his gaze for a moment before she realized the reason for the silent admonishment.

"Oh!" She bowed and covered her face before looking at him again. "Baba Sama, what is wrong with you?"

"Don't you have a class to attend?" he asked.

Tisha shook her head. "My classes are complete for the day."

"Then you should be on your way to prayer," Ihecha said.

Tisha looked away. "I am."

"You are a bad liar. Now go before you are late."

"Not until you tell me what is wrong with you."

Ihecha couldn't help himself. He chuckled. "Now you are my master?"

"Forgive my words, Baba, but your mood concerns everyone. You are so distant that the students are talking. They wonder what is distracting you so and why you keep your encouragement from them. It is not good for the mood of the temple. How can we learn when we are concerned about you?"

If he had a child, her name would be Tisha. He touched her cheek with his palm and she shared the glowing smile for which she was known.

"I'm grateful that Cha gives me students that care so much

for me," he said. "I am fine. There are always things that distract a baba and sometimes they are hard to keep hidden. Spread the word among the students that I am watching them, even if my words or attitude seem otherwise."

"I will tell them," she said.

Ihecha began to walk away but Tisha grabbed his sleeve again.

"What is it now, Tisha?"

"Maybe you should share your thought with the acolytes," she suggested. "An issue shared is an issue solved."

Tisha's words made Ihecha smile. "Now you share my own words with me."

"I am a good student," Tisha said.

"Yes you are. Now go to prayers."

Tisha bowed, covered her face then scurried away.

Ihecha watched her go, making sure she entered the prayer room. He headed for his sanctuary to pray as well. He'd thought the balcony view would inspire him, but it was the opposite. He was a boy when Cha touched the priests before him, telling them of a land waiting for them beyond the mountains. They heeded Cha's words, packing everything they owned and selling all they could not carry to follow Cha's word. Many died along the way; the mountain crossing was a terrible experience that still scarred the memories of them all. Ihecha lost both his parents during the treacherous ordeal. He was taken in by the priests with whom he remained the rest of his life. But when they finally emerged into the lush valley Cha granted them, they realized that those who perished were a necessary sacrifice for their reward.

But Cha still tested them. A people inhabited the valley; they called themselves the Mosele. They were cattle-raising folk, following their herds across the vast grasslands at the whim of the rainy seasons. At first they welcomed Cha's folk, giving way to their farming lifestyle, but as the Adamu thrived the Mosele suffered. Adamu farms prospered at the expense of open grazing land, inciting confrontations during the dry seasons. Then the wars began. The Mosele proved formidable foes, driving Cha's folk to the edge of the mountains and threatening to push them back to their old homeland. But the Adamu would not be denied. They built Djenna, and learned to be warriors themselves. With new vigor and Cha's blessing they drove the Mosele across the plains and into the desert. It was a brutal war of attrition. Though his people had been victorious, the ferocity of the Mosele resistance scarred them. They remained near the mountains, building their cities and farms close the land from which they escaped.

Ihecha entered his sanctuary. He trudged to his prayer carpet and sat cross-legged before the simple pedestal crowned a bundle of sorghum stalks and a worn scythe, the symbols of Cha. He covered his face with his calloused hands and prayed, hoping for clarity to a vision that had plagued him for months.

The revelation struck him like a hard fist. He fell backward, his head striking the stone floor hard. He opened his eyes to Cha's vision. He soared over Adamuland like a raptor, the landscape streaking under him in a blur. He crossed the grasslands in seconds, leaving the cool abundance for the hot desolation of the desert. Bleached bones littered the sands, the detritus of the hapless people they had driven into the dead land. The sand turned darker and coarser until he glided over a gray rocky landscape which ended abruptly against the highest mountains he'd ever seen, their pinnacles hidden by gray clouds. The Mosele huddled at the barren foothills, shivering, half naked in despair. Then the mountains trembled and Ihecha saw movement in the clouds. A being appeared, a figure gray like the mountains it descended and whose eyes glowed like the sun. It approached the people and they gathered around it.

"I am Karan," it roared. "Why have you come here?"

"Grant us the power to revenge and we will worship you!" they cried.

The being looked directly at Ihecha.

"So be it," it growled.

Ihecha jerked up into a sitting position. His head

throbbed, but any physical discomfort paled to the stinging truth Cha revealed to him. He came to his feet and stumbled out of his sanctuary to a solitary rope hanging from the temple bell. Ihecha yanked the rope, the sharp tolling reverberating throughout the building. Acolytes came from every direction, trailed by curious students. They gathered close to him; Ihecha continued to ring the bell until they were all present.

He regarded them with serious eyes.   "Follow me," he commanded.

The acolytes followed him into the sanctuary. Ihecha took a stance before them and they immediately sat cross-legged, forming rings around him that extended to the sanctuary entrance. The students crowded outside the portal, none of them allowed entry. At the front of the crowd was Tisha, her eyes and ears attentive. Ihecha smiled when he saw her. What he was about to say was for all of them.

He waved to them. "Come in, children. Join us."

Shocked expressions took hold of the acolytes' faces. The children looked just as dumbfounded, all except Tisha. She strode in boldly, heading directly toward Ihecha. The priest held up his hand, stopping her determined march.

"Students will stand against the wall," he added.

Tisha went immediately to the wall, taking the position closest to him. The other students trickled in, their steps hesitant and unsure. They lined the granite walls, each staring at Ihecha with questioning eyes.

"For months I have struggled with a vision Cha bestowed upon my heart," Ihecha began. "It vexed me, for unlike Cha's other visions this one remained unclear. It was as if his word was being interfered with. Worse still, I began to question my worthiness. Was I losing my faith? Was Cha losing his trust in me? How else could I explain failing to receive a vision from whom I live for?"

There was worry in the eyes of the acolytes as he looked among them. He imagined how he would feel if the priest he looked up to questioned his own faith. If he was not worthy, then who was?

"But moments ago Cha's message filled my mind with purpose," he continued. "Today I lifted myself to Cha's demand and understood the message he sent to me. It is a message of peril, one that threatens us. It is a message that enlightens us to the error of our ways and warns us of the consequences. It is one that we must share outside the temple, a message that we must share with our people and with our mansa."

Silence pervaded the sanctuary. Every acolyte leaned forward, waiting for his next proclamation. The students stood rigid, their faces tight with fear and worry. Ihecha looked at Tisha. She was so young, a girl of whom he would be proud if she was his daughter. What he had to share could mean devastation for her and those of her age group if they failed – if he failed.

"The Mosele are coming back," he said.

A collective gasp filled the sanctuary. Ihecha stood silent as the murmured response swept the room like a dry-season fire. When the babble died down, he continued.

"Our enemy did not perish in the desert," he said. "They suffered, but they survived."

Ihecha closed his eyes, summoning Cha's vision to clarity. "They found themselves pressed against the dark mountains at the edge of the world, desperate, naked and alone. There was no food, no shelter; nothing left for them. So they prayed, not to the god of this land for it had abandoned them. They prayed to anything that would lift them from such despair. They cried out to anything that would end their suffering. And when they reached the limit of their suffering, when they began to die at the foothills of the cold mountains, something answered."

Ihecha struggled to hide his fear of the image forming in his mind. He swallowed hard before continuing. "It came from the mountain where it had been banished long ago, before there was a Mosele, or our own. It rose, fed by the desperate cries of a people without hope. It grew, fed by their pain and suffering. It descended from its lofty crypt, a being of rock and fire, an ancient creature, a remnant of a race whose time had come and gone. The

Mosele knelt before it and promised to serve it if it would grant them hope, strength and revenge."

The sanctuary fell completely silent. Ihecha looked into their fearful eyes with sadness. He did not want to burden them with his vision, but they must know for they would be the salvation of their city.

"It calls itself Karan. As we have prospered in peace, the Mosele have prepared for war. They are coming, and we must stop them."

It did not surprise him that the first person to speak was Tisha. "Then we will fight again!" she shouted. Her fellow students and senior acolytes did not share her apparent enthusiasm.

Ihecha grinned. "No, Tisha, we will not fight. I will take my vision to the mansa. He will decide what we will do."

Ihecha stood and the audience covered its face with trembling palms.

"Misganna and Jabilo, you will accompany me to the palace," Ihecha announced. "Everyone else please return to your duties and chores. I know it will be difficult because of what I have shared, but you must show your discipline. It is important that we do what we are called to do. Everything matters."

Misganna, a lean woman with midnight skin and piercing eyes, stepped forward. Jabilo, a shorter man with a round face and nervous smile, followed. They halted before Ihecha while the others filed from the sanctuary, filling the air with nervous murmurs. Ihecha's attendants appeared at his side with his golden staff and amber medallions, his required accoutrements for meeting with the Mansa.

"This is most irregular," Misganna said. "Will the Mansa meet with us without a formal request?"

"The fact that we come without a request will indicate the graveness of our visit," Ihecha replied. "I'm sure he has seen what I have. My concern is that he has not contacted me."

Ihecha felt a tug at his robe. He looked down into the face of Tisha.

"I should go with you," she said.

Tisha's inquisitiveness had become irritating.

"This is not a teaching moment," Ihecha said. "Serious matters must be discussed, situations far beyond the comprehension of a student."

"But who will tell the other students?" she asked.

"Their teachers," Jabilo scolded. He pushed Tisha aside as he took his place beside Ihecha, who gave him a hard look. "She should be with the others studying instead of being a nuisance," Jabilo explained.

"I will go," Tisha snapped. She stomped away.

Ihecha watched Tisha until she left the sanctuary. She would make a fine acolyte, maybe even a high priest. But Jabilo was right. She needed to keep her place for now. Her time would come.

The Mansa's palace was not far from the temple. Although Ihecha held the highest rank among Cha's teachers, it was the Mansa who was closest to Cha. His lineage had been favored for as far back as the gesere, the history keepers, could sing. It was his ancestors who led the Adamu over the Old Men and into this land, who fought the Mosele and pushed them into the desert.

The Mansa's palace differed little from the temple. The wide circular structure was carved from the same granite and capped with white marble. Four stone corridors extended from the central dome like spokes from a wheel, each ending at wide based towers that narrowed as the ascended into the sky. The major difference between the temple and the Mansa's abode was the enormous entrance gate, a thick ebonywood door decorated with ornate carvings chronicling the Adamu's journey over the Old Men. Ihecha and the acolytes stopped for a moment to admire the detailed work.

A palace guard approached them, a stout man carrying an oblong shield and tall broadleaf spear. He wore a metal helmet with a flaring nose guard dividing his intense brown eyes. The man placed his shield and spear aside as he covered his face in respect.

"Welcome, Teacher," he said. "Baba Fesseha said you would come."

Ihecha eyebrows rose. So Fesseha had seen the vision.

The guard gripped the thick door handle and pulled. The muscles of his arms and legs rippled as he opened the ponderous portal. Ihecha and the others entered and were immediately met by Fesseha's gesere, Nzali.

There were some who whispered Nzali was queen of the Adamu. Many believed that a woman of such beauty could not be so close to such a powerful man without one day bearing his children. But Ihecha knew different. Fesseha and Nzali were like brother and sister, their love for each other familial rather than romantic.

The deep blue head-wrap bordering her oval face accented her beauty. She shared a smile with Ihecha. "The palace is always a brighter place when you arrive, Ihecha," she said.

The high priest grinned. "I wish the news I bring was just as bright."

Nzali's smile faded. "We are aware. We have much to discuss."

The gesere led them down the wide corridor to the Mansa's receiving room. Baba Fesseha sat on a large tasseled cushion, his thick arms folded in his lap. Fesseha smiled at the trio as they approached, his cherubic face revealing the ease of his rule. The mansas of the past were warriors, men and women with hard bodies forged in constant battle within and without Djenna's walls; first against the Sesu, then against the Shamfa, and finally against the Mosele. Fesseha was the first Mansa to know peace throughout his rule. His mother, Mansa Nokora, drove the Mosele into the desert, ending their threat once and for all; or so she'd thought.

"Ihecha my friend," he said in a warm, resonant voice. "You have finally come to discuss our dream."

Ihecha and his acolytes covered their face before Fesseha as Nzali joined the Mansa, sitting beside him on his cushion. Servants brought cushions for the visitors and they sat in unison. Ihecha took a quick look about; with the exception of servants there were no others in the room. Fesseha no longer kept bodyguards close by. Such was his confidence of the peace over which he ruled.

"I have come to discuss Cha's vision," Ihecha finally said.

"And how is it that you know this is a vision sent from the Most High? Could it not be a dream tainted by your faith?"

"There are times that I am amused by your doubt," Ihecha said sternly. "This is not one of them."

Fesseha's smile transformed into a hard line. "I don't mean to aggravate you, Ihecha. What I express is a wish. I know what you saw and how it came to you. It was difficult for me to discern what I was seeing until only recently. At that point I awaited your visit. It seems we have a war to wage."

Fesseha's conclusion caught Ihecha off guard. He'd come ready to discuss the interpretation of the vision but the Mansa had arrived at a solution.

"Are you sure this must be our response?" Ihecha asked.

"Nzali and I have discussed it at length."

Nzali nodded as she touched Fesseha's sleeve, a gesture that was more personal than he'd seen exchanged between them. Maybe the rumors about them were true, Ihecha thought.

"Karan is an old god," Fesseha said. The mention of the deity's name chilled Ihecha.

"It savors the praise of men and feeds off of their offerings. It grows stronger every day, and each day its demands increase. The Mosele will do what they must to gain its favor and its help. We must strike before both Karan and the Mosele are strong enough to challenge us."

Fesseha's words held wisdom.

"But what of the journey?" Ihecha asked. "The Mosele were driven into the desert, the same desert we must enter to find and defeat them. Such an expedition takes much planning and we still may not be certain if we have enough provisions to last us. Besides, we do not know what direction they took once in the desert."

"The songs say the Adamu never fought the Mosele with

large armies," Nzali replied. "They say we always fought them with an army of champions led by a High Priest of Cha. We defeated them with skill and faith. We will do so again."

Ihecha's eyes widened. "Are you saying that I must go?"

Fesseha frowned. "You are surprised? Of course you must go. You are Cha's beacon. You will lead us to the Mosele. Cha will show you the way."

"And what of you? You are the highest of us all, the closest to the ancestors and to Cha. Will you march with us as well?"

Fesseha closed his eyes and nodded slightly. "If Cha chooses me."

Ihecha waited before asking his next question to be sure his anger did not reflect in his voice.

"And why would Cha not choose you? Your forefathers have always led the Adamu into battle. Many times we faced defeat, but the spirit and vigor of the Mansa took us to victory." Ihecha stared at Nzali. "So the songs say."

"Do you reject Cha's judgment?" Fesseha asked.

"No." Fear ran rampant through Ihecha's mind. He was not prepared for what was happening. "If Cha calls me to lead his champions, I will."

"Good. Then we must prepare."

"Will you lead the champions?" Ihecha asked again.

Fesseha's eyes narrowed. "We will see."

Nzali rose and approached Ihecha. "We value your visit, as always."

Ihecha and the acolytes stood, and Nzali led them out of the audience chamber and to the door. The acolytes went outside, but Ihecha hesitated before exiting.

"You know this is wrong, Nzali," he said. "You carry the songs in your soul. You know what Fesseha must do."

A hint of worry marred Nzali's solemn countenance. She looked away. "What if he is killed? What if the champions are not enough?"

"If that happens, then it is Cha's will," Ihecha replied

sternly. "Do you think I am unafraid? I am ashamed to say I am not. But if Cha deems it so, I will go. Fesseha is the Adamu. If he does not go our failure is sure. He must go!"

Nzali did not answer. Iheca realized that the rumors about them were true.

"Don't let your emotions cloud your mind," Ihecha continued. "You are his council. You must demand that he do what is best for the Adamu. You must."

Nzali finally looked at him, her eyes glistening. "I will try, Ihecha."

Ihecha covered his face and left the palace. He stormed by the acolytes, burning with anger. The acolytes scurried to his side.

"Misganna, go to Dama and ask for an audience with Balogun Jetade."

Misganna gasped. "The war chief? Why?"

"Fesseha will fail us," Ihecha replied. "When our champions go into battle they will need more than spiritual leadership. They will need a warrior leading them."

"Jetade will lead them?" Jabilo asked.

"No," Ihecha replied. "I will."

-2-

Balogun Jetade Akinkoye strode through the temple to Ihecha's audience chamber so quickly the acolytes accompanying him had to run to keep pace. A tall man with dusky brown skin and bald head, Jetade was a striking example of his family's blood line. A leather jerkin gripped his broad muscular torso, his rank necklaces jangling with his heavy gait. Loose fitting pants fell to his sandaled feet. Jetade's bloodline were a folk born to be warriors; tall, muscular, agile, intelligent and fearless. They were known as the yaala jara, the Walking Shumbas, a moniker they accepted proudly.

Ihecha waited patiently on his cushion, flanked by Misganna and Jabilo. This would be an awkward discussion. Jetade would not be easy to persuade.

The Adamu war chief stood before Ihecha and quickly covered his face with his large hand. "What do you want with me, priest?" he growled.

"Thank you for coming," Ihecha said, attempting to inject some respect into the meeting. "I apologize for taking you from your duties."

Jetade's face seemed to relax. He folded his arms across his chest.

"These are dangerous times," he replied. "I'm sure you are aware of the Mosele threat."

"I am," Ihecha said with a nod. Threat was an overstatement at this point, but Jetade was a military man.

"It is why I won't waste any more of your time. I would like you to assign one of your warriors to train me and my acolytes."

Jetade leaned his head back. "Train you to do what?"

"To fight."

A slight grin came to Jetade's face, which for him was equivalent to hysterical laughter. "Do not joke with me, priest. I have serious matters to attend to."

"I do not joke," Ihecha said. "You know I will accompany you on this journey."

Jetade nodded in grudging agreement.

"Since it is not certain the Mansa will come with us, someone must assume leadership of the expedition."

Jetade raised an eyebrow. "You assume that someone will be you?" he said.

"Believe me, Balogun, it is not a position that I relish. But the person leading us against the Mosele must have the blessings of the ancestors and Cha with him or her. The person most qualified for that is Fesseha. In his absence the responsibilities fall on me."

"And I am not to be considered?" Jetade growled.

"Of course you are," Ihecha said. "But it is not for me to choose."

"And since you are Cha's Voice, he would naturally choose you."

"Don't make this something it is not," Ihecha warned. "I seek no glory or honor in this. It is a duty, nothing more. If I had my way I would bless you all and pray for your victory and safe return. But there is something that must be given that Cha will give only to me and I must have the skill to use it. So let us get back to our previous situation. Will you assign someone to train me and my acolytes?"

Jetade wasn't ready to give up so easily. "One hundred warriors will be chosen from our army, one hundred men whom I have personally trained since birth. These are men who respect strength, skill and unwavering leadership. These are men who, when confronted with the terror of battle, will wish to look to a man who can get them through. Pardon my words, but I do not think you are that man."

Ihecha sighed. "How many wars have you fought, Jetade?"

The question was meant to cut deep and judging by Jetade's expression, it did.

"I come from a line of proud warriors. I have studied their songs since I was a child. I am the best warrior in this land. No one has ever defeated me in competition. I may not have fought any wars nor won any battles, but I'm more than sure the warriors under my command would rather follow me into battle than you."

"Your words are inspiring, but the fact remains that for now our battle experience is equal," Ihecha replied.

"Be glad I did not bring my sword," Jetade snapped.

"Your warriors will follow you," Ihecha continued. "But you will follow me?"

Jetade did not reply.

"It is the way Cha will have it. We will need him with us, Jetade, and the only way that will happen is if I lead the warriors."

"I will send my weapons trainer," Jetade finally said. "You will give him your full attention and effort. If I hear anything otherwise he will not return."

"We will give you all we have," Ihecha said.

"You have no idea," Jetade said.

The balogun stomped away without formality. Ihecha waited until he left the temple before he slumped into his cushion.

"I think you have made an enemy," Jabilo said.

"No, I think not," Ihecha replied. "I hurt his pride, but he knows what I say is true. He will not make it easy. His trainer will push us hard, hoping we will give up. We will spend much time praying for Cha's strength."

Ihecha's words were prophetic. Jetade's weapons master, Fanus, was younger than Ihecha expected but no less harsh. Ihecha and the acolytes conducted morning prayers and spent the remainder of the day under his hard eye being pushed to their physical brink. By day's end they were totally drained, barely able to drag themselves to rest. As the priests trained in the temple, the warriors competed in their compound. Jetade was the first, as expected, but some of the other selections were surprising. Fesseha did not limit the competition to warriors. The announcement carried throughout the land and thousands answered. Among those selected were hunters, craftsmen, traders and entertainers. It seemed warriors lurked among the throng, waiting for the opportunity to show their skills. Those with spouses and children were not allowed to participate, which narrowed some of the untrained ranks, but in the end Jetade was faced with a force of two hundred warriors. It was twice the amount originally planned and almost half of those were not trained warriors. There was much work to be done.

By the third week of their training the acolytes were beginning to show some skill. Injuries were far less common and the training sessions went quickly. Everyone improved except Ihecha. He prayed nightly for strength, but the toll of time would not let his skills advance in step with the younger acolytes. Doubt seeped into his mind; was he truly meant to lead the Adamu against the Mosele?

He opened his eyes on the fourth week of training with the question on his mind. The sun pressed against his bone-white curtains, filling his bedchamber with muted light. Morning chill lingered; he wrapped his body in his robe and dropped his face into his palms.

"If I have turned your words the wrong way, please tell me," he prayed. "I am not a young man. My spirit exceeds my physical ability. If it is Jetade's place to lead our warriors, then let it be so. But if it is my place, please give me the strength to do your will."

Ihecha attempted to rise from his bed but could not. Comforting warmth encased him as the light in his room increased. He knew not to lift his face from his palms. Instead he waited on the words of Cha to answer his plea. But none came. The light subsided and the warmth gave way to the morning chill. He slowly lifted his face, puzzled by what occurred until he saw the sword.

It stretched across the foot of his bed, a weapon of beauty and terror. The golden pommel shone like the sun. The dark metal blade widened as it extended from the hilt, ending in a sharp-edged curve. It was an executioner's sword, a blade fashioned to fit the neck of the hapless victim. Cha had answered his plea. He was to lead the Adamu.

Ihecha reached out and grasped the sword's hilt. A surge of energy passed through him and he picked up the sword. It seemed surprisingly light for its size. He weaved it as Fanus taught him and a smile graced his face. This was a good blade as far as he could tell, a blade which seemed made for him.

"Judgment," he said. He'd never thought of naming a weapon, but this sword deserved such a moniker. It was given to him to judge those who stood against Cha, those who would call to false gods to answer their failed prayers. There would be judgment, and he would deliver it.

He entered the training room holding the sword in hand. The acolytes looked at him in astonishment; Fanus looked at him with wonder and skepticism.

"Where did you get that?" he asked.

Ihecha smiled with new confidence. "From Cha."

Fanus's eyes widened.

"Do not be alarmed," Ihecha said. "It is a gift to help us against the Mosele."

"How?" he asked.

Ihecha's smile faded. "I don't know."

Fanus transformed from astonished believer to stern trainer. "A weapon must be tested." He raised his sword and Ihecha took the guard position.

Fanus attacked with skill and fury. Normally such an attack would wear down Ihecha quickly, but the high priest kept pace with quick but jerky motions. Ihecha was too astonished to understand what was happening, but Fanus was more observant. He stopped his attack.

"It is leading you," he said.

Ihecha didn't understand; a frown appeared on his face.

"Cha is guiding your hand. You must relax and follow his will."

Fanus took his stance. The irritated look he'd carried throughout their training was gone, replaced by a respectful look. "Again."

Fanus attacked. This time Ihecha's response was smoother and much sharper. He repelled Fanu's stabs and slashes with ease, his limbs moving with a grace far beyond his skill. There was no pain in his joints, no fatigue in his muscles. He moved as if dancing.

Fanus broke off his assault. His chest heaving and his hair matted with sweat, he sheathed his sword, fell to his knees and covered his face.

"Cha is within you," he said.

So this is it, Ihecha thought. This was how he would lead the Adamu's chosen warriors against Karan and the Mosele.

"Rise, Fanus," he commanded. "Continue training the others."

Fanus came to his feet and nodded. Ihecha left the training room and returned to his chamber. He summoned a passing student before he entered. "Find Tisha and send her to me," he said.

The student bowed and hurried away. Ihecha sat at his desk and removed a sheet of parchment from his drawer. The note he wrote was brief but sure to bring Jetade and Fesseha to the temple. As he rolled the scroll, Tisha entered his chamber and covered her face.

"You summoned me, Teacher?"

"Yes, Tisha." He extended the scroll. "I need you to take this scroll to the palace and deliver it to Baba Fesseha."

Tisha's head jerked up, her eyes filled with wonder and shock. "You want me to take this to the mansa?"

Ihecha laughed. "Yes, I do. I would think you would be pleased."

"I am, but I am just a student!"

"You are not just a student," Ihecha replied. "You are our

best student. With the acolytes in training you must rise to a higher responsibility. I'm sure you can handle the delivery of a scroll."

"Yes, yes! Of course I can!" Tisha's joyful expression dissipated into doubt. "But why would I be allowed into the palace?"

"Because you will carry my staff." Ihecha stood and went to his closet. He returned with his staff, a thick length of ebony wood crowned with a golden leopard.

Tisha gripped the staff with her small hands, her face as serious as a young girl's could be. "I will not fail you, Teacher," she announced.

"I am not asking you to wrestle an ukombe," Ihecha replied. "I'm only asking you to deliver a message."

Tisha grinned as she took the staff and backed out of the chamber, bowing her head since she couldn't cover her face. As soon as she stepped over the threshold she spun and ran as fast as she could across the atrium.

Ihecha suspected she ran the entire way to the palace. Jetade, Baba Fesseha and the chosen warriors arrived at the temple at dusk. The acolytes still practiced, Fanus leading them in light sparring. Ihecha clapped his hands, ending the session. The acolytes and Fanus prostrated before the Mansa. Fesseha and Jetade approached Ihecha, their eyes falling to the unique sword at his side.

"Your messenger almost died delivering your message," Fesseha joked.

"Tisha takes her duties seriously, which is why I sent her."

"So is this it?" Jetade asked. He gestured to the sword.

Ihecha lifted the sword, making sure his motions were meant for display. He was not certain how the weapon would react.

"This is Judgment," he said.

Jetade grinned. "A sword with a name promises great things."

"It is Cha's will."

"Show me what that means."

"Shouldn't such a demonstration be held in private?" Nzali asked.

"No," Jetade answered. "Our champions are ready to make this journey. Fanus tells me the acolytes are as prepared as they will ever be. The only question left to answer is who will lead us."

Apparently Jetade had had a change of heart in respect to Cha's wisdom. He seemed eager to prove that he should lead the Adamu against the Mosele. Ihecha did not answer. He lowered the sword and took a stance.

"Then let us answer the question," he said.

Jetade took out his blade. "Yes, let us."

Nzali pulled Fesseha away from the men. The warriors and acolytes formed a circle, the adversaries in the center. Ihecha braced himself. Even with Cha's guidance he was not prepared for the fury that was Jetade. The war chief literally jumped the distance between them, descending on the shocked high priest like a bird of prey. Judgment jerked upward, almost flying from his hand as it met Jetade's blade and deflected it to the right. Ihecha instinctively stepped to the left as Jetade's blade cleaved the stone floor. Judgment streaked at the war chief's head; Jetade managed to roll away as he yanked his sword free.

If Jetade was surprised that Ihecha deflected his attack, it did not show in his determined face. He attacked again, a probing attack of stabs and slashes. Ihecha stood his ground, refusing to give way as he took Fanus's advice to heart. He let go completely, embracing the sword's control. Jetade struck hard and fast but Ihecha did not move. After what seemed like an endless barrage Jetade, hesitated, his well of strength and attacks exhausted. Ihecha and the sword sensed the moment; Ihecha stepped in, touching the edge of his sword against Jetade's neck.

The balogun's eyes widened and a smile slowly formed on his face. "This is truly a gift from Cha," he said. "How else would an old priest defeat a yaala jara?"

The warriors raised their weapons and cheered. The acolytes covered their faces and mumbled prayers through their fingers. Fesseha and Nzali approached both men. Fesseha seemed relieved. "It seems Cha means this song for you," he said.

"You are closest to him," Ihecha replied. "You can still lead us. I am sure Judgment would honor your hands much more than mine."

Fesseha flinched. "No, no. The honor is clearly rested in your hands." He turned to the others and raised his hands upward. "With the sword of Cha and our fearless champions, we will defeat the Mosele once and for all!"

Warriors and acolytes converged on Jetade and Ihecha, chanting their names in a powerful rhythm. Ihecha looked at the war chief and Jetade looked back, his face full of confidence and acceptance. There would be no issues with the warriors as long as Jetade believed in Cha's will, and at least at this moment, he did.

"Go ahead," Jetade said. "Give them their display. You are their leader. They will follow you into fire."

Ihecha stepped forward and raised Judgment over his head. "Cha's will be done!" he shouted.

Acolytes fell to their knees, their hands over their faces. Warriors raised their weapons with one hand and beat their chests with the other. The rooms vibrated with the sound of young melodic voices; Ihecha looked over the warriors and acolytes to see the students surrounding them all. Tisha looked back at him like a proud daughter, her voice rising over them all. Ihecha smiled, but inside his emotions were in turmoil. He was chosen, yet he fought to keep his sword arm from trembling with doubt. Was he the savior of Djenna? He still was not sure.

-3-

Djenna's champions left their city on a day designated for celebration. The dry season sky was clear of clouds, the sun granting pleasant warmth on the city and the surrounding farmlands. Drummers stood side by side on the city ramparts, their calloused hands beating out a defiant and hopeful rhythm accompanied by the voices of trained and untrained singers. Cha's temple shimmered with hundreds of red flags, resembling the pulsing flow of blood in the veins of the Adamu and their fierce champions. Once again they were called to march. Once again the few were called to sacrifice for the many.

Ihecha fidgeted in his armor, Fesseha's words incomprehensible through his helmet. The iron cap rested low on his head, the nose guard biting into his skin. His chain mail jerkin rested heavy on his frame despite his months of training. How warriors fought in such clothing baffled him, but he was destined to find out. Again a wave of doubt swept him despite hours of prayer and meditation. Was he worthy of this task? Would he succeed?

A heavy hand rested on his shoulder and he turned left to see the smiling face of Jetade.

"The speech is over," he said. "Time to give the throng its show."

Ihecha flashed an embarrassed smile. "I must admit I did not pay attention to our Baba's inspiring words."

"Most warriors don't, at least that is what I was told," Jetade replied. "Most of us are either praying or hoping someone would come to their senses and call the whole thing off."

Ihecha laughed. "The Mosele are not likely to, and we can't.

So we will fight for the glory of the Adamu and Cha's blessing."

Jetade's smile faded. "Excuse me, priest, but I'm in no hurry to meet our master. I'd rather come back in victory rather than martyrdom."

"That is Cha's will," Ihecha replied.

Jetade's face grew even darker. "Not if I can help it."

Their march from the city was more like a stroll. It was a gesture of confidence that the Adamu enjoyed, a show of nonchalance toward the coming battle. The people sang a song that had not been uttered for two generations, a song of a nation fighting to prove its right to exist.

The city gates opened as the last notes faded away. Ihecha strode out first, followed by the warriors as flower petals and ululations rained down upon him. Before him stretched the Mansa's Road, a hard-packed highway that cut a straight line through the surrounding farmlands, gradually dissipating into the surrounding savanna. A column of ox-drawn wagons followed them, brimming with supplies, talismans and gifts. It would be a luxurious march until they reached the desert's edge. For three days they walked and sang and ate, building up the reserves that would dwindle away as they crossed the Mosele's greatest weapon, the desert. The Adamu had driven them there, hoping for their demise. Instead, their enemy waited at the edge of mysterious mountains, emboldened by a false god who promised them victory.

On the fourth day the Mosele's prison stretched out before them, a barren bronzed land taunting them to enter. A great feast was held the following night; the oxen were killed and their flesh smoked to preserve it for the crossing. Each man gathered as many water gourds as he could carry. The next morning, Ihecha led the warriors in prayer, fighting hard to keep his voice from trembling. Though Judgment rested at his side, his doubt still loomed large. He looked into the eyes of each warrior and was steeled by their visible resolve. They were at the cusp of their journey and they each held the confidence of determined men. He hoped he possessed the same resolve on the fateful day.

Cha was truly with them. Wisps of clouds passed overhead and the normally torrid temperature was tempered by cool winds blowing from the east. Scouts hired from villages that rimmed the desert's edge led them to oases to fill their quickly emptying water gourds and supplemented their provisions with the hidden bounty of the desert. It was also a blessing that they were a small group. A larger army would be doomed to run out of supplies long before they reached their destination.

When that would occur, no one knew. For weeks they trudged across the stale landscape, searching the horizon for any sign of the gray peaks, let alone the people waiting in defiance of them. They traveled during the night to avoid the draining heat, but fatigue still settled on their weary bones. Ihecha ignored the questioning stares and remarks which grew with each day past. He may have doubted his worthiness to lead the expedition but he did not doubt its purpose. The desert would eventually end and at its end would be the Mosele and their false god.

That end came abruptly. The band of warriors were finishing their morning meal when an acolyte noticed an undulating line of moving objects advancing rapidly across the horizon.

Jetade unsheathed his sword, walking toward the image without his armor. "We have visitors!" he shouted.

The warriors reacted to his voice immediately, dropping their food platters and donning their armor with precision. The acolytes were much slower. They looked to Ihecha first, whose attention was locked on the strange sight before him.

"Teacher?"

Ihecha turned to see Jabilo at his side.

"What do we do?" he said.

"Arm yourselves," Ihecha replied. "And pray."

Ihecha donned a cotton undershirt then slipped on his chain mail and helmet. He hung his baldric across his shoulders and unsheathed Judgment. The blade felt eager in his nervous hand. Its purpose was finally clear and it seemed anxious to fulfill it. "Cha be with us," he whispered before striding toward Jetade and the warriors.

"Stay back, priest," Jetade ordered.

"You seem to forget who is in charge here," Ihecha shot back.

Jetade looked back at Ihecha, his expression respectful but stern.

"Your time will come with the main attack," Jetade replied. "This is the Mosele's vanguard. They are testing our strength and hoping to test our will. Besides, look closely at what comes. These are not Mosele."

Ihecha covered his eyes. The advancing line was not composed of Mosele, but some type of creature resembling a mix of dog and simba. "What are they?" he said aloud.

"Pets of their false god, no doubt," Jetade said. He stood stoically, seemingly unnerved by the strange beasts. A grim smile came to his face. "I don't know how they live, but soon we will see how they die."

The warriors formed a line on either side of Jetade. Ihecha now realized why Jetade did not argue with him about who led the expedition. Jetade knew that when the time came he would command, for only he had the blood and the experience to do so. Judgment stayed calm in his hand. Apparently Cha knew so, too.

The warriors did not speak as they formed a solid line. "Do not let your brother down!" Jetade shouted. "Protect the flanks! Acolytes, form a line behind us. If anything gets past the first line, kill it. If a man falls before you, replace him."

The acolytes began to pray. Jetade's head jerked about. "Stop it!" he shouted. "The time for praying is over. It's time to fight!"

The first running beast reached the line, its maw wide and anxious. Its narrow body was covered with splotchy fur resembling the wild dogs of the savannah, but its over large head spoke of a feline persuasion. Jetade stepped from the line, swinging his large sword with both hands and cleaved the beast's head in half. The other beasts were close behind and the warriors went to work. Grunts, howls, cries and screams rose from the wall of warriors reaping beasts like ripe sorghum. Ihecha worked the hilt of Judgment nervously, eying portions of the slaughter taking place before him.

A warrior fell, a beast on his chest biting at his face and neck. Jabilo leaped forward, kicking the beast off the man and stabbing it with his sword. He glanced at Ihecha and took the man's place among the warriors.

"Circle!" Jetade shouted.

The warriors on either moved back until they stood side by side, facing outward. The warriors had formed a circle around the acolytes, continuing to beat back the four-legged onslaught. But it was obvious they were tiring. More warriors fell, replaced by acolytes. A beast somehow leaped over the line, plunging toward the inner circle with its mouth wide. Ihecha jumped toward it, Judgment held high. With one stroke he clove the beast in half from head to tail. The dead beast's carcass fell to either side of him, its blood splattered on his blade, face and armor. He'd drawn his first blood.

Ihecha quickly assessed his comrades and gave orders for what needed to be done. The onslaught of creatures waned; soon the attacked ceased. Jetade raised his sword and the warriors responded with a cheer. The acolytes were more subdued. They wandered about, stunned by the carnage about them and tending their wounded comrades. A few dead lay among them, mauled by the sharp teeth of their attackers.

The silent lull was shattered by a crescendo of rumbling drums and shrill ululations.

The Mosele were coming.

Ihecha's eyes went to the horizon just as a wave of energy surged through him. Judgment warmed in his hand as he marched to Jetade's side.

"This is the main attack," the balogun said without looking at him. "The beasts were meant to wear us down."

"And they have."

"No matter. We will prevail. Cha is with us. We will form the circle as before. It is a good strategy."

"No," Ihecha replied. "It is my time."

Jetade finally looked at the priest. "What do you mean by that?"

Ihecha gave Jetade an unreadable expression. "You will know when you see it."

Ihecha sprinted toward the advancing Mosele, his legs fueled by currents of energy pulsing from Judgment. Serenity overtook him at that moment as the realization of his purpose emerged. He would never see Djenna again. He was never meant to. He would leave his all on this battleground and by doing so save his people. The doubt which rode his shoulders ever since the day he received Cha's message was gone, replaced by resolve.

As he neared the Mosele, he could see the hate in their eyes. It was deserved; the Adamu had driven them from their land to certain death. But that was their fate. Cha had decreed it so. And now Ihecha was here to complete it.

He leapt over the first line of warriors and landed in the midst of the horde. Ihecha closed his eyes and gave himself over to Judgment. The Mosele surged around him and he cut them down like bothersome weeds, Judgment shattering shields, spears and swords like dry sticks. Flesh was far less durable. He weaved about, never allowing them to trap him in one place, constantly cutting, stabbing and striking with ceaseless energy.

Ihecha swung Judgment like a scythe. The blade met resistance, vibrating his hand. He stumbled from the impact, almost falling into the pile of bodies forming a ring around him. He opened his eyes, his melding with the celestial sword broken. Before him stood a creature of stone resembling a heavily muscled man. It towered over him, not a giant, but much taller than any man Ihecha had yet encountered. Its face was blank except for four slits, two where eyes should be, one which would have been the nose, one for the mouth. This was the creature the Mosele worshiped as a god; the thing that they hoped would help them reclaim their land.

Ihecha attacked. The thing met his blade stroke by stroke with its stone hands, the shock of the blows sending aches through the warrior priest's hands and wrists. Slits appeared on the creature where Judgment bit; cuts quickly filled and healed by molten rock oozing from inside the creature. They fought for hours, a stalemate that brought silence around them save for the ringing of Judgment as it met the creature's stone-like limbs. All the while Ihecha's confidence waned. Shouldn't this beast be done by now? Why would Cha let this thing resist him? Was it truly a god?

With doubt came fatigue. Judgment weighed heavy in his hands. He struggled to keep paced with the tireless creature, his attack becoming an overburdened defense. In desperation Ihecha leaped at the creature, raising Judgment high as he aimed a blow to its head. "Cha help me!" he yelled.

The creature's massive hand crashed against Judgment, sending it flying away from Ihecha's hand then shattering into shards of light as it struck the ground. The creature caught Ihecha with its other hand, hot stone gripping Ihecha's neck and searing his skin. The priest did not notice. He stared, stunned, where Judgment had fragmented, a deep smoldering hole where the blade struck. He slowly scanned the battlefield. Everyone was dead. Acolytes and warriors lay strewn among celebrating Mosele. One warrior raised a spear crowned by Jetade's head.

"Ihecha." The voice speaking his name grated like stone against stone.

Ihecha looked into the sparse face of the creature.

"Is this what you expected? No, of course not. You thought you would stand on my corpse as the Mosele fled into my mountains, broken and defeated. Your god failed you. No, you failed your god. You were not worthy of his blessing. You were too weak."

Ihecha nodded. It was his fault. The doubt hiding inside him had grown with this creature's resistance. He'd failed Cha and the Adamu.

"Yet, there is strength in you," the creature said. "You came despite your fears and you fought knowing you might fail. It is a valuable thing to have such strength."

"Kill me," Ihecha said.

The slit that served as the creature's mouth rose at both ends. "No, Ihecha. I will not kill you," it said. "I am Karan, god of the Grey. I have need of you."

BOOK II

The Shosa's Child

Hazeeta stumbled through the dense trees, her rough hands gripping her swollen belly. A powerful contraction surged through her in waves and she collapsed to her knees. Pain clutched her lower back; she fell forward, supporting herself with her outstretched arms. The contractions came closer and more intense.

"Not yet," she moaned. "Not yet!"

She rolled onto her side and gritted her teeth, breathing deeply until the contractions subsided. As soon as they diminished, she struggled back to her feet and continued to her destination. Her baby would come soon. She had no idea of the outcome, but she knew she had a better chance if she reached her goal. Despite the traditions of her calling she would not let her baby die. Her child was no mistake.

She smiled when her hut came into view. Hazeeta was a planner, which was why she rose rapidly in the ranks of the Shosa. The moment she realized she was pregnant, she knew she would not kill her child. She petitioned Baba Longi to assign her unit to a frontier post so the reaction to her violation would not be so severe. When her sisters discovered her condition they were disappointed but supportive. She was their Padume; it was not as if they could tell her what to do. She promised them she would do what was demanded when she bore the child and they believed her. Everyone except Asli. Only she knew how much Hazeeta loved the baby's father, another violation of the Baba's edicts.

"I know you cannot kill the child," Asli told her one night.

"But you know you cannot keep her."

Asli's words haunted her as she stumbled into the hut. Another contraction racked her body and she fell to her knees, then onto her side again. She lay still while the pain consumed her, the pressure stronger about her loins. Her baby was coming soon.

The contractions subsided. She secured the hut door, undressed, and then lay on the blanket-covered mat. Her provisions rested within reach on either side. Hazeeta closed her eyes, whispered a prayer and braced herself for the next contractions. They were strong, the strongest yet. She tried to be quiet but the scream was out of her mouth before she knew it. The pain about her loins increased to a level she'd never experienced. The contractions were successive; Hazeeta wasn't sure if she could stay conscious. She was at the brink of her endurance when the pain subsided and her screams were replaced by a strange sound. She sat up on her mat, her breath heavy, her body covered with sweat. The strange sound coalesced into a strident, piercing cry. Hazeeta lifted up her head and looked between her legs. A baby sprawled before her, its small arms waving, its legs kicking. Hazeeta grasped the knife by her side and bent closer, ignoring the burning agony. She cut the umbilical cord and tied it closed with a thin thread. Hazeeta examined her baby and her face brightened; it was a girl.

"My daughter," she whispered. "My beautiful daughter."

Hazeeta held her close as she wiped her clean with a cloth. Fatigue swept over her and her eyes became heavy. She reached out for a large blanket and pulled it over her and her child. She closed her eyes and let sleep take her.

-1-

The touch on Hazeeta's forehead was not welcomed. She grabbed the knife by her side and lunged. Someone caught her wrist and forced her arm back to her side.

"I don't think you want to do that."

Her eyes snapped open upon hearing the familiar voice. Asli knelt before her, a welcoming smile on her face. Her smooth black skin and easy smile disguised her deadly fighting skills and experience. Hazeeta touched her own face, felt the pock marks mingled with ragged scars: a face that revealed a life of struggle. Her constant squint formed wrinkles about her eyes that aged her beyond her years. Asli's eyes drifted to Hazeeta's baby and the smile dissipated.

"So it lives," she said.

"She lives," Hazeeta corrected. Asli let go of Hazeeta's wrist then shuffled across the birthing hut, allowing Hazeeta room to sit up.

"Her name is Sadatina," Hazeeta announced.

"You named her?" Asli said, surprise in her voice.

"Of course I did."

Asli reached to her side and lifted a bowl of goat stew. "You should eat. She should, too."

Sadatina gazed into Hazeeta's eyes and realized the wisdom in Asli's words. The more time she spent with her daughter, the harder it would be for her to do what she had to do. She guided Sadatina's mouth to her nipple and instinct led mother and daughter to that quiet, nurturing space which only they could find. Sadatina sucked vigorously.

"How did you find me?" Hazeeta asked.

"You are my sister," Asli answered. "Did you think you could hide from me?" She lifted a spoonful of stew to Hazeeta's lips. The aroma sparked her hunger and she ate with her daughter.

"You endanger yourself," Hazeeta warned.

Asli fed her another spoonful. "There is no danger in knowing that you bore a child. You are not the first Shosa to fail Baba's commands."

The word fail struck Hazeeta hard, as Asli meant it to.

"The danger is knowing what you do afterward."

"So why did you come?"

"To make sure you lived," Asli replied. "I'll stay until you are strong enough to ride. Then I will go. You will return alone and everyone will know you fulfilled your duty. "

"I will not kill my child," Hazeeta said. "You know this."

"As long as you don't come back with her, it doesn't matter."

They were mostly silent for the next week. Asli took care of Hazeeta and Hazeeta nursed Sadatina. At the end of the week, they tore down the birth hut and burned it. They spread the ashes among the surrounding bushes and brushed the site smooth with branches. Hazeeta carried Sadatina in a sling before her, whispering and singing to her child as she worked. Asli fed and saddled the horses. W,hen it was all complete she mounted her horse. Asli did as well.

"We leave for Wangara within the month," Asli said. "If you are not back, everyone will assume you died in childbirth. That is what I will tell them."

"I will return," Hazeeta said.

"You don't have to, you know." Asli's voice was pained. "You could stay with your child wherever you have chosen to take her."

"And how long could I hide?" Hazeeta shook her head. "I'm safer among my sisters and Sadatina is safer without me."

The sisters reached out, grasping each other's hands.

Asli smiled. "Be safe, sister." To Hazeeta's surprised her sister stroked Sadatina's head. "Was he worth it?" She asked. "Is she worth it?"

Hazeeta grasped her hand. "Yes. I've never known such happiness, however brief it has been."

Asli squeezed her hand, turned her horse and rode away. Hazeeta waited until her sister disappeared in the bush before setting off in her own direction. She was behind schedule; her recovery had taken longer than she'd expected. On the other hand, she had not expected to have a horse to ride, and gave silent thanks. With the horse she would make good time. ` She could encounter danger along the way to her destination, but the further she strayed from Wangara, the less chance there was of such an encounter occurring. The ginangas, Karan's dog-like nyokas, seemed focused on the city for now; their terror had not spread into the countryside. She had hope that it never would, but she knew it was a just a matter of time until the ginangas expanded their range. Still, her daughter would have a chance, which was all she could ask.

It took months for Hazeeta to find the village which met her exacting standards, and weeks more to locate the family that would suit her needs. They owned a farm near a cluster of wooded hills, a small river forming a natural barrier between the hills and farmland. The livestock appeared healthy and the fields looked well cared for, promising ripe harvests every rainy season of sorghum and yams. The farmer's wife recently had borne a son and was near the point of weaning him. It was possible they would reject her plea, but Hazeeta had prepared to make her offer hard to resist.

She approached the farm from the hills, taking care to remain in view of any who noticed her. She did not want the farmers to think she was sneaking up on them.

A chill hung in the air, a morning mist drifting among the treetops. The horse waded into the cold river, issuing a grunt in protest. By the time they crossed the waterway, the farmer and his helpers had trotted across the fallow fields toward them, weapons in hand. The farmer carried an oiled throwing iron, a crude weapon but deadly in experienced hands. His helpers brandished spears with long broadleaved heads. They were shumba hunters; they carried little fear of a woman and a child riding a horse. She reined her mount to a halt a good distance away from the three. The shumba hunters stopped as well.

The farmer approached her. "Hello, sister," he said, his greeting polite despite his armed approach.

"Hello, brother," she answered. "I and my child have been on the road for most of the day and seek rest. I beg your hospitality for the night, lest we are forced to camp in the bush once again."

"Where is your husband?" he asked.

The sadness that came to Hazeeta's face was real. "He is dead."

The farmer lowered his weapon. "Come with us." He grabbed the horse's bridle and led them to his house. His wife emerged from the home holding their baby, a welcoming smile on her young face. Hazeeta wondered if that smile would remain once she revealed her intentions.

The farmer looked at the youngest hunter, gave a brief head nod. "Take the horse to the stable."

Hazeeta dismounted and handed over the reins.

The farmer and his wife approached Hazeeta, their eyes on Sadatina. "She is beautiful," the wife said. "She looks like you."

"She has her father's eyes," Hazeeta said sadly.

The wife pulled at her sleeve. "Come, there is food inside."

The home was modest yet neat. A small table occupied one side of the one-room house, a bed and cradle near the fireplace against the opposite wall. An iron kettle hung over the fire, an aromatic stew simmering inside. Hazeeta sat at the table as the farmer's wife sat her child by the bed. The boy protested, his whine raising doubt in Hazeeta's heart. How would this woman raise two small children? What would happen if she could not manage? Would she take Sadatina and leave her in the bush?

"Shh, little one," the woman said. The boy obeyed, his

lips poked out in disapproval.

The farmer's wife nodded and went to the fire. She took a bowl from her cupboard and filled it with stew. "This is good stew," she said. "It will give you good milk."

"Thank you." Hazeeta tasted the stew and closed her eyes in pleasure. "This is very good."

"I am Kiden," the farmer's wife said. "My husband is Abay. You must forgive him. We don't get many visitors. We live far from the village."

It was time, Hazeeta, thought. "I am Hazeeta," she said. "I am from Wangara."

Kiden's eyes widened. "It is such a long way for a woman with a newborn child to travel. Why did you come so far alone?"

"You have shared your home with me, so I must speak truth to you," Hazeeta said. "I am a Shosa."

Kiden's hand went to her mouth as she leaned away from the table.

"Do not fear, Kiden. I mean you and your husband no harm."

"You are a nyoka-hunter," Kiden said. "Are there nyokas about?"

"No, this is why I am here."

She was about to continue when Abay entered. "Husband, come sit. Hazeeta has something to tell us."

Abay sat beside his wife, his eyes narrowing. "What is wrong?" he asked.

Hazeeta began again. "I am a Shosa from Wangara."

Abay sprang to his feet. "Are there nyokas?"

"No, Abay, there are no nyokas here. Your valley does not interest them. They seem only determined to destroy Wangara, which they will not do as long as the Shosa ride."

Abay sat down slowly. "So why are you here with a child, warrior woman?"

Sadatina began to whine and Hazeeta rocked her quiet. "This is not my first time seeing you. I have watched you for months. I had to be sure you were the right ones."

"The right ones for what?" Abay asked.

"I needed to be sure you were the right ones to raise my daughter."

Both Abay and Kiden's mouths dropped open.

Hazeeta continued to speak. "It is forbidden for a Shosa to have children. Normally we are punished when it is discovered we are pregnant, and then forced to take certain herbs to end our pregnancy. If the herbs do not take, the child is taken away and killed immediately after birth. I will not allow either to happen to my child."

She saw sympathy in Kiden's eyes but protest in Abay's. He raised his hand before Kiden could speak. "We cannot do it," he said. "Whatever would befall you would befall us if others discovered we took the child."

"That will not happen," she said. "I plan to return to my sisters if you take my daughter. I will tell them I killed her myself."

"No one will believe a mother killed her own child," Kiden said.

"They won't question me as long as I return alone."

"How will we provide for another child?" His question was more for Kiden than Hazeeta. "I had to hire men to do my wife's work. She has a child. We can't raise another."

"I understand it would be difficult," Hazeeta answered. "Come with me."

She led the curious couple to the stable. Sadatina slept against her breasts, oblivious to the importance of the conversation. Hazeeta opened a satchel strapped to her horse, reached inside and took out a small bag.

She gave the bag to Abay. "Here."

Abay opened it and his eyes went wide. He showed it to Kiden and she gasped. The bag was filled with gold dust.

"I have ten more bags in my satchel. I will also leave you my horse."

Abay broke his gaze from the bag. "That is a big horse. She

will eat too much."

"She will make up for it by plowing your fields," Hazeeta assured him. "She is not a workhorse, but she is gentle and obeys."

"Are you sure of this?" Kiden asked.

Hazeeta wasn't sure, but she had no choice. If she didn't return, her sisters would search for her. If they found her and Sadatina alive, they would kill them both. "Yes, I'm sure."

"We will have to hire a wet nurse to help you with them both," Abay said.

"Terte is almost weaned," Kiden said. "I can nurse them both until then."

Abay looked at Kiden for a long moment. Then they faced Hazeeta with smiles.

"We will accept your child," Abay said.

Hazeeta was filled with relief and sadness. Kiden sat Terte down and approached Hazeeta, arms extended. Hazeeta looked into her daughter's eyes and tried not to cry. This was the last time she would see her first and only child. Sadatina would only remember Kiden as her mother.

She took Sadatina from her sling and handed her to Kiden. No sooner did Kiden take her did Hazeeta turn and hurry away.

"I thank you," she said as she walked away. "Take good care of her."

Hazeeta kept walking, her eyes focused on the wooded hills before her. She plunged into the river, wading through the cold waters. Still, she did not look back. As she climbed onto the opposite bank she cried, tears shaping rivulets down her cheeks like rain. At the crest of the first hill, her legs failed, and she collapsed, her sobs paralyzing her. When she finally decided to look at the farm, Kiden and Abay were gone. A brief panic flashed through her, but she soon calmed herself. They were safe inside their home, living in a valley far from the dangers of nyokas and Wangara.

She stood and wrapped the control and discipline of her sisters around herself She had done all she could for her daughter. It was time for her to return.

-2-

Sadatina brushed back her damp braids and sighed. She looked down into the ironwood mortar at the powered sorghum and over to the half-full basket waiting for her arduous attention. Mama said she was a strong girl, but the work still seemed hard; dry season made the sun bright and hot in the clear sky. She lifted the pestle and continued pounding, humming a song to set her rhythm.

"Sadatina!" Baba's voice broke her pace and she felt a shiver of excitement. Before she could move her mother stepped from the house.

"Leave her alone!" she shouted. "She's pounding sorghum!"

"She can do that later," her baba shouted back. "There are shumbas about."

Her mother frowned as she looked at her. "Go ahead. I'll finish here. Be careful."

Sadatina's joy showed in her smile. "Yes, Mama!"

She dropped the pestle into the mortar, slipping by Mama to get her shield and spear. In a larger village, only men dealt with shumbas lurking about the livestock. Here, far from the nearest village, it was up to their family to deal with the opportunistic predators. Baba and Terte were good hunters, but it helped to have another spear when dealing with shumba. For the feline to stalk their herds meant either it was old or had been driven from its pride. The reason did not matter. Their livestock had to be protected.

She bundled her hair and covered it with her head wrap to

keep her braids out of her eyes, then sprinted to catch up with her brother and father. At thirteen seasons Sadatina had grown into beautiful woman with an athletic body that both women and men admired and envied. She stood at least a foot taller than Mama and almost as tall as Baba. Terte challenged her in height but not in skills. She frustrated him with her strength and quickness when they were younger, besting him in wrestling, running and climbing games. Baba always comforted him, telling him that when he became a man everything would take its rightful place and he would be Sadatina's superior in such manly things. But a year had passed since Terte took his initiation rites and Sadatina still surpassed him physically. It was an annoyance to him but nothing more. Their bond as siblings was stronger than an annoyance.

She caught up with them as they reached the pen. Sadatina counted the goats with her father; they were one short. Her father crouched to look at the tracks and frowned.

"The good thing is that it's only one shumba. The bad thing is that it is a female. If she is with cubs, she will be even more difficult to kill."

Terte frowned. "Can we drive her away?"

Her father stood, his expression hard. "No, she has found easy prey. She will not be forced to leave."

Sadatina scanned the ground and picked up the shumba's spoor. "She went this way," she said. "The blood is fairly fresh."

They set out immediately, following the blood trail to the river. They waded to the opposite bank and tried to pick up the trail again. Sadatina entered the edge of the forest, her eyes trained on the ground while listening for any sounds that might betray the shumba's proximity. She was stepping deeper into the foliage when a strange sensation enveloped her, drawing her eyes to the dark shadows between the dense trees. She seldom ventured into the wooded hills; she had more than enough to keep herself busy on the farm. Their fields and livestock provided all the family's needs. They occasionally hunted bush meat for variety, but the woods were mainly a pretty sight, nothing more. Now, there was something more in the woods, something that seemed to be watching her.

Baba's hand on her shoulder broke the sensation. "What is it?" he said. "Do you see something?"

"No, Baba. I feel something."

She expected to see a skeptical look on Baba's face when she turned to face him. Instead she was greeted by a concerned frown.

"Come. We've done enough today. We have late nights ahead of us. We need to guard the stables until our shumba shows up again. I can't afford to lose any more goats."

Sadatina followed Baba back to the river. She looked back into the woods one last time before wading back to her home.

That night as she prepared for bed her mother came to her. "You should not go hunting with your baba and brother any longer," she said.

Sadatina looked at her mother, careful to control the confusion and anger fighting to speak. "Why?" she managed to ask calmly. "Our meals can be better when I can help them."

"What about me?" Mama asked. "You runoff with them and the chores don't get done."

"I don't see why they can't help us," Sadatina snapped. She covered her mouth with her hand, surprised at herself.

"It is our work," Mama scolded. "Not theirs. Just like hunting is their work. Not ours. Besides, it is time you considered other things."

Sadatina's eyes narrowed. "What other things?" she asked.

"You are a woman now. You should be thinking about a husband and a family. We live far from the village so it is difficult for you to meet bachelors. Difficult, but not impossible. We will spend more time at the market; maybe attend a few ceremonies..."

"Mama!" Sadatina had never experienced the fear she felt at that moment. "I'm not ready to marry!"

"Maybe not now, but you will be. You should spend more time with the village women as well. You can learn many things from them about which bachelors are more desirable."

Marriage was the last thing Sadatina wished to discuss, but her mother was focused and would not relent.

"I'm tired," Sadatina said. "Can we talk of this tomorrow, mamma?"

Mama looked at Sadatina with curious eyes. "Of course we can, and we will. Good night, Tina."

"Good night, Mama."

Later that evening Sadatina lay on her cot trying to sleep but her mother's words would not let her rest. Marriage. Family. Two things she had no interest in whatsoever. She could not deny her interest in boys; last rainy season she had watched the bachelors who helped with the harvest, their lean bodies pleasing to her. A few of them returned her gaze, smiling and waving. They did not approach her, however. Most worked for her father to raise a dowry for the women they were promised to when they were boys. It didn't matter to Sadatina. They were a passing interest and no more.

Mama and Baba slept in a separate room but their voices carried clear to Sadatina's cot.

"You must talk to your daughter," Mama said.

"About what?" Baba asked.

"It is time she considered marriage and family."

"She's too young."

"Too young? She's a woman. She is the same age I was when you drank beer with my baba."

"That was different. Besides, Sadatina is not like us. Marriage may not be in her future."

Sadatina sat up. Not like them? What was different about her?

"She is the same as any other girl in the valley. I am her mother and I will decide."

"Don't be disappointed if you fail."

"I will fail if you don't talk to her. She listens to you."

"I'll talk to her tomorrow. Tonight I'm tired." Baba complained.

"See, she's just like you. It's as if she is your child."

Sadatina stood now. Baba was not her father? She walked to her parents' room ready to confront them with this sudden revelation. Before she could push the curtain aside Mama stepped through. They both jumped.

"Sadatina! Is something wrong?"

The strength that brought her to the threshold fled at her mother's stern glance. "No, Mama," she squeaked. "I was going to get water."

"I was, too," her mother said.

Sadatina followed her mother to the water gourd, trying to muster the courage to confront her. She mumbled to herself as her mother poured the clear water into a wooden cup. Mama turned to hand Sadatina the cup and her courage failed her again. She drank quickly, water streaming down the sides of her cheeks.

"Slow down, girl!"

Sadatina handed the cup to her. "Sorry, Mama. I'm going to sleep now."

She scurried to her bed and closed her eyes. Mama stood there for a moment watching her, then went back into the sleeping room. Sadatina had no intention of sleeping. She would wait up until her father came from the room to feed the horse and goats. She would talk to him.

When she awoke the sun had breached the horizon. Sleep had slunk up to her like a snake through rocks. She jumped from her bed, running from the house as fast as she could to the stables. A moan escaped her lips; the goats had been fed and the horse was gone.

"Sadatina!" her mother shouted. "What's wrong with you girl? Get back here. We have work to do."

Sadatina stormed back to her mother, her anger clear on her face. Her mother's face transformed to match.

"Don't you look at me like that! What is wrong with you, girl?"

"You said Baba is not my father!" Sadatina shouted.

Mama's angry countenance fell away to shock.

"I heard you last night," Sadatina continued. "You said Baba is not my father."

Mama reached for her hand but she jerked it away. Her anger was full upon her now. The truth was in her mother's eyes. Baba was not her father. Mama had betrayed him.

"Sadatina, listen to me. You heard something that was not for your ears. There is..."

"How could you!"

There was puzzlement on Mama's face, then clarity. "No Tina, it's not what you think."

"Tell me, Mama," Sadatina sneered. "What am I thinking?"

Mama dropped her head. "You are not your baba's daughter. Neither are you mine."

Mama's words reeled her as much as the words she'd heard the night before. She slumped to her knees, looking up into her mother's eyes for an explanation. Her mother knelt before her and grasped her hand, leading her into the house and to the table. Sadatina sat absently staring at her mother as she poured her a cup of water. Sadatina took the cup and drank it just a bit slower.

"We were going to tell you later," her mother said. "Thirteen years ago, a woman came to us from the hills. She came with a child, asking us for lodging. We brought them into our home. The woman's husband had died and she could not keep the child. She asked us if we would take the child and raise her as our own."

"That was me," Sadatina whispered.

"Yes," Mama answered. "She gave you your name."

"Who was she?"

Mama moved her chair close to Sadatina and hugged her. "She made us promise we would not tell you."

Sadatina pulled away from Mama. "Why? Did she despise me so much?"

"No, no," Mama replied. "She loved you very much. I was a mother then as well. Terte was almost one year old. I could see the love and pain in her eyes. Leaving you with us was a very difficult thing for her to do. She was a very important woman whose position would not allow her to have a child. Knowing who she was would put her life and, more importantly, your life in danger."

Sadatina said nothing. In a few hours, her life had shifted as a handful of sand slides down a dune. She looked into her mother's eyes again.

"You are our child," Mama said. "You became our daughter the moment I took you into my arms. I love you as much as I love Terte. Never doubt that."

"And Baba?" she asked.

"Of course he loves you! You shouldn't have to ask. I think he favors you."

Sadatina managed to smile.

"Stay inside today if you wish," Mama said. "Your father will be back soon. You can talk to him when he arrives."

"No, Mama," Sadatina replied. "I will work."

Much waited to be done during the dry season; the house needed repairs, the livestock required constant care, seeds for new plantings had to be sorted.   The sun had already begun its descent toward the western horizon when her father and Terte appeared. They'd been hunting; their game bag bulged with a successful day's work. Normally Sadatina would have rushed to them to see what they had bagged, but that day she stayed with her mother, her eyes focused on Baba. His smile diminished as he saw her expression; his face turned grim when he looked and Mama nodded at him in a certain way.

"Terte, take the bag to the smokehouse and clean the game," he said.

Terte looked at Mama, Baba and Sadatina. "Am I to do this alone? I'm tired!"

Mama went to him and grabbed the bag. "Come, I'll help you." Mama walked to the smokehouse. Terte followed, peering back at Sadatina and Baba.

"Mama told me," Sadatina said. "I am not your child."

"Yes you are," Baba replied.

"You know what I mean, Baba. I was given to you."

"That doesn't make you any less than ours," he replied. "Your mama fed you from her breasts. We love you and care for you every day. In my heart and in yours you know you belong to us."

Sadatina smiled. She knew her father's words were true. Still, uncertainty remained.

Terte's loud yell broke the day's peace. Baba and Sadatina ran to the stable, both with the same thought on their mind. When they reached the stable they saw what they dreaded. Mama stood against the fence, the game bag clutched in her hands. Terte crouched before her, his spear pointed at the female shumba standing guard before them. A dead goat lay under her paws, and her ears flattened on her head. She roared and Mama flinched, dropped the game bag and snatched up her cutting knife.

"Sadatina, go to the hut and get your spear, now!" Baba shouted.

Sadatina sprinted to the house before Baba could finish his words. She burst into the house, ran to her cot and grabbed her spear and shield. Her feet barely touched the ground as she dashed back to the stable. Baba was inching closer to the shumba, yelling and waving his throwing knife. The shumba's head jerked back and forth between Terte and Baba, roaring with each swing of her head. Sadatina rushed by her father.

"Sadatina!" he shouted.

She paid him no heed. Her shield before her, she charged the shumba. "Hah!" she shouted.

The shumba swiped at her shield. Sadatina inched closer, jabbing her spear at the shumba, fighting back the fear threatening to send her running back to Baba's side. Instead she looked at Terte and motioned her head toward the shumba. Terte yelled and shook his spear as well. The shumba looked his way and roared. Sadatina closed on it, yelling and jabbing with her spear.

Baba needed no encouragement from her. He took advantage of her distraction to work his way slowly behind the big cat. Sadatina watched him from the periphery, continuing to press the shumba. The beast began favoring her actions, so she inched her way to her mother and brother, hoping to help protect them with her shield and spear. A few steps away, Mama and Terte were almost near enough to touch when she saw the shumba's ears shift backwards. The shumba spun, facing Baba who was almost to the beast, his throwing iron raised. Time seemed to slow; the shumba's mouth gaped as it sprang, its front legs spreading wide, its paws flared and claws extended. Sadatina dropped her shield and grasped her assegai with both hands, lunging at the shumba and praying she would reach it before it reached her father. The broad leaf blade sank into the shumba's body. It howled and twisted, dragging Sadatina off her feet as she held on to her assegai. She lost her grip and slammed into the dirt. She rolled with her momentum, attempting to distance herself from the wounded predator, ending the roll on her hands and knees. The shumba loped toward her, the assegai protruding from its side. Then Baba appeared, striking down with his throwing iron behind the shumba's head. The feline howled and dropped where it stood, the ferocity in its eyes giving way to a solemn, blank stare.

"Tina!"

Mama ran to her, Terte close behind. Baba loomed over the shumba, striking it one more time to make sure of its demise. Sadatina tried to stand and a stabbing pain at her side sent her back down to her hands and knees.

"What were you thinking, child?" Mama hugged her and she winced. "You are hurt?"

Sadatina nodded.

Baba pushed past Mama and lifted Sadatina into his arms. He carried her to the house, Mama and Terte running before them. "You are your mother's daughter," he whispered to her.

"Which one?" Sadatina managed to ask.

Baba smiled at her. "Both." He carried her inside and set her down on her cot. Mama came to her and immediately pressed her hard about her sides. She winced where Mama's hands landed.

"Her ribs are not broken, only bruised," Mama said to Baba. "She will need a poultice to help her heal. You'll have to go to the village. I don't have the proper herbs here."

"I will go soon," Baba said. "Our job is not done."

Sadatina and Mama looked at him in puzzlement.

"The shumba had teats, which means she has cubs."

Sadatina shivered unexpectedly. She understood now the expression on the shumba's face before she died. She had failed her children. She was leaving them alone.

"What will happen to them?" she asked, although she knew the answer.

Baba smiled and patted her shoulder.

"We won't have to worry about them. Without their mother they will either starve or be killed. Either way, our livestock is safe."

Baba's words did not make her feel better. There was no reason she should be concerned about the lives of shumbas, yet the mother shumba's final expression seemed to lay a burden on her.

"Be still, Tina," Mama said. "It's too late to go to the village. Your baba will have to wait until morning. Terte, you will help me with chores today."

Terte's face dropped. "Me? Do woman's work?"

Baba cuffed his head. "There is no men's or women's work on this farm, only work. Do as you're told."

Terte smirked at Sadatina. "Next time do your chores before you get hurt."

Sadatina stuck out her tongue. "Next time you kill the shumba."

She spent the rest of the day under her mother's care and thinking about the shumba's offspring. How many cubs had she left behind? Why was she not with a pride? At least with a pride another mother might take on the cubs. On the other hand, the cubs might be killed by a rival female, especially if her shumba challenged the dominant female. That may be why she was alone with her cubs. She may have been driven from the pride.

Her thoughts did not end during her slumber. She dreamed of the cubs mewing desperately as they waited for a mother who would never return. A faceless woman appeared before the cubs and took them into her arms. She lifted her shirt and fed the cubs from her breasts as she sang a song familiar to Sadatina, although she had never heard her mother croon such a tune. The woman stopped singing, and then turned to face Sadatina.

"They are yours now," the woman said. "They belong to you."

Sadatina sat up, her blanket flying from her shivering body. The morning sun seeped into the house through the roof fronds, illuminating the cramped interior. Her dream told her what she must do. She had to find the cubs. She had to save them.

-3-

A week passed before Sadatina could do light chores, two weeks before she was strong enough to be useful. Mama complained that the village herbalist gave her bad herbs and threatened to return to the village for the goods they traded for them. Terte was grateful to see her up and about again. He was happy to get back to what he considered "men's" work, no matter what Mama chose to call it. Sadatina spent the entire time anxious, her head filled with all types of disasters that could have befallen the cubs. When she was well she worked relentlessly, trying to gain time for a chance to search the woods for them. But Mama had more than enough chores for her. She finally decided she had to take more direct steps.

Sadatina waited for her parents to come from their room. As soon as her mother stepped through the threshold she announced her intentions.

"I want to go hunting," she declared.

Mama swiped at her with her hand. "We have too much to do for you to go playing in the woods. Rainy season is coming and we need to plant."

"Baba is going to the village to hire bachelors for the planting," she answered. "We'll have plenty of help."

"You have to wait for him to return anyway," Mama said.

"I want to go hunting alone."

Mama looked at her as if a tembo sat on her head.

"What is wrong with you?"

Sadatina clinched her fists. "I just want to go."

Her father emerged from the room, ambling by her and Mama. "You can't go hunting alone. You know that," he muttered. "Finish your chores for the day, and then take Terte with you."

The tembo now sat on Baba's head.

"You're letting her go? With Terte?"

Baba sat at the table and rubbed his eyes. "They are not children. Besides, she killed a shumba. I think she deserves some space."

"I seem to remember three people involved in killing that thing," Mama argued.

Baba looked at Mama with an expression Sadatina was familiar with but had never seen directed to Mama. "She must be who she is."

The words came heavy from his mouth. Mama's shoulders slumped. She looked at Sadatina, the weight of Baba's words in her eyes.

"Finish your chores like your baba said and you can go," she said. Her voice was almost a whisper. "Be careful, Tina."

She touched Sadatina's face and fled from the room. Sadatina gazed into the room for a moment before she sat at the table with Baba. "What do you mean, be who I am?"

Baba looked into her eyes with apprehension and pride. "Your first mother was a special type of person. She was a woman who would prefer hunting to farm work. It seems the same trait runs in your blood as well." He stood and Sadatina stood with him. "You have always displayed a special skill. We should not stand in the way of who you are meant to be."

"So why does Mama try?"

Baba smiled. "Mama loves you as I do. She wants to protect you."

The shumba's dying countenance appeared in Sadatina's head. "Thank you, Baba." She didn't wait for a reply, but rushed from the house to begin her chores. She was breaking the ground for planting long before Terte arrived, pounding the tough dirt with her iron blade.

"What's wrong with you?" he said as he fell in beside her. Their work took on an unconscious rhythm.

"Good morning, frog face," she said.

Terte grinned. "Good morning, fish mouth. You really like to work, don't you?"

"I have other things to do," Sadatina commented.

"Like what, going into the village to get a man?"

Sadatina glared at Terte and he laughed.

"That's what Mama said. She said you needed to be stringing your beads instead of running around in the woods like a man."

Sadatina said nothing. The thought of finding a husband made her stomach churn.

"If it makes you feel better, I'd rather hunt than find a husband, too."

Sadatina swung at him with her hoe. Terte jumped away in mock anger.

"You should be in the village looking for a wife," Sadatina snapped.

"No need to," he replied. "I've made my choice."

Sadatina eyebrows rose as she ceased her work. This was news. "Have you? Who?" It did not matter what he told her, for she didn't know any women other than Mama. She was never very sociable when they visited the village; she actually didn't like it. Too many people, too much distraction.

"You wouldn't know her," Terte said. "Her family has a farm down the river. Baba and I visited a few time while hunting last season."

"He never took me there," Sadatina said.

"They don't have sons," Terte explained. "The only reason he took me was to meet her baba and to see her."

Sadatina blinked in relief. She wanted to avoid any courting and marriage arrangements as long as possible. She was not ready. Still, it would have been nice to know there were other people close by.

"Are there other families close to us?" she asked.

"There are farms all along the river," Terte said. "Most are closer than ours and some are in the hills. The folks in the hills raise cattle."

"And I knew nothing of them," Sadatina mused. She was not concerned with the other people. Her concern was that the others may have already discovered the cubs and killed them. She worked faster.

"I've never seen anyone so anxious to hunt. Slow down and I'll go with you."

"No!" she blurted.

Terte jumped, dropping his hoe in surprised. "Are you sure there's not a man waiting for you in the trees?" he chided.

"Shut up," she snapped.

They finished in early afternoon. Sadatina dropped her hoe in the fields and sprinted to the house. She brushed by Mama to get her hunting bow, spear and throwing knife.

"Are you sure you wish to go by yourself?" Mama's voice strained with concern.

"Yes, Mama." She placed her hand on Mama's shoulder. "I'll be fine. I'll be just across the river. Maybe I'll get a guinea or two for the stew pot tonight."

Mama smiled and patted her hand. "You be very careful."

"I will." She sprinted out the door and across the fields. She waved at Baba, stuck her tongue out at Terte and jumped into the cold river water. She waded across and disappeared into the foliage. The shumba's trail was long cold. She would have to try to think where a mother would hide her cubs. There were places she knew from childhood, but would a shumba use them as hiding places? Perhaps the cubs had been found and killed by a larger predator. A pang of guilt tightened her chest and gave gravitas to her efforts. She decided she would try her old hiding places first, and then expand her search later.

But first she had to hunt. She made her way to the top of the nearest hill, near a field that guineas frequented. Sadatina slowed her pace as she neared the field, crouching low as she took her hunting bow from across her back then nocked a blunt arrow from the quiver hanging from her waist. Guineas could fly but they preferred the ground. They only flew if they were threatened and only as a last resort. As she neared the forest edge, she heard the familiar chirping of a guinea flock. Their sound made her pause. The sharp chirping was a danger signal. Something was nearby. Could they have sensed her so soon?

A strange growl broke the silence and the guineas exploded into the air. Sadatina smiled as two shumba cubs tumbled into the clearing, leaping in vain at the fleeing guineas. Hunger had apparently spurred the cubs' hunting instincts. They were trying to fend for themselves but were obviously doing a poor job. They meandered where the guineas had been, sniffing the grass and occasionally mewing in frustration. Sadatina watched them with patience and sorrow. They were thin, their ribs visible through their skin. They were starving. If she tried to approach them they would run, so she decided she would wait and follow them to their lair. Once she knew where they took refuge she would hunt and bring them food.

The cubs plodded across the grass field. They began to play, swiping at each other's tails and engaging in a full romp. Sadatina was fascinated with how they frolicked despite their dire plight. Maybe they were too young to understand. Maybe they held onto the hope that their mother would return. Her thoughts were interrupted by a commotion to her right. She crouched lower, replacing a sharp arrow for the blunt one meant for small game. A forest hyena came slinking through the grass, its eyes on the frolicking cubs. Shumbas and hyenas were natural enemies, and neither would miss the opportunity to kill the other. Sadatina waited to see if there were other hyenas with this large beast, for hyenas were not known to often travel alone. Luckily this one seemed to be hunting solo.

She inched closer to the forest edge and the hyena stalked into the open, its eyes fixed on the cubs. They continued to play, unaware of the threat approaching them. Sadatina knew her arrow could not kill the beast, but if she could strike the hind legs she could slow it down. The predator was so focused on its enemy she was able to get closer to it than under normal circumstances. The hyena stopped, preparing to sprint and overtake the cubs. Sadatina raised her upper body, aimed and loosed the arrow. The arrow struck the hyena's hind leg and it howled. The cubs froze, looking in the direction of the beast. Sadatina quickly shot a second time, hitting the hyena in the foreleg. It fell to its side, thrashing in the grass and howling. Sadatina heard other hyenas answer in the distance. The cubs still stood frozen.

She jumped up and ran at the cubs, waving her arms. They looked at her and ran. Sadatina followed. Hopefully they would flee to their hiding place. She also did not want to be near when the other hyenas came to find their wounded comrade. A lone hyena would not attack a person, but a pack would have no such hesitation.

The cubs were quicker than she expected, but she soon caught up with them. They led her to a dense patch of shrubs where they crawled through and fell silent. Their instincts were good. Sadatina backed away and surveyed the area around her. She'd never been in this part of the forest, but it was easy for her to get her bearings. Now that she knew where the cubs hid, she could get about finding them food.

Her search did not last long. She came upon a group of monkeys feeding on fruit a few yards away from the cubs' lair. Two quick shots and two monkeys fell before the others fled. She set them down near the shrubs before retreating and hiding a distance away. Sadatina waited patiently; the cubs would have to emerge eventually. A cub poked its head out of the hiding place, its nose flaring as it sniffed the unexpected bounty. It darted out and grabbed one monkey carcass and dragged it into the lair. The other cub emerged more boldly, searching the area and striding about proudly before picking up the carcass in its mouth and crawling back into the lair.

Sadatina smiled. "The bold one, I see," she whispered.

No sooner had the words slipped from her lips did the cub

emerge again, its ears flattened on its head and snarling. It looked in her direction and mewed.

"The feisty one, too," Sadatina said. She stood, revealing herself to the shumba. It crouched and backed into the hiding place.

Sadatina eased away and resumed hunting. She tracked down the monkeys and felled two more to take home. She then worked her way back to the grass field. The hyenas were gone, including the wounded one, but the guineas had returned. She took down two with fortunate tosses of her throwing knife. It wasn't a great outing, but it was enough to show she'd actually spent some time hunting. The monkeys she gave to the cubs would have made it a good day. As she bagged the guineas she wondered how she would feed the cubs. They were definitely hunting on their own but their condition revealed they were not very good at it. She was sure that Mama would not let her go hunting every day despite Baba's intervention. An idea came to mind, one that made her laugh with its absurdity. She could teach them how to hunt.

"You're losing your mind," she said to herself.

Still, she thought on it as she made her way home. She would have to win their trust first, just like the young animals at the farm. But these were shumba cubs, not goats. Though they were young, they were also fierce, which the bold one clearly displayed. She thought on it a moment more and grinned. The young animals at the farm always came when they were fed. They were docile then, and they came to trust her and Mama as their own parents. She would have to feed the cubs but she would have to let them see her as well. Maybe then they would trust her and she could teach them to hunt.

She returned to the farm just before nightfall. Mama stood before the house, a torch in her hands. Sadatina sighed as she prepared for a stern scolding.

"Where have you been?" Mama said. "You were supposed to be back long ago!"

"I'm sorry, Mama," Sadatina replied. "The hunting

was hard today."

She held up her game bag with a smile. Mama took the bag from her and looked inside. A slight smile came to her face; it was gone when she looked at Sadatina again.

"It is almost too dark to clean all this. If you had been a moment later this would have been a waste. Don't take life so lightly. These creatures have given up their spirits for you. You must show more respect."

Mama grabbed her hand and led her to the smokehouse. They quickly cleaned her game under the waning light and began the smoking process. After washing in a nearby water gourd they strolled to the house.

"I worry for you, Tina," her mama blurted. "You are so different; I don't know how to treat you."

Mama's revelation stunned her.

"You treat me fine, Mama," she said.

"You don't understand. By now you should be preparing your dowry, yet you show no interest in marriage or children."

"Is that so strange?" Sadatina asked.

"Yes...I mean, no." Mama stopped walking. "When I was younger I knew many women who did not want to marry. A woman's work is hard, much harder than a man's. Taking care of a husband and a family consumes all of our time. I was lucky to have your father ask for me. Unlike many of my friends I actually liked him, and he works beyond his need."

"Am I like my other mother?" she asked.

Mama looked at her sadly. "In some ways."

"Please tell me about her," Sadatina asked.

Mama looked away. "There is not much to tell. We did not know her long. Only moments, actually. She was a strong woman and she was determined to..."

Mama stopped talking. Sadatina waited for her to continue, but she didn't. She knew better to ask her to continue so she bit her lip in frustration as they walked the rest of the way to the house in silence.

-4-

Mama shook Sadatina awake. She sat up, rubbing her eyes, her hands still sore from the late-night cleaning.

"Good morning, Mama," she croaked. She felt as if her head was in thick fog.

"Come eat your breakfast," Mama said. "We are going into the village today."

Mama's words quickly cleared Sadatina's head. "The village? Why?"

Mama frowned. "Do not ask why. Just get ready."

Sadatina trudged to the table with worry. A journey to the village would be an all-day affair, which meant she would have no time to hunt for the cubs. There was no way she could sneak away, so they would have to go hungry. Hopefully the monkeys she fed them the day before would sustain them; it was possible they would be luckier and bring down their own kill.

After she finished her meal she went to her bed to gather her things. Mama's hand caught her shoulder.

"Come with me," she said.

Mama led her into her room. Sadatina's eyes widened with foreboding. If Mama was allowing her into the parents' room, something serious was afoot. Her father sat on the bed, a mischievous smirk on his face. Mama looked and him and scowled.

"Get out," she snapped. "This is woman's time."

Baba left without protest. Mama reached behind the bed and dragged out a wooden storage box. She opened it, reached inside and revealed an outfit that sent a shudder through Sadatina.

"You will wear this today," Mama said.

"Mama, I am not ready!" Sadatina exclaimed.

"You are past ready," Mama snapped.

"But Mama!"

Mama pointed at the door. "Go, child! You're wasting time and trying my patience."

Sadatina slunk out of the room to her corner of the house and put on the beaded outfit. The short skirt barely covered her buttocks and the beaded top highlighted her breasts. She felt like a mating guinea, all bright and colorful. Her mother came to her.

"Stand up and let me see," she said. Sadatina stood. Mama smiled and her eyes glistened.

"You are so beautiful!"

Sadatina heard a giggle to her right. She turned and flashed a scowl at Terte.

"You look like a tigerfish!" he laughed.

"Be quiet, boy," Baba said.

Sadatina looked at Baba with pleading eyes. Baba's look was as stern as Mama's.

"Come help me load the wagon," Mama said.

Sadatina trudged behind Mama. Together they loaded the wagon with goods to trade. Sadatina checked to make sure the oxen were properly hitched before climbing in the back.

"We'll be back before dark," Mama said to Baba.

She snapped the reins and the oxen plodded forward. Sadatina watched as the farm and hills faded into the distance. They followed the winding road to the village and Sadatina pulled her arms tight around her. She did not visit the village often and was always aware of the stares she and her mother drew. Now, wearing her mother's courting beads, she was sure to draw even more attention. She looked at Mama angrily. If she noticed, she gave no indication.

They rode through the small farms surrounding the village. Most of the farmers worked their fields, planting seeds in anticipation of the upcoming rainy season. A few glanced up at them, but most remained focused on the job at hand. The village wall soon appeared on the horizon, a ragged rim of patchwork wood mounted on thick columns of ironwood. It was a remnant of a time when the nondescript village was an important outpost of Wangara. The geseres said there was a time when their land was at war with the people who once lived on this land, a people called the Mosele. The Wangarans were invaders, led to this land from the country over the mountains by their god's divine decree. Cha willed the land to them and they followed his word. Sadatina had always felt sorry for those who once lived where their wagon now tracked. What had their god told them? It was no surprise to her the Mosele fought so hard against the Wangarans. It was also said that the old warriors drove these people into the desert. If that was so, it was a cruel way to die. She wondered sometimes what those people had done to deserve such a fate. She wondered if anyone deserved such a fate. But she would not say such things aloud. Cha was good. Whatever Cha decreed was done ultimately for good. But still, she wondered.

Sadatina was so distracted by her musing and worry that she didn't notice when they entered the village.

"I'm going to the storehouse to sell our grain," Mama said. "I need you to go to the market for bowls and beads."

"You want me to go by myself?" she exclaimed.

"Of course," Mama answered. "You're a woman, Tina. Besides, no bachelor will look at you when you're with your mama."

The village storehouse stood just beyond the gates. Mama steered the oxen to the cylindrical thatch-roofed building. Three narrow towers rose above the main building, crowned by ironwood roofs. Three men emerged from the main building, an old man wrapped in the plain robes of an elder and two dusty, younger bare-chested men. Their eyes immediately fell on Sadatina and they both smiled in unison. Sadatina looked away, embarrassed by their immediate attention.

The older man glanced at her and greeted Mama with a grin.

"Kiden!" he said. "Do you bring me good grain?"

"Always," Mama replied. "What do you have for me?"

"Come, I will show you," the man gestured.

Mama stepped off the wagon and Sadatina followed. The young men's eyes widened when she stood and Sadatina felt like shrinking away.

"Well, well, Sadatina," the mill owner said. "Cha has blessed you!"

Mama frowned. "Youth is for the young," she snapped. "Let us get on with our business. Sadatina?"

She tiptoed to her mother side. She was normally not so demure but the sudden attention shook her confidence. "Yes, Mama?"

Mama handed her a small bag of cowries. "Bowls and beads. If the kola nuts look good get a few of those for the ride back home. Take your time."

"Yes, Mama." Sadatina took the cowries and headed to the market. She tried to keep her eyes focused on her destination but they kept darting side to side on their own. She was drawing much attention, more from the men than the women. The more looks she drew, the more her feelings changed from shyness to anger. Everyone seemed to be judging her, assessing her worth like a bag of yams. They knew nothing about her. She was more than a bead dress and a body. She made up her mind that if anyone came to her and mentioned how she looked, she would punch them like she punched Terte. The thought brought a smile to her face. By the time she reached the market she strode confidently, her head raised and her fists clenched.

She was not displaying herself as Mama wished. She cut through the crowd and went directly to the first bowl stand she found. The woman standing beside the stand was a stout lady with a smile as bright as her dress. Her bracelets jangled as she raised her hands to Sadatina as if she was a long-lost relative.

"Ah, lovely daughter! You have come to share your cowries with me?"

Sadatina did not miss the woman's comment on her looks, but she was too polite to punch. Instead she settled into bargaining mode.

"I doubt it," she said. "I have broken bowls better than these."

The woman's smile remained but her eyes narrowed. The game was on. "Then your bowls must have been fashioned by Cha's angels themselves. No mortal hands craft bowls better than Gakee." She touched her ample breasts with her hands.

"No one in this village, perhaps," Sadatina said. She browsed the bowls unemotionally. They were excellent bowls, much better than the ones she and Mama made from the nearby river clay. Not only were they well shaped, the colors and patterns were lively, just like Gakee's dress. She picked up a larger bowl and was surprised by its lightness.

"This thing would break if I coughed," Sadatina commented.

Gakee took the bowl from her hand and dropped it. Sadatina skipped back, expecting it to shatter. The bowl hit the hard-packed ground and bounced several times before spinning still. Sadatina fought hard to hide her surprise.

"This is not river clay," Gakee said. "My family holds the secret of bowl making from long ago. This is knowledge from beyond the mountains. I shouldn't be wasting my time here. It would be better if I took a wagon to Wangara and sold them all to Baba Sekou."

Sadatina picked up the bowl. "I'll pay three cowries per bowl. One for this one. It's damaged."

Gakee laughed. "I should charge you three cowries for looking at them as long as you have. Eight cowries a bowl and six for the one you hold."

"I would buy you a dozen bowls!"

Sadatina saw Gakee's frown before she turned to the source of the gruff voice behind her. The man she set eyes on was much older than her but not as old as Baba. He was shirtless, his hair matted against his head. A damp net hung over his left shoulder; in his right hand he held a bag of fish. Sadatina knew now why Gakee frowned. He was a river man.

"I have my own money," Sadatina said.

"But I would have to buy the bowls for your loloba," the river man said.

"Keep your insults, river man!" Gakee exclaimed.

"I don't believe I was talking to you, bowl woman," the river man retorted. He reached into his damp pants pocket and extracted a handful of river pearls.

"Jewels for a queen, which you would be if you marry me," he said. "I am Kasamba."

"Enough, river man."

Three tall men approached each holding stabbing spears and war clubs, leopard skins covering their chests. Their eyes raised slightly when they fell on Sadatina, then narrowed as they settled on Kasamba. The men were older, excepted for one man in the rear holding the weapons of the others. He looked to be her age, his smooth black face and bright eyes revealing his youth. His eyes lingered longer on her as a slight smile came to his face. She did not mind his attention.

"Time for you to leave," the tallest man said. "You have what you need, now go."

"I don't have everything," he said as he leered at Sadatina.

"You have all that you will get," she said.

Kasamba frowned. "Another time."

One of the leopard men placed his hand on Kasamba's shoulder and he shrugged it away. The river man stomped into the crowd.

"Thank you," Sadatina said to the men.

"You are to blame," the man said.

"I did nothing!"

The man looked Sadatina up and down. "Do you see anyone else dressed like you? This is not the season for such clothing, especially when river men are about."

Sadatina's embarrassment reached full crescendo.

"I...I did not know. Mama told me to wear this."

The man smiled. "Your mama should know better. Is she anxious to marry you off?"

"She underestimates you," the younger man offered. "You need no embellishments."

"Be quiet, Teshome!" the elder man barked.

Words that would have angered her coming from the river man felt flattering coming from this Teshome. She smiled.

"Thank you. I will go to my mother now. I will cause no more trouble."

"Wait!" Gakee handed her the bowls.

"Here. Your prices are good." Sadatina took the bowls and gave Gakee the cowries. She bowed to the leopard men and scurried to the mill, glancing over her shoulder at Teshome. With her extra cowries, she stopped and bought a bag of kola nuts.

Mama and the mill workers were loading the wagon when she reached the mill. Mama looked up, her face serious. "Did you get the bowls?" she asked.

Sadatina held up the bag. Mama took the bag and took out a bowl, inspecting it closely.

"This is a very good bowl! How much did you pay for them?"

"Nine cowries," Sadatina answered.

Mama's eyes went wide. "Only nine? I should bring you to market more often."

Sadatina decided she would not tell mother of the incident with the river man and how it affected her price.

They climbed into the wagon and set out for home.

"So did you meet anyone?" Mama asked.

"I met a river man," Sadatina replied. "He asked me to marry him."

Mama eyes went wide. "You're lying!"

Sadatina cut her eyes at Mama. "No, I'm not. A river man came to me and offered to buy me bowls and give me a handful of river pearls to marry him."

"Why didn't you come to me?" Mama fussed.

"You dressed me in this," Sadatina said, shaking her beaded skirt. "It's not even market season. I look like a fool."

"You look like a beautiful woman." Mama handed her a kola nut. "Besides, who notices one flower when all the others are in bloom?"

Mama's compliment dulled her anger. "I was embarrassed."

"Don't be. Those village folk think they know everything. It's a village, not Wangara. Now the young men know you. Come market season they will remember you first."

Sadatina was not in full agreement with Mama's scheming. There was one face she would remember come market season: the weapons bearer Teshome.

They traveled a good distance before stopping by an open field to let the oxen rest. Mama busied herself about the wagon while Sadatina lounged in the grass enjoying the bitter stimulation of her kola nut. Her mind drifted to the shumba cubs. It had been hours since she fed them last, but not long enough for them to starve in her absence. Most of all, she hoped they had not forgotten her.

Sadatina's attention drifted to the road behind them. Someone was coming, moving at a running pace. She sat up and strained her eyes. What she saw chilled her blood.

She jumped to her feet and ran to the wagon.

"Mama! River men!"

Mama looked up, her face twisted with dread. She jumped into the wagon at the same time as Sadatina and cracked her whip at the oxen.

"Run!" she shouted at them.

Sadatina scrambled among the grain and found her bow and arrows and Mama's muder. She turned to face the road. The river men were coming fast, much faster than the oxen could run. She looked back at Mama working the reins and the whip and made her decision. She grabbed the weapons, took a deep breath and leaped from the wagon. Her feet hit the dirt and she tumbled, rolling the way Baba taught her long ago. She came to her feet and trotted toward the men.

She recognized the man from the market immediately and a fearful chill ran through her body. He had come for her despite her refusal. The men flanking him stared at her coldly and she began to realize she'd made a grave mistake.

"See?" the man said to his cohorts. "She comes to greet her new husband!"

Something in his tone pierced her fear and transformed it to intense anger. She raised the bow and aimed. It was a small bow only meant for hunting, but a well-placed shot could kill the most formidable of beasts, and Sadatina was a very good shot.

The river man was still laughing when her arrow found his throat. It took him a moment to realize what had happened. He clutched the arrow and fell to his knees, blood running from the wound and his mouth. His cohorts ignored his gurgling, springing toward her like dogs released from their chains. Sadatina only had time to let loose one more arrow before the men were upon her with nets and knives. She swung at them with her muder, careful not to get it tangled in their nets. The hungry smiles on their faces faded as they realized she would be no easy catch. They stepped away and circled her, one man waving his net, the other holding a knife in each hand. Sadatina turned with them, her hands sweating against the warm iron of the muder. She had no idea what to do. She'd practiced with Baba and Terte, but never had she hit them with the sharp edge. But never had she shot a man with her bow either. She looked at the river man writhing on the ground and felt sad for him despite his intentions. She did not wish death on anyone, but it seemed death was the only way to keep these men from claiming her.

The man with the net moved in. He feinted at her head then swung the net at her ankles. Sadatina almost jumped over it, but the wet cords wrapped about her left foot.

"Ha!" the man exclaimed. He yanked the net toward himself and Sadatina crashed onto her back. Her grip loosened on the muder but she did not lose it. The knife man appeared above her and she jabbed. His face crunched and blood burst from his mouth and nose. He cried as he clamped his hands over his wound and stumbled away. The net man kept pulling at her but wouldn't come close. He watched the muder intensely as he scowled. He raised a trident, a wicked weapon with a three-pronged tip. If he had any intentions of claiming her as a wife, he had apparently forgotten them. He pulled at the net and jabbed at her with the trident. Sadatina winced as the tip scraped her neck, barely deflected by the wavering muder. She twisted and turned as she dodged the spear. Tears welled in her eyes; she was getting tired but the river man seemed relentless. His strikes drew more blood; she bled from her shoulders and the side of her head.

"Sadatina!"

Mama's wail ripped through the deadly silence of her struggle. She turned to her right to see Mama charging toward the river man on the back of one of the oxen, flailing her whip against the bovine's flanks and forcing it to run faster than it probably ever had. The river man was quick, but his instincts were flawed. He twisted about and threw his trident. The spear bounced harmlessly off the ox's horns as the river man crumbled under hooves and ox flesh. Sadatina watched Mama tumble off the ox then lay back on the ground. She dropped her muder and threw her arms open. Her breath came heavy, her chest heaving as her wounds began to sting. By the time Mama reached her side she labored for breath.

"Sadatina? Sadatina!"

Sadatina could not speak. Her throat felt like it was packed with cotton. The fire from her wounds had spread throughout her body; sweat ran from every pore. She barely felt something being shoved in her mouth and her mouth worked by familiar hands. Moments later the burning subsided although she still felt terribly weak. She drifted in and out of consciousness, her body vacillating between hot and cold. She remembered throwing up at least twice, once a food-filled spewing and again a painful dry heave. Then she rested, her mind wrapped in a fog of peace, while voices whispered from what seemed far away. She strained to hear them but the fog muffled the words. She knew it was Baba and Mama, but she could make out nothing they said. She gave up and released herself to the fatigue reaching out to her.

-5-

When Sadatina awoke, Baba sat beside her, his rough hands holding hers. He smiled as she looked into his eyes, but there was something different in the way he looked at her, something interesting yet disturbing.

"You have come back to us," he said.

"Where did I go?" she replied in a raspy voice.

"Only the ancestors know." He handed her a bowl of liquid. "Your mother said you should drink this as soon as you woke. It will strengthen you."

Sadatina took the bowl to her dry lips and sipped. It was guinea broth, but there was something in it that gave the otherwise soothing solution a sharp bite. Whatever it was, it served its purpose. She immediately felt better. She tried to sit up but Baba gently forced her back down. "She said you would try to rise. The broth makes you feel stronger than you are. You still need lots of rest before you are truly healed."

"Am I so weak that the prick of a river man's trident would wound me so?" she fussed.

"It was not the trident's bite that wounded you, it was its sting," Baba explained. "River men are known for their poisons. It is how they catch big fish in those poor nets they carry."

"Still, I was almost killed by a poison meant for a fish."

Baba's eyes took on that strange look again. "No, Sadatina, you don't understand. The river men's poisons are the most potent. It is their specialty. It is amazing that you are still alive."

Sadatina closed her eyes as she absorbed Baba's words. So

the look in his eyes was admiration? She opened her eyes again and saw something different in his eyes. She finally realized what it was: respect.

"Where is Mama?" she asked.

"She and Terte are planting. The rains are near and the seeds must be sown."

Sadatina managed to laugh. "Terte probably hates me."

Baba smiled. "Terte will do as he's told."

Sadatina's humor faded as the incident with the river men emerged in her mind. "Baba, have you ever killed a man?"

Baba's head sagged with her words. He sighed as he took her hand in his. "Yes. It is a terrible thing."

A wave of guilt washed over her. "I shouldn't have killed them."

"You had no choice," Baba answered, his voice stern. "If you hadn't, your mother would be dead and you would be just as good as dead. The river men work their women like slaves. If there is anyone who should feel guilt it's me. I should not have let you go into the village alone."

Sadatina squeezed Baba's hand. "You were there in me. You taught me to wrestle."

"I wish I could take credit," Baba said. "You did things that no one should be able to do. It is because of your mother's blood that you live."

Her mother. The mysterious woman who left her with Mama and Baba was now responsible for her skill and strength.

"Tell me about her," Sadatina asked.

Baba rubbed his chin. "There's not much to tell. We did not know her. She brought you here and she was gone. We have not seen her since."

"You must know something!" Sadatina's desperation showed in her voice.

"I know something of her kind," Baba admitted.

This was something new. "Her kind?"

Baba's eyes darted about and he shifted on his stool. He

looked at her and opened his mouth, then closed it and looked away.

"Baba, please tell me," she said, squeezing his hand.

"I will tell you what I've heard, nothing more," he finally said. "I cannot say if it is true because it is village talk, and most villagers don't distinguish truth from fable. They say that Wangara is still at war, but it is a war of a different kind. We do not fight the men who lived here before us. We fight the minions of their god, nyokas who strength goes beyond that of normal men. The only warriors who can stand up to them are warriors specially trained by Baba Sekou himself and imbued with the spiritual strength of Cha. Only they can confront the nyokas and win. They are called Shosa."

"And my mama was a Shosa?"

"I believe so."

"So if she was a nyoka killer, why would she abandon me?"

"She had no choice," Baba said. "Of this I am certain."

"Why are you so certain of her reasons when you are not certain of whom she was?"

"Because she told us. The Shosa are not allowed to be married nor have children. If they do bear a child, that child is killed and the mother punished. I do not think she cared if she was punished. She cared about you."

"How could she care for me yet abandon me?"

Baba smiled and patted her hand. "She cared about you so much she brought you to us."

Sadatina's hand trembled. She felt weak. "Do you and Mama love me as much as you love Terte?"

"Of course we do. You are our child."

Sadatina smiled at the truth in Baba's words and expression. She could not worry herself on the feelings of a woman whom she had never met. She could only be certain of what was before her, which was a family who loved her. That was more than enough.

After a few more days of rest she was able to walk about

the farm. She did what she could, tending the goats and walking with the cattle to pasture and back. Baba left the farm after a week and returned with a wagon filled with bachelors from the village to help with planting. Despite everyone's hard work there was still planting to be done and the rainy season was fast approaching. He paid in gold dust, which was eagerly sought not because of its value, but because it was the preferred means of payment to those who sold cattle.

She watched from the house as they unloaded and then caught her breath when she recognized the weapons bearer of the Leopard Men, the man they called Teshome. The other men followed Baba immediately to the fields for their seed bags. Teshome hesitated, glancing about the farm with a serious face. Sadatina backed away from the door. Was he looking for her? Had he come to court? She felt a different weakness this time, one that seemed to please her as much as it worried her. Mama's plan had apparently succeeded. Sadatina had a suitor.

Baba looked back at Teshome and he followed the others to the field. Sadatina waited until he was full involved in the planting before she joined her mother at the stables.

"Your father is back with the bachelors," Mama commented.

"I saw them," Sadatina replied.

"A few of them are your age."

"I know, Mama."

"Today is a hot day. They will need water soon."

"I wish to go hunting," Sadatina said.

"There's no need to," Mama replied. "We have plenty of food."

"Maybe for us, but not the bachelors," Sadatina said. "We should reward them for coming so far to help us."

Mama smirked. "They need no reward. They're getting paid good gold to plant. Your father is too generous with his pay. They'll have their loloba before the end of the week."

"We should be generous," Sadatina insisted.

"Then take them water when they need it," Mama said. "You can go hunting later."

Sadatina paced until her father called out for water. She trudged to the river and filled the water gourds, then met at the edge of the field.

"Thank you, Sadatina." He noticed the quiver on her back. "Going hunting?"

"Mama said I could go."

Baba nodded. "You should spend more time hunting. You're good and it adds variety to our meals. It is probably good for you, too."

Baba's last statement seemed strange, but before she could ask for an explanation she saw Teshome hurrying over to them, an eager smile on his face.

"I must go, Baba," she said. "It will be dark soon."

She trotted to the river and waded across. She didn't look back until she was hidden by the trees. Teshome stood by her father drinking from his guard and looking in her direction as if he could see her although she knew he couldn't. She hoped the planting would go quickly; otherwise Teshome was going to be a problem.

She pushed such thoughts from her mind. The shumbas were her concern now. It had been weeks since she saw them and their fate had gnawed at her conscience every day. She quickly made her way to their makeshift den. The sight of it struck her with foreboding. There were no signs they had hunted, but at least there was no sign they'd been found. She edged closer and heard a weak growl emit from the tangled bushes. A cub appeared, its face fierce despite its obvious weakness. It was probably the same one that challenged her before.

"Be patient, brave one," she whispered. "Food is on the way."

She hunted with a sense of urgency, quickly downing two monkeys and a small bush deer. She detoured to the river to fill her water gourd and returned to the cubs. She placed the game and water before the bush, but this time she did not leave. She stood in full view. The brave cub emerged first, growling and posturing as before, but this time the other cub emerged. It pushed by its sibling and bit into the bush deer. The other cub forgot its fierceness and joined in. Sadatina watched them until they were done. They took turns lapping water from the gourd until it was empty. The quiet cub looked at her, yawned and slipped back into the bushes. The brave cub took its stance and growled, its voice much stronger. Sadatina edged closer, pushing the rest of the game toward the cub.

"Don't be greedy," she said. "I don't know when I'll be back."

Sadatina slipped back into the woods. She brought down another bush deer and monkey and bagged them for the trip home. The sun was descending into the western horizon by the time she reached the farm; the bachelors were gone. She went to the smokehouse and cleaned her kill, then hung it inside. Mama was waiting when she entered the house.

"You've been gone a long time," she said.

"Hunting was tough," Sadatina replied. "I brought a bush deer and a monkey back. I put them in the smoke house."

"I could have used your help. The bachelors did a fair job in the fields but there was much to do in the house."

"I'm sorry, Mama."

"No hunting tomorrow. You will help with the planting tomorrow."

Sadatina's eyes went wide. "But the bachelors can do that!"

Mama grinned. "Exactly."

Sadatina was trapped. "I won't wear that beaded thing."

Mama walked away. "I won't ask you to."

Sadatina tossed and turned all night on her cot. The shumbas should be content for at least two days. She'd left them enough food to sustain them, unless a jackal or hyena caught the scent and stole it from them. The thought made her sit up with worry. In her haste to help them she might have exposed them to more danger. She would have to figure out a way to see them tomorrow despite her mother's orders. Her biggest worry was the planting. Mama was putting her on display again, but this time her actions were more direct. Baba wouldn't protest; he would see nothing wrong with her working the fields. She lay back on her cot, her eyes wide. It wasn't the fact that she would be working with them; she was nervous that she would be so close to Teshome. There was no doubt he would work his way toward her. What would she do if he spoke to her? What would she say to him? Should she say anything to him? She knew nothing about such things. Her stomach growled with nervousness and she wrapped her arms around it. She decided she did not want to court, let alone marry. She would defy Mama and run off into the woods. She would be punished, but she didn't care. She was not ready to be a wife.

Sadatina's night-time bravado left her with the morning light. She ate breakfast slowly with her family, Mama watching her with narrowed eyes, Baba looking at Mama curiously, and Terte oblivious to the tension around him.

"So, Tina, which one of the bachelors will you marry?" Terte asked.

Sadatina threw her bowl at Terte and he laughed as he dodged it. Terte's humor fled quickly when Baba smacked the side of his head.

"Clean up that mess!" he shouted.

"But she threw it!"

"Do as your baba says," Mama ordered.

Terte scowled as he left his seat to clean up Sadatina's breakfast.

Mama turned to Sadatina. "You come with me. Breakfast is over."

Sadatina followed Mama out of the house to the pen to feed the goats. The bachelors were already in the fields. This was their last day of planting. The clouds were more frequent now, with more overcast days than clear. The rainy season would begin soon and they wanted to be done in time to receive good pay. Sadatina glanced at them, searching the sleepy faces for Teshome. Then she saw him. He rubbed his eyes and looked immediately at her. Sadatina jerked her head away and concentrated on her duties.

Sunlight was full upon them when she and Mama joined the others in the planting fields. They worked side by side, a synchronized tandem used to the repetitive work. Sadatina lost herself in the routine, her mind wandering to the cubs.

"Hello."

Sadatina look up to see Teshome standing beside her. Mama had worked away, placing herself among the other bachelors. Teshome's smile calmed her nervousness.

"Hello," she answered.

"I am Teshome."

Sadatina looked away. "I know."

"You do?" There was joy in his voice and Sadatina's nervousness increased.

"I remember you from the village. You are the weapons bearer for the Leopard Men."

"Not anymore," Teshome answered.

Sadatina looked at him in surprised. "Why not?"

"They did not think I listened very well," Teshome said. "The truth is that they are not very good fighters. They didn't like it when I beat them."

"My brother doesn't like it when I beat him."

It was Teshome's turn to be surprised. "You wrestle?"

Sadatina nodded. "Baba taught us both. We can't depend on Leopard Men out here."

Teshome stopped planting. "Show me."

Sadatina kept planting. "Don't be silly."

"No, show me. I've never met a girl who could wrestle."

"I cannot wrestle you," Sadatina insisted.

"It won't be a real match," Teshome explained. "I would like to see what your baba has taught you."

"Then talk to my brother," Sadatina said. "He taught him the same things. It would be more appropriate."

Teshome grinned but didn't answer. They worked the rest of the day side by side in silence, falling into a smooth rhythm. One of the men chanted and the others fell in. It was apparently a working song that Sadatina did not know, but it was easy to learn and she soon sang along. Before she knew it they were done. The field was planted. By the end of rainy season the barren patch of land would undulate with sorghum.

The workers trudged to the house for their pay. Sadatina trudged as well. It was a fruitful day but a hard one, and she couldn't wait to get to the house for water, food and rest. She wanted to steal away to check on the cubs but she was simply too tired.

She saw the arm appear over her right shoulder and reacted instinctively, raising her right arm to block it and twisting simultaneously as she thrust her elbow behind her. She heard a grunt as her bone met flesh. She spun, thrusting out with both hands. They smacked into Teshome's bare chest and he fell onto his back. "What is wrong with you?" she shouted.

Teshome rolled backwards onto his feet and came at her again with blows and kicks. He was faster than Terte but not as fast as Baba. She dodged and deflected his strikes, getting angrier with each move. Finally she yelled and snapped out a vicious kick to Teshome's stomach that doubled him over. Before he could wince she swept his feet and he collapsed onto his side. Sadatina kicked him onto his stomach, sat hard on his back and pulled up his upper body as she wrapped him into an air-robbing choke hold.

"Do you think I can wrestle now?" she hissed.

Teshome patted the ground. Sadatina let him go with a shove. When she looked up, Baba and the others were running toward them. By the time they reached them Teshome was sitting, massaging his neck and grinning.

Baba ran to the young man. "Are you hurt?" he asked.

"No, I am fine."

Baba nodded and looked at Sadatina. His scolding stare demanded an explanation.

"It was his fault!" she blurted.

Teshome stood. "It was, uncle. She told me she could wrestle and I didn't believe her. Now I do."

"I don't," one of the bachelors said. The others laughed at his implied meaning. Teshome walked to them, and then waved his hand toward her.

"Let's see how you fare," he challenged.

"Enough of this," Baba said. "Everyone back to the house." He gave her a sideways glance before turning his back and heading to the house. The bachelors followed, laughing and talking under their breath.

Teshome remained, his smile even wider than before his unexpected trouncing. "Goodbye, Sadatina. It was very good meeting you. I hope you will come to the harvest festival next season."

Sadatina was surprised by his words. "I…I may be there."

Teshome nodded, turned to walk away, and then hesitated. "I hope you wear your beaded dress as well."

Sadatina could not answer, nor could she move. A knot of emotions held her in place and took her breath. She didn't notice Mama's approach until she was beside her.

"Well, that's not the way I envisioned it, but it is good anyway."

Sadatina slowly turned her head to her mother. "What do you mean?"

Mama grinned. "When you go to the festival next season, I believe someone will have loloba waiting for your baba."

Sadatina turned away from Mama to hide her smile. She hoped he would.

-6-

Rain finally claimed its season, spreading its life giving-substance over the hills across the river and the planted fields surrounding the farm. Sadatina sat on the small porch of their home, watching sheets of precipitation roll over the hilltops and into their shallow valley. The thin rain clouds came in smoky waves, sometimes releasing heavy torrents, other times spreading an annoying drizzle. There were even moments of respite, but they were few and lasted moments. This was the heavy rainy season, a time of constant wetness and occasional floods. The fields closest to the river had been left fallow for such a reason. The floods were damaging but they left the fertile silt that would make those same fields crowd with sorghum and yams the next planting season.

Sadatina's mind drifted beyond the stables and fields to the dense forested hills barely visible through the liquid haze. The cubs probably crowded in their lair, protecting themselves from the downpour. She wondered if they hated the rain as much as she did. She spent most of the time confined to the house except when tending to the animals or repairing the roof for leaks. She still hunted, but tracking was difficult with the constant rain washing away sign. Mama, Baba, and even Terte wondered why she continued despite the difficulty, even though they had plenty grain and meat from their goats. She always said it was because of her love of bush deer, but she could tell her explanation was not convincing. Baba's suspicions showed in his eyes; Mama's was more vocal.

"You should pay more attention to what I do rather than run into the woods whenever you can," she argued. "The harvest festival is not as far away as you think."

Sadatina pounded the sorghum kernels with constant persistence.

"Teshome did not ask me to marry him," she replied. "He just said he would like to see me."

"This is not just about Teshome," Mama said. "When one man shows interest, other men do. Why a man would want a woman who would wrestle him I do not understand, but if one man does, others will. When you go to the festival the word will have spread. There will be other men just as interested. Some of them may make better husbands than Teshome."

Sadatina stopped pounding. She never imagined that other men would be interested in her. "Other men?"

Mama sucked her teeth. "Of course! You are a beautiful woman, Sadatina. You would know if you didn't spend so much time in those woods. Why do you think Teshome came to the farm? He saw you in that bead dress. Which reminds me; we need to make you a new dress. You will need something more noticeable for the festival. You will not be the only flower blooming in the field."

"I'm not interested in anyone else," she said. She immediately regretted her words. She wasn't sure if she was interested in Teshome. She liked him, but did she really want to marry him?

"Don't set your sights on that boy," Mama warned. "He is a handsome man, but beauty doesn't fill bellies. You want to marry a man like your baba."

"There is no man like Baba," Sadatina said. Of that she was certain.

Mama nodded. "That's true, but you must try to find someone as close to him as you can. Your baba will teach him the rest, as my baba taught yours."

"So Baba wasn't always like this?"

"Of course not," Mama said. "He was a village boy like Teshome, all pompous and knowing. My baba had to be very patient with him. He did so for my sake."

They talked and worked throughout the day, the rain playing a soothing drone behind their banter. By the time they were done the sun had set. Sadatina felt guilty that she had not had a chance to feed the cubs, but she was thankful for the time with Mama. They spoke as women, and it felt good that Mama was beginning to see her as such. Still, she was nervous of what lay ahead for she knew she was not like other women. Whatever man entered her life would have to be very special.

She woke the next day determined to go into the woods. The weather was conducive to her desire. Though it still rained, the downpour had momentarily reduced to a drizzle. She dressed quickly and grabbed two pieces of hard bread Mama had managed to bake the day before. She was exiting the door when Mama called out to her.

"You're going hunting?"

"Leave her be," Baba answered. "It's her way."

"I don't care if it's her way or not. We have things to do."

"Terte will help you."

"No, I won't!" Terte shouted.

"Yes, you will," Baba shouted back.

"I hate you, Tina!" Terte yelled.

Sadatina splashed across the muddy field toward the river, careful to avoid the sprouting sorghum. She reached the river and followed the swollen waterway to its shallowest point. The cool water penetrating her leather garments gave her a brief chill as she waded across. She smiled as she stepped onto the opposite bank. No sooner had she entered the woods was she greeted with a familiar growl. The cubs emerged from the wet foliage and loped to her. She knelt to tussle with them. The bold one nudged her with her snout as the timid one brushed against her side. They were bigger now, much bigger, almost full grown shumbas. They were hunting much better as well. Sadatina suspected they no longer needed her nurturing, but they were bonded now. They were a sisterhood.

After a few more moments of socializing, they hunted.

The bold one took the lead now, disappearing quickly into the bush. The timid one stayed close to Sadatina, her nose close to the ground at times and lifted into the air at others. Sadatina did not possess their sensitive sense of smell, but her eyesight and hearing made up for the shortcoming. Still, hunting in the rain was more of a challenge. Scents were muted, movement blurred by the motion of rain-pelted fauna. Prey tended to stay still during such weather, making them harder to detect. But hunger knows no respite.

A strange growl came from up ahead. Sadatina knew it came from the bold one, but it was a sound she'd never heard emitted from her sister. The timid one knew, for she immediately sprinted ahead. Sadatina followed as fast as she could. When she reached them they circled around a patch of ground, their movements agitated and uncertain. Sadatina approached the area and stood over it. It was sign, an obvious print but one she'd never seen before. She knelt to get a closer look. It was a paw print of some kind, but not of any animal she knew of in these woods. Baba told her of animals that migrated during the seasons. He told her of the gnus, thick-bodied beasts that came in the thousands, migrating through their country with the rains. She had never seen such a sight; the migrations no longer passed through their valley since the village had grown in size to block the path of the living river. But the animals Baba described to her were four-legged beasts. Whatever made these prints was two-legged like a man.

Sadatina continued to study the odd footprints. Another creature came to mind. The old men of the forest once called these hills home, but this too was before her time. Baba said they resembled men but were much more powerful and wiser. They kept to themselves and were mostly gentle unless threatened. Some said if you were patient they would reward you with words of wisdom or a bit of nyama. But they were gone now, some said to the hills beyond the mountains.

Sadatina searched about for more prints but found none. She decided not to waste any more time with this mystery. She had to return home soon, and to return empty-handed would raise suspicions. She coaxed her sisters away from the strange sign and they continued their hunt.

A few moments later they all stopped in their tracks. Her sisters raised their heads, nostrils flaring and ears rigid. Sadatina's senses were attuned to different signs. She saw the bushes ahead shifting slowly and heard the familiar grunting of a bush hog. This would be a grand prize, for bush hogs were intelligent and belligerent, difficult to catch unawares and to come this close to one and not be detected was a rarity. Sadatina surmised that the rain worked in their favor.

The bold shumba's ears flattened on her head as she stalked away to the right. The timid one sauntered to the left. Sadatina continued to move ahead. It was the pattern of their hunting, a ritual that developed naturally to exploit their strengths and weaknesses. She ignored her bow in favor of her spear because of the close proximity of the hog. She didn't like approaching a bush hog so closely; they were ferocious when cornered and their tusks could kill quickly. It was unlikely it would be her role to kill it though. The hog would hear her before the others. It would flee either right or left, which would drive it into the fangs of either of her sisters. If it ran directly away from them, there would be a race that the hog would win due to the dense forest and its short stature.

A sharp grunt stopped her advance. The hog grunted again and squealed. The bushes about it exploded with activity and the hog ran directly toward her. Sadatina barely had time to position herself before the bush hog was upon her. It seemed just as surprised as she when it appeared, its wart-filled face and sharp tusks covered with mud. Sadatina took advantage of the confusion, darting to the right and plunging her spear into the hog's side, piercing its lung and heart. The hog collapsed where it stood, letting loose a shrill squeal as it died. Sadatina let go of her spear; the hog collapsed onto its side onto the wet foliage.

Sadatina took out her knife, looking left and right as she approached the bush hog. She expected to see her sisters any moment to join with the kill. This was usually the difficult part. Her sisters would be eager to feast, but she would have to keep them away until she was able to get a portion for herself and her family. She knelt by the hog, looking again for her sisters but they still did not approach. Something was wrong.

Sadatina pulled her spear from the hog and crouched low. She closed her eyes, concentrating on the sounds around her. Her sisters were close by; she could hear their breathing over the patter of drizzling rain. She also heard something else. There was another creature near them. It panted a quick steady breath like a drum. She slowly realized that it was not her or her sisters that startled the hog and sent it fleeing in her direction.

But the creature did not pursue its prey, nor did it challenge her for the prize. It sat still, breathing and watching. She heard the bold one growl and move toward the breathing. Still the creature did not move. The timid one moved toward it as well, the only indication the slight rustle of the vegetation to her right. The creature remained still. An ominous thought entered her head. This creature was not hunting the bush hog. It was hunting them.

Sadatina joined her sisters and crept forward, her spear gripped tight in her hands. Finally there was movement. The creature shifted, disturbing the bush only a few yards in front of her. The bold one lost its patience. She let out a roar and charged, quickly joined by her silent sister. Sadatina stayed motionless, spear at the ready. The creature responded, letting out a cry that stunned her in its pitch. It leaped into the air and Sadatina caught a glimpse of it. At first glance she thought it was a large monkey, for its body resembled that of one. But then she saw the gray fur and the head that reminded her of the wild dogs of the grasslands beyond the hills. It landed on the ground and fled, running faster than any creature she'd encountered. Her sisters pursued it briefly, and then turned away. They had chased away a challenge to their kill and they were satisfied. When they finally appeared Sadatina still stood in place. She had no idea what she had witnessed.

Her sisters returned to her and sniffed their conquest.

Sadatina continued to stare where the creature had been, her heart racing. She tried to dismiss the encounter as some odd distraction but an strange feeling would not let her. She left the hog to her sisters, walking slowly to where the beast had been. She found its prints, identical to the print they discovered weeks ago. She continued to walk until she found where the creature landed from its leap. Two footprints side by side were before her, both deep with the weight of the beast. She bent close as sniffed them. The biting odor made her wince and recoil. It was like nothing she'd ever smelled, a stench she would never associate with a living being. She suddenly felt uncomfortable, as if she was in an alien place. The woods she'd grown up around and inside became strange to her. She stepped away from the prints and hurried back to the kill. She was too late; her sisters had begun feasting and ruined the portion she planned to take to her family. She squatted beside them, steadied by their presence but still not quite calmed.

The bold one lifted the hog's remains in her mouth and the three of them returned to their lair. Sadatina did not linger as usual. She headed for home as soon they reached the stand of dense shrubs. Her sisters called out to her but she continued on. She needed to be out of the woods; the longer she stayed the more fearful she felt. At one point she felt as if she was being watched. She turned suddenly and saw her sisters standing behind her.

"Go away," she whispered. "Baba will come hunting for you if he sees you."

She waved them away but they refused to move. Sadatina shrugged and hurried to the river. She splashed across and hurried to the house, looking behind her to see if her sisters still lingered. To her relief they were gone, but her nerves did not ease. She still felt watched, so she hurried across the field to the house. She burst through the door, startling her family.

Mama's surprised expression quickly transformed to annoyance. "Look at you!" she exclaimed. "Go get out of those wet clothes."

"Yes, Mama," she said as she scurried by to her cot. She

stored her weapons under her bed and redressed quickly. When she was done, she turned to see Terte looking at her curiously.

"What's wrong with you?" he asked.

"Nothing," she answered.

"No, something's wrong. Mama told you to do something and you did it right away."

"Leave me alone, Terte. I'm tired."

"What did you do wrong?"

"Leave her alone, Terte." Baba looked at her and smiled. "Bad hunting day?"

"Yes." She sat on her cot and rubbed her hands together. "It is more difficult when it's raining like this."

"Rain does not stop hunger," Baba said.

Sadatina managed to smile. "No, it doesn't."

"But we don't need bush meat." Baba rested his hand on her shoulder and his eyes widened.

"You're shivering!"

His hand went quickly to her forehead. "How do you feel?"

"I'm fine, Baba, really I am."

"No you're not. What happened? Did you see a shumba?"

Baba's mention of a shumba made her shiver again. He could never find out about her sisters for he would surely hunt them down and kill them.

"No," she replied. "It was something else."

Baba gave her a curious stare.

"I've never seen anything like it. It was shaped like a monkey but it was too big. And its face seemed more like a dog's. We...I was stalking a bush hog when I came across it."

Baba frowned. "Sounds like you saw an ngun," he finally said. "It's unusual for them to be in the bush, and it's especially unusual for one to be alone. They are usually on the savannah and they normally travel in groups."

Sadatina felt more at ease now that she had an idea of what she'd encountered. The way the creature looked at her still made her nervous. "It did not seem to be afraid of me," she said.

"Nguns are very bold, especially in groups," Baba explained. "It is a good thing it didn't attack you. If it had been a group..." He nodded decisively and stood. "It is best you not go hunting alone for a while, Sadatina. An ngun troupe can be as dangerous as a shumba. We must also keep an eye out here as well. It is not past them to try to break into our granary. Not only are they fearless, they are smart."

Sadatina nodded. She said nothing else about the creature the remainder of the day as she fell into the pace of maintaining the house. Though Baba's explanation calmed her, it still did not remove her apprehension. She decided she would not hunt for a while. Her sisters were not cubs anymore and did not need her to feed them. She would miss them, but they would be fine.

Her absence from the forest extended from days to weeks. Mama was happy with her sudden disinterest in hunting but Baba seemed concerned despite his advice for her to stay out of the woods. Once he offered to take her but she refused. As much as she tried to fight it, fear grew in her mind. She finally decided she would not return to the woods until the dry season. Hopefully by then the ngun would have returned to its normal haunts and the woods would be as she remembered them.

The season's end arrived with infrequent rains and thinning clouds. Sadatina would do her chores for the day and sit before the house staring into the hills. She was losing her fear to the changing season and was anxious to get back among the trees to see how her sisters fared. It had been a long time since she hunted with them. A thought came to her that worried her. Would they remember her? If not, her predicament would be more dangerous than confronting a mysterious beast. Shumbas did not hunt people unless they were old, but they attacked when threatened. Maybe it was time for her to move on and leave her sisters to their life. She'd fulfilled her silent obligation to their mama; the cubs were now adult shumbas, full grown and hunting on their own. She hoped they would continue to stay away from the farm.

She went inside and was greeted by Mama's smiling face. She worked on Sadatina's harvest dress, the dress she would wear to the festival. It was a much different dress, a shimmering blend of red and white beads accented with expensive cowries. The cowries were a symbol of their wealth; the planting had gone well and the fields were bursting with sorghum, yams and other vegetables. Their goat and cattle herds had expanded as well. Any man wishing to join with their family would have to provide a generous loloba, to prove he was able to provide for Sadatina in the way to which she was accustomed.

Teshome's image came to her. She wondered, no, she hoped his family fared as well. She'd made her decision during the rains that he was the man she would marry. If he baba's permission, of course. He was a good man and seemed not to notice her differences from other women. She couldn't be sure; men and women were known to change once they became husbands and wives, at least that's what Mama said, but she felt Teshome was an honest man. He showed no shame when she defeated him. As Mama said, any man who would want a woman after she beat him up is a unique man indeed.

The decision to marry Teshome also confirmed another musing. She smiled at Mama as she went to her cot and got her weapons.

Mama frowned and Sadatina continued to smile. "One last time," she said.

Mama dropped the dress and clapped her hands. "You will marry Teshome!" she exclaimed.

"Yes I will, if he asks."

Baba entered the house, his clothes smeared from the filth of the stables. He stared at Mama's grinning face, and then watched Sadatina securing her weapons. "What's going on?"

"Sadatina is ready to marry!" Mama blurted.

Baba was not amused. "What? Who are you taking about? What is going on here? Where are you going, Tina?"

"I'll talk to you when I return," Sadatina told him.

She hurried through the tall sorghum to the swollen river. She waded across gleefully, happy with her decision. She would marry Teshome. She would visit her sisters for the last time to say goodbye. The forest belonged to them. It was time for all of them to get on with life.

She was halfway to her sisters' lair when she heard the sound. She stopped and crouched, scanning the brush for its source. Something was close, but she could not discern exactly what. Nervousness seeped into her as the strange sound released a memory of the ngun. She nocked an arrow to her bow and crept backwards toward the river. She heard the grunt again, but this time it came from behind her. She slowly sank down to her knees, turning her head from side to side. She was being hunted. Sadatina breathed deeply and slowly, forcing down the panic threatening to overwhelm her. She searched the forest and located an ironwood tree a few paces to her left. She tiptoed toward it as she listened for her stalkers.

Once she reached the tree she pressed her back against it and listened again. They were coming toward her, their grunts louder. She strained to recognize the sound but nothing came to her. She knew that bush hogs would sometimes attack if their young ones were threatened, but these were no bush hogs. These were predators, for only hunters would approach so cautiously. A spark of hope entered her mind.

"Sisters?" she called out softly.

The bushes to her left exploded into motion. Sadatina caught a glimpse of what she dreaded, a beast similar to the one she encountered weeks ago. It leapt toward her, paws wide and mouth agape. Sadatina let loose an arrow and lunged under the beast's body. It slammed into the tree, her arrow protruding from the back of its head. She rolled to her knees, her muder in her hands as the other beast charged from its hiding place. She sidestepped and swung the sharpened iron blade, striking the beast on the side of the head and sending it reeling into the bushes.

More grunting rose from the dense bushes and Sadatina

slumped. She dropped the muder and raised her bow, steeled by a sudden rush of fatalism. She was going to die, but she would die fighting. She raised her bow and fired, each arrow hitting its mark. Beasts howled and rolled in the brush, some killed instantly, some writhing on the ground and gravely wounded. Sadatina fired her last arrow into the throat of a beast to her left and snatched up her muder. She swung the blade two-handed into the head of a beast on her right and continued the swing to bury the blade into the flank of another beast. The creature wrapped its arms around the blade as it fell away, snatching it from her hands. She was unarmed when another beast charged her, slamming into her and knocking her onto her back. She raised her left arm instinctively and grimaced as the beast bit into her forearm. The beast pulled at her arm as she struggled for and found the knife at her side. She freed it and plunged it into the beast's abdomen. She stabbed again and again but the beast would not let go. Then suddenly it was gone and Sadatina heard a familiar roar. Another beast leaped at her but was knocked aside by a blur of brown.

Sadatina sat up, leaning on her good arm. Her sisters circled her, facing off dozens of beasts who grunted and swayed from side to side. Her sisters answered with roars and false charges that sent the beasts scattering. A loud series of grunts emerged from the distance, and the beasts backed away and melted into the brush.

Her sisters paced around her for a few more moments, then came to her. The bold one immediately went to her wounded arm, sniffed it and began licking it.

"No, sister," Sadatina said. She reached into her bag and took out a salve which she spread across the wound. It was bad, but not as bad as she'd imagined. When she returned home, she would ask Mama to tend it.

The thought of home sent a chill through her. These beasts were moving in packs. She struggled to her feet, picked up her muder and loped toward the river. Her sisters followed as she crashed recklessly through the brush, jumping over the bodies of the dead beasts as she rushed to the river. She emerged from the bush and saw the sight she dreaded. The beasts swarmed the farm. She plunged into the river, high-stepping through the slow current to the opposite bank.

"Mama! Baba!"

Her shouts drew the beasts' attention. They ran toward her, their grunts replaced by hysterical howls and barks. Sadatina raised her muder and howled back, her fatigue and pain drowned by her desperate anger. Her sisters ran alongside her, their roars matching her howls. They met the beasts with equal fury, tearing through them like a dry-season fire. Sadatina barely saw the creatures she slayed, her vision fixed on the house and what she hoped she would not find when she entered. Her path finally cleared and she ran to the house, jumping up the stairs and pushing past the door. Mama lay on her back, blood running from her ripped throat. Terte lay face down on his cot, his back torn apart. She could not move, she could not cry. Her sisters brushed by her, sniffing her mother and brother, the sounds coming from their throats mournful.

"Baba," she whispered.

She stumbled out of the house to the stables. All the goats and cattle were dead.

"Baba!" she cried.

"Sada..."

She rushed into the shed. Bab lay near the hay pile, surrounded by dead beasts. There was a large bleeding hole in his chest, his arms limp by his side, his muder just beyond the reach of his clenched fingers. Sadatina fell on her knees by his side, cradling his head.

"I knew," he whispered. "I knew you would be alive."

Sadatina cried.

"You are your mother's child," he said. "Your mother's child." He closed his eyes and let out a final breath as he died.

Sadatina did not remember how long she held her father and cried. Her sisters stayed by her side, moaning low and nudging her from time to time. She finally relented, duty overcoming her grief. She dragged her father's body to the house. There she laid him beside her mother, and moved Terte's body beside theirs. She trudged back to the shed and returned with a shovel. Then she dug for the rest of the day and into the night until the grave was wide and deep enough for the three of them. She had no burial shrouds, so she used the sheets Mama made for the four of them for the chilly nights. She cleaned them as best she could and placed them side by side in the grave. She had no words, for she had never attended a burial. She had to say something.

"I wish I was with you," she finally said. "Your company among the ancestors would be paradise compared to this world alone. I will join you soon. But first, I have something to do."

It took her the rest of the night to cover them. When she was done, she felt neither hunger nor fatigue. Anger infected her overnight, burning through her like a fever by morning. She gathered her weapons, securing them about her body. When she stepped outside the house, her sisters were waiting. They both stared into her eyes. There was a mood about them, an agitation that revealed they knew her intent.

"Come, sisters," she said. "We're going hunting."

The Shosa training room vibrated with the sound of exuberantly played djembes. The drummers formed an inner circle a few feet from the wall, their hands slapping the goat skin drumheads in a vibrant and lively rhythm. They stepped in time with the beat, wide smiles gracing their faces. Behind them their cohorts stood near the wall, clapping in time with the drummer and occasionally letting loose a loud shriek or prolonged ululation. All wore simple black tunics that fell to their knees, the garment pulled tight to their waists by turquoise beaded belts. Some wore their hair braided while others sported close-cropped hair, the sign of the elite warriors. Wooden swords lay at their bare feet, ready to be snatched up in case they were summoned to the center of the circle. One woman claimed the space, pacing and striking her swords together in time with the drummers and the singers. She was their best. It was to her the others hoped to prove themselves.

Hazeeta studied the eager faces of her sisters, wondering who would be the first to challenge her. She was answered almost as soon as the thought entered her head. A familiar shout rose over the drumming and Sardah broke the drummers' circle, spinning her swords over her head. Hazeeta grinned at her; if anything she was persistent. Their swords clacked together as Sardah began her vigorous and haphazard attack. Her enthusiasm did not improve her poor form and inconsistent technique. Still, it was good enough for the ginangas and the washakas they fought. Against other sisters, however, it was easy to defeat.

Sardah was still full of fight when the telltale red welts appeared on her arms just before Hazeeta knocked the wind out of her with a jab to her chest. Sardah winced and collapsed, her swords clattering beside her. A cheer went up among the sisters as two of them lifted Sardah to her feet and carried her back to the line. The young Shosa managed to look at Hazeeta and smile while she was taken away. Hazeeta mouthed the word 'practice' to her sister.

Two more entered the circle to try their skills. Hazeeta handled them with different levels of difficulty, sending them away with welts, smiles and a silent recommendation. Soon half of the sisters had been fought and advised.

The drumming stopped abruptly. The sisters clapped; Hazeeta rubbed her tired arms for a moment and worked her head from side to side to relieve her sore neck. She was getting too old for this. She would have to pick a successor soon, allowing herself to be defeated by the sister she deemed worthy to lead weapons training. But her pride would not yet let her give up her station. The sister taking her place would have to send her to the perimeter with welt and a word, just as she had done to others so many times.

The drummers watched her, waiting for her signal. She surveyed her sisters, her eyes lingering on the senior fighters as they moved forward. The smile faded from Hazeeta's face as she nodded to the drummers. They played again, but this rhythm was slower and serious. The sisters' lively vocalizations were replaced by a slow, repetitive chant as solemn as the drummers' cadence.

> *"We are the arms of Wangara,*
> *We are the daughters of light.*
> *We hold the weapons of Cha,*
> *We slay the nyokas of night."*

Asli stepped into the circle, accompanied by the low coo of anticipation by from the sisters. Hazeeta took a stance, waiting for her to complete her stretching ritual. It was ironic that her best friend was her best challenger. It was also comforting, for if she had to give up the training dance to anyone, Asli would be the one she would pick.

They traded respectful nods, and then attacked. For an uninitiated observer their battle was a wild fray, but to the women watching it was a rapid test of technique and stamina. Asli was unnaturally quick, able to best most opponents within a few strokes. Hazeeta was the only Shosa who could match her speed, but only because of her experience. Her well-timed counterattacks kept Asli cautious and slowed her tempo. They broke away from each other for a moment, a move that was frowned upon by both but necessary when they faced each other. The monsters they fought gave no respite. A Shosa did not stop attacking until either she or her foe was dead. No quarter was necessary for nyokas.

Asli surprised Hazeeta with an unexpected counterattack. Her wooden sword slid across Hazeeta's right cheek, leaving a red welt. Her victory was short-lived; Hazeeta immediately stuck Asli's left forearm, causing her to drop her sword. She attacked Asli's weak side for the kill. Even Asli was not fast enough to protect herself from a person as skilled as Hazeeta wielding two swords. The welt appearing on her chest was inevitable. Instead of her usual yell of defeat, Asli gave Hazeeta a sly grin and danced from the circle. Hazeeta prepared for the next challenger until the drummers parted again, revealing her next challenger.

The drummers fell silent. Hazeeta was puzzled; she hadn't signaled a rest. Then Nana Isabis entered the circle accompanied by her young attendants. Her purple robe weighed heavily on her shoulders, her golden head wrap sitting low on her head. Her aged face creased with worry, she nodded to Hazeeta. Hazeeta fell to her knees, her palms pressed together before her chest.

"Nana, I diminish in your presence," she said.

"Rise, daughter," Nana replied. "I apologize for interrupting your dance. Cha's business calls us."

Hazeeta looked into the matriarch's eyes. Nana Isabis was the second most honored person of Wangara. Only Baba Zenawi held higher respect.

"Gather your sisters and follow me to the sitting chamber,"

Isabis commanded. "We have much to discuss."

Isabis left the room, her attendants trailing behind. Hazeeta did not need to inform her sisters. They knew as well as she that Nana's presence meant something sinister was afoot. They replaced their training weapons and djembes in their storage places then followed Hazeeta out of the hall, through the narrow passageways of the dormitory to the sitting room. The other sisters were already present, sitting cross-legged in a semi-circle around Nana's raised platform. Nana climbed to her place with the assistance of Adande, her acolyte and a high-ranking Shosa. To attend Nana Isabis was a great honor, one that Adande took very seriously. Hazeeta frowned as she saw Adande's condescending eyes scan her sisters. Some people did not deserve the rank they claimed, she thought.

"Daughters of Cha, our Baba has spoken to me," Nana said. "Praise his words, for it is he who guided our feet to Wangara and made us Men among Men. It is he who took the sword of the Moi and placed it in our hands, for only those who give birth to life will protect it without fail."

Hazeeta's eyes narrowed with the utterance of those last words. Every day she thought of the child she had to give up for her duty. Was she still alive? If so, did she look like her or her father? A light touch on her elbow broke her musing.

"Watch yourself, sister," Asli warned. "Nana Isabis sees all."

"For many seasons we have fought Karan's evil," Nana Isabis continued, "ever since that day the Priest of the White Tower failed. We have sacrificed and held him at bay, but today my words will not bring joy. Cha tells me that Karan's children have spread like locusts throughout our lands. They no longer concentrate their hate on Wangara. They roam the valleys and hills now, seeking the blood of our unprotected kin."

Hazeeta stiffened. She cut her eyes at Asli, who looked at her, then away.

"We must ride out to protect our own," Isabis concluded.

"Our sisters and brothers need our protection. I have received word from Tuso Valley. Karan's children have appeared among the hills. They have ravaged the farms and laid siege to the village. Who will go to help our brothers and sisters?"

Hazeeta was on her feet before Isabis's last words escaped her lips. Her sisters rose soon after, their determined expressions confirming their resolve.

Isabis gazed at Hazeeta for a moment before smiling. "Cha will carry you swiftly to the Valley. Time is not our friend. You must leave at first light."

Hazeeta and her sisters knelt before Nana in farewell before they hurried from the meeting room. Their dormitory section swirled with activity as the sisters gathered their weapons, talismans and armor for their journey. Hazeeta and Asli worked silently for a time, each focused on collecting their gear.

Asli broke the silence. "You left her in the Valley?" she asked.

Hazeeta nodded. "A farm family close to the river. They recently had a son so the mother's milk was good. I gave them gold and cowries."

"How far from the village?" Asli's voice was tight.

Hazeeta stopped for a moment. "It doesn't matter. The valley folk have no way of fighting Karan's children. Ginangas maybe, but not washakas."

"They could have survived," Asli offered. "Nana says they are present, but she did not say how many. She did not send us all but only asked for volunteers. The threat may not be as dire as you imagine."

"Don't treat me like a neophyte," Hazeeta snapped.

Asli shrugged. "I meant only to speak what I'm thinking."

"We must hurry," Hazeeta answered. "Nana will wish to meet us in the temple."

It was late when Hazeeta led her sisters to Cha's main temple. The streets of Wangara were empty for the procession of sisters, their black tunics making them difficult to see in the dark night. Hazeeta's trembling hands held the bright torch lighting their way.

Cha's temple towered over the city center, second in height only to the Mansa's palace. It was the first building built in the walled city, raised with stone from the buildings destroyed in the city that occupied the hills before the arrival of the Adamu. The road snaked in wide avenues lined by family compound walls, each homestead silent under the night sky. Hazeeta knew these were the people she was chosen and trained to protect, but that night none of them mattered. She though only of the daughter she had not seen in 12 years, the daughter who, if still alive, was threatened by an evil only she and her sisters could confront and defeat. Impatience melded with her fear; her pace quickened as she led her sisters onward.

The temple doors were open, the gilded entrance illuminated by five torches. Temple caretakers joined their procession, leading them to the main sanctuary. Nana Isabis stood before a large marble dais covered with grains, fruits, and incense. Two of her acolytes flanked the dais, each holding golden torches. The sisters filed in and separated into ten rows, ten sisters for each row. The first row was one short; Hazeeta left the ranks of her sisters to stand before them as their leader.

Nana Isabis raised her hand and the sisters knelt in unison, leaning forward to place their foreheads on the cool stone. Hazeeta knelt as well; instead of prostrating like the others, she stretched out her arms and cupped her hands together.

Nana Isabis closed her eyes. "Once again we come to you for your strength. Make our arms like iron, our legs like stone, and our will as everlasting as Uhuru."

She lowered her arms and the acolytes set fire to the offering. Hazeeta watched the flames and imagined all of Karan's vile creations burning just as vigorously, consumed by Cha's judgment and her fury. The smell of incense slowly filled the room. Nana Isabis strolled to the fire and lifted her arms again.

The fire flared into an enormous blaze, its heat warming Hazeeta's cold face and steeling her heart. Cha was with them; they would be victorious. She wished she was as sure about those in the Valley.

The fire died quickly after Cha's confirmation. The acolytes returned with jeweled gourds in which they swept the ashes of the offering. They carried the gourds to Nana Isabis, who brought them to Hazeeta. It was then that Hazeeta took the position of her sisters, prostrating before Nana. Isabis dusted her head with the ashes and touched her head, signaling her to rise. When Hazeeta regained her feet, Isabis handed her a gourd. There was a look on the priestess's face that unnerved Hazeeta so she looked away. She proceeded to her sisters, dusting each of them with Cha's offering and, hopefully, Cha's blessing. When she was done she returned the almost empty gourd to Nana Isabis, who still looked at her curiously.

Her sisters stood and followed her out of the temple. They proceeded back to their dormitory, this time led by Isabis's acolytes who sang as they returned. Hazeeta was about to enter the domicile when one of the acolytes clamped her wrists. The woman's eyes were serious.

"Nana Isabis wishes to speak to you alone," she said. Hazeeta nodded, remaining at the dormitory entrance until all her sisters were inside. Asli glanced at her curiously and Hazeeta didn't respond. It was beyond them now.

The acolytes doused their torches. Hazeeta followed them back to the temple, two questions on her mind: did Nana Isabis know? What would she do?

She found herself in the sanctuary again, kneeling before the dais. Nana Isabis sat on a thin silk pillow facing her. "You may leave us," she said to her acolytes. They bowed and exited the room. Nana tilted her head slightly. "You volunteered quickly for this expedition," she finally said. "Why?"

"The time between us receiving the summons from the Valley and now has been too long. We must respond quickly if we wish to save our brethren."

"It may already be too late," Nana Isabis admitted. "We know the fury of Karan's children. They spare no one."

Hazeeta struggled to keep her emotions contained. She refused to believe her daughter might be dead. "If you believe this, Nana, why are you sending us there?"

"This is a war, Hazeeta. You know this. We need to confirm if Karan's children are in the Valley and, if they are, whether this is an attempt for a permanent occupation or just a random incursion. Moving into the Valley could be an attempt to encircle Wangara. This cannot occur."

"So we are not seeking survivors?" she asked.

"Of course not," Isabis answered. "Should we?"

Hazeeta knew full well the meaning of Isabis's question. "No," she answered.

"You seem to be upset by my news. Have you family in the Valley?"

Hazeeta almost smiled at the question. Isabis was approaching the question from a different angle. "No, Nana. I am a Soma of Wangara, but that does not keep me from feeling remorse for our brothers and sisters beyond the Wall."

Isabis nodded in agreement. "Truly spoken. You have always been a sensitive daughter. I apologize if my suspicions have upset you. I know what you had to do was not easy to do."

"I am a Shosa," Hazeeta replied. "I do what Cha asks."

"It was not Cha who asked that we give up our right to bear children," Nana Isabis revealed.

Hazeeta's eyes went wide.

"That was an order from Baba Nema, the mansa disgraced by the White Temple. Cha gave Baba Nema the words that his blessing would be among women to protect our people, since the priest of the White Temple failed to follow Cha's commands. It was up to Nema to implement Cha's will. He organized the Shosa and declared that they could not bear children as long as they served Cha. Baba Nema believed that a woman could only serve one family and a Shosa's family is her people. Every Adamu is her sister and brother."

"Which is why we cannot marry," Hazeeta finished.

Isabis nodded. "If you have something to share with me, do so now. I do not want my daughters compromised by a sister who is in conflict with her duty."

"There is nothing that will affect my duty to Cha," Hazeeta answered. On this she was certain.

Isabis was silent for a moment. "Go with Cha's blessing and protection, daughter. I hope we are in time. I doubt it, but it does not still my hope."

Hazeeta touched her head on the stone floor before standing and leaving. Nana's words were gone from her mind before she stepped into the dark streets, her trembling more from anxiousness than the chilly night. She would not sleep this night; she doubted she would sleep at all until she knew the fate of her daughter.

-8-

Sadatina peeled a mango absently with her small knife as she stared at the land that was once her home. She fought back the urge to cry again; every time she thought she had no more tears they came again. Her sisters would press against her, soothing her with their humming, but it would not take away the knot of pain that rested in her chest like an assegai. When will the pain stop, she wondered. When will it end?

She bit into the fruit, barely noticing its sweetness. The world seemed to carry a gray haze like a rainy season sky. She thought of going to the village, but she knew no one there except Teshome. Although she once considering marrying him, in reality, she barely knew him. So she waited in the woods with her sisters, crammed into the bundle of shrubs they claimed as their own since they were cubs. The beasts that killed her family still roamed the hills and occasionally crossed the river to the farm. She did not know how many of them there were or from where they came. But she would stay until she killed all of them, or until they killed her.

She gazed at her sisters, both cats lounging in the small space. The bold one slept on her back, her legs folded against her body. The timid one licked her fur. She was constantly primping, like a woman unsure of her looks or a man wishing to impress his friends. Their ways were so much like people. She wondered if they mourned their mother like she did hers.

"I must give you names," she said. "You are my family now. You must have names."

She looked at the timid one as she continued to preen, oblivious to Sadatina's words. "Your name is Pausa," she announced. She looked at her other sister, sprawled her back and oblivious to the naming ceremony. "You are Nokofa," she decided. The naming made her feel bittersweet. Having names would make her more comfortable, but the names she used were for the children she would probably never have.

There was nothing she could do for the moment. Once her sisters were rested, they would hunt for the nyokas. They were better at it now. In the beginning they fought desperately, stumbling into victory and barely surviving. But that was months ago. They knew the ginangas now and their larger brethren, the washakas. The ginangas were pack animals, always attacking in groups. They were vicious but they were not very smart and easily frightened. The washakas were much different. They hunted either alone or in duos. They were intelligent and elusive, usually shadowing the ginangas and making their move when the ginangas had worn down their victim. But she knew them now, and she was aware of all their traits; after all, they were nyokas. They could out-power a human, but they could never out-think one.

She didn't remember falling asleep, but she was on her feet and had her weapons in hand as soon as Nokofa issued her familiar growl. Sadatina peered from her hiding place to the barren land that was once her home. The nyokas traveled a familiar pattern which always brought them sooner or later back to the farm. They would search about for more to kill and relieve themselves to mark their territory. Sadatina expected to see the ginangas nosing about, but instead was startled by a group of men from the village. They were armed with assegais, shields and short swords. Their eyes were alert yet afraid as they crept across the fields to the ruins of the house. Teshome was with them. He looked older than the last time she saw him, yet he was still as handsome as she remembered. Unlike the others she didn't see fear in his eyes; she saw concern.

"Come sisters," she said. "They don't realize what danger they are in."

The trio ran from their hiding place to the river's edge. Sadatina emerged from the woods first, followed by Nokofa and

Pausa. Teshome saw her first. He yelled to the others and they ran to the river, weapons at the ready. Sadatina was almost to the river when she realized what the hunters thought. She stopped abruptly, waiting for her sisters to catch up with her. By the time the men reached the river's edge Nokofa and Pausa lounged beside her, cleaning themselves. The men froze, unsure what to do. Teshome waded into the river without hesitation, and strode directly to her. He was about halfway away from her when her sisters took notice and stood, their ears flat on their heads.

"No," she said. "He is a friend."

Sadatina was about to go to Teshome when Nokofa charged at him. Teshome raised his assegai and shield in a fighting stance. "Teshome, no!" she shouted. She grabbed Nokia's tail and pulled her back. "I said no, Nokofa!"

Nokofa turned and roared at her. Apparently she did not like her tail pulled.

"Go back with Pausa," she said, pointing the way.

Nokofa sulked back, roaring again as she passed Sadatina.

Sadatina smiled at Teshome. "You can put those down now," she said. "They will not harm you."

Teshome kept his weapons high. "What is this, Sadatina? What is going on?"

"The shumbas are mine," she said. "It's a long story, but they are mine."

"Where is your family?" he asked, his voice still suspicious.

"They are dead," she said with a trembling voice. "The nyokas killed them."

Teshome lowered his weapons. "I'm so sorry, Sadatina. They attacked the village as well. We came as soon as we could. You are the only person we've found alive so far."

"Teshome!" one of the men shouted. "Nyokas!"

Sadatina looked past Teshome and saw the nyokas charge from behind the farm buildings. "Come to us!" she shouted.

The men hesitated, looking fearfully from the nyokas to the shumbas.

"Come on!" Teshome shouted. "The shumbas will not hurt you."

The warriors leaped into the water and half swam; half ran to the other side. The nyokas were right behind them. Sadatina and the shumbas met them in the water, the young woman stabbing and slashing, her sisters biting and clawing. Teshome joined them, his efforts nowhere as effective. By the time he killed one nyoka, Sadatina and her companions had killed the rest.

They waded from the river together, Teshome eying Sadatina with amazement.

The other warriors' looks were not so generous. "She's not one of us!" one of them exclaimed.

"What are you saying, Rezene?" Teshome said.

"She is a witch!" Rezene replied. "How else do you explain how she fights nyokas with shumbas?"

Teshome couldn't answer.

Sadatina shook her head slowly. "I am not a witch," she replied weakly.

"Every farm we encountered has been destroyed. Everyone we found was dead."

Mequanent stepped forward. The only Leopard Man among them, he was the de facto leader.

"There is something wrong here," he continued. "Can you explain why you are still alive, Sadatina?

"My parents told me I am the daughter of a Shosa. Maybe that is why..."

"She is a witch in league with the nyoka!" Rezene shouted. "We should kill her now!"

"And how do you suppose we do that?" Mequanent asked. "She killed the nyoka like they were goats."

Rezene backed away. Teshome remained beside Sadatina. At least he doesn't believe I'm a witch, she thought.

"I am glad you live," Mequanent said. "But we can't bring you back to the village until this is resolved. You have survived so far. I feel you can survive on your own a little longer."

The Leopard man's words angered her. "Don't worry," she said. "I have no intentions of going to the village."

"What are you saying?" Teshome blurted. "You have to come back. You are not safe here alone."

"Like the Leopard man said, I have survived so far," she said.

Teshome took her hand. "Sadatina, please."

Sadatina came close to him. "Go back with them," she whispered. "You are the one who is not safe. If you stay here, the nyokas will kill you. If you continue to defend me, your friends will think you are possessed by me and they will kill you."

"But I want to marry you," he whispered back.

"And I you," she replied. "But everything has changed."

And then he kissed her. His lips felt good against hers and she kissed him back hard.

"I will come back," he said. "You can't stop me."

Sadatina didn't want to stop him. She simply smiled, which was all the answer Teshome needed.

Teshome joined his companions; together they waded the river and hurried down the road back to the village. Sadatina watched them leave, but there was gladness in her heart. Teshome would come back, and she would be waiting for him.

Weeks passed and Teshome had not returned. Sadatina, Pausa and Nokofa continued their deadly routine, hunting nyokas during the day then resting at night. Though revenge still burned in her heart Sadatina missed Teshome. One morning she awoke with a decision.

"Come sisters. We are going to the village."

Sadatina did not take the road for fear of being exposed to a nyoka attack. Instead she paralleled it from the woods, taking short cuts whenever possible. They traveled half the distance in one day then hunted for food before resting. The next day they continued their journey, keeping close to the woods. The noon day sun was high overhead when they came across nyoka spoor.

"No!" Sadatina blurted. "No!"

She ran and her sisters followed. Speed was of the essence now, so she took to the road. As she neared the village he heard the sound she dreaded. The farmhouses along the way were destroyed, some smoldering from recent fire. The yelping of nyokas reached her ears, mingled with the cries and shouts of the villagers. Ginangas leapt at the walls while the washakas hung back waiting for their chance to strike. The village warriors jabbed at the nyokas with their spears while other folks poured hot oil onto them. Sadatina's attack was sudden. She cut off a washaka's head before it knew she was near. Nokofa and Pausa each dragged down two more, ripping out their throats with practiced ease. The other washakas attacked them, howling out to their lesser brethren. The ginangas left the walls to join in the attack on what they thought was easier prey.

She'd never fought nyokas in the open. The beasts were their own obstruction, tumbling over each other to get to the threesome slaughtering them. Her muder turned red with their blood as she hacked and sliced with blind fury, never once thinking her situation hopeless. All she thought of was Teshome. She would not lose another person she loved.

The nyoka broke away. They fled toward the river, apparently realizing that this was not their day. Sadatina and her sisters gave chase; killing three more ginangas before the pack crossed the river then faded into the hills. They stood at the river's edge, making sure the horde did not double back. Once they were satisfied they performed their ending ritual, plunging into the river to rid themselves of the foul stench and blood.

When Sadatina emerged a small contingent of village folk emerged from behind the wall. Teshome was among them. He was accompanied by the same men who had come to her home. There was another man among them wearing the ornate pange and talisman signifying him as woleab, chief of the village. He walked up to her, Teshome at his side.

"You are the witch they told us about," he said.

"I am no witch," Sadatina replied. Her eyes fell on Teshome.

"You are good, I see."

Teshome smiled. "I meant to come back, but the nyoka attacked the village three days after we returned from your farm. We've been trapped inside since then."

"Will you come with me?" she asked.

Teshome came to her then grasped her hand. Together they walked down the road.

"Wait!" the woleab shouted. "You saved our lives! We must thank you!"

"I did not come to save you," Sadatina shouted back. "I came to see Teshome. Be thankful he lives in your village."

She squeezed his hand. "How long will you stay with me?"

"As long as I can," Teshome replied.

"That is all I ask."

She kissed him and they continued their walk back to her hills.

-9-

Hazeeta was first to rise to the morning drums. Their rapid cadence echoed throughout the dormitory as she sat upright and swung her legs off the bed then donned her undershirt and chain mail. "The day is fleeing, sisters!" she shouted. "Cha calls us to duty!"

Her sister warriors responded with alacrity, dressing as quickly as they could. Asli marched up to her fully dressed; her talisman-bedecked cloak draped over one forearm. It hadn't taken long for the early Shosa to discover that Karan's children's remains were the best protection against them. Each Shosa wore a cloak fashioned from ginanga skin, decorated with the teeth and bones of their unfortunate donors.

Hazeeta inspected Asli's cloak and her other gear with her usual scrutiny.

"You met with Nana," Asli said.

"I did."

"What did she want?"

"She was unsure about my focus. She sensed that I was disturbed by this mission and she wanted to know why."

"I see you convinced her that everything was fine."

Hazeeta lifted her head, her annoyance clear on her face. "I did. Do I have to convince you, too?"

Asli gestured to Hazeeta's cloak with a nod of her head. Hazeeta put on the garment and Asli began her inspection.

"No. I trust you even though you are taking this mission for the wrong reasons."

They completed the rest of their inspection in silence.

Hazeeta took her place in the middle of the bunk area, Asli standing beside her.

"I don't have to tell you that we are pressed for time," she told her assembled sisters. "Nana's vision was blurred by Karan's nyama, which means the valley folk are probably in grave danger. We will have three mounts per rider. We ride hard until we reach the valley. Understood?"

Her sisters nodded in silence. It would be an exhausting journey. Hazeeta struggled with the decision, knowing that if they were too exhausted when they reached the Valley any immediate confrontation would cause high casualties among them. But if they lagged, the Valley could be wiped clean. She decided in the end to push hard and take the chance they would have time to rest before any nyokaic confrontations.

"We will be tired when we reach the valley," Sardah commented. "Tired and vulnerable."

Hazeeta nodded to Sardah's concern. "Let's hope that Cha protects us until we can protect ourselves."

They bowed in unison to her words.

"Come," she said. "The day escapes us."

One hundred Shosas streamed through the dormitory, down the narrow hallways to the spiraling stairway which led to the armory. They acquired their poisoned arrows, lances, and sabers then marched on to the stables to receive their mounts. Each horse was trained since birth for battle and then selected not only for fearlessness but aggressiveness. This made them hard to control at times, but there was more than one Shosa that owed her life to the sharpened hooves of a Shosa equine. Rishan the stable master met Hazeeta before the stable doors, her face a reflection of Asli's. She was a thick woman with strong arms and a gentle heart, the perfect sister to raise and train horses.

"Are you sure you want three mounts?" she asked.

"Yes. Is there a problem?"

"No. We have the horses. It's just that I know the lands between here and the valley and the forage will be sparse despite the rains. You may find yourself leaving a few of them behind."

"We'll deal with that if it happens," Hazeeta said.

"Don't dismiss my horses so lightly," Rishan warned.

"We all sacrifice for Cha's will," Hazeeta answered. "Now bring me my horses."

Hazeeta mounted her horse, and then waited for her sisters to do the same. She raised her saber. Her sisters repeated her gesture and together they unleashed a high-pitched ululation that echoed from the city walls. The sound was repeated in the distance, the call from their sisters wishing them well. A deeper call rose soon after, the call of their brothers, the Baba's elite guard. Hazeeta lowered her sword and the Shosas galloped away to the valley.

Hazeeta was true to her word. They rode hard all day, stopping only to eat and relieve themselves. They would sleep easy with a night watch, for they were confident in the area near the city. Other sisters patrolled their encampment, which dismissed them of any diligence. That changed once they crossed the Jambila River, the natural boundary of the Shosa controlled lands. Cha's minions had not been known to cross it, but that was no longer a surety.

The Shosa waded across the river and made camp. Once the tents were secured Hazeeta summoned her sisters. "We must be wary from this point on. I will select scouts to ride out ahead for nyoka sign. We'll post night sentries in rotation from here on out. Stay diligent! We are Cha's sword in this land."

The scouts set out at daybreak. Hazeeta and the others followed at a slower pace. Each scout checked in with Hazeeta, relaying their information as they advanced into what now had become hostile territory. Hazeeta was not ignorant of her surroundings; this was the route she took delivering her daughter to the family whom she hoped still lived. Her daughter would be thirteen seasons in age, old enough to take a husband. She hoped she would have the chance to find out.

By nightfall, they reached an outcrop of wooded hills separating the flat savannah from the Valley. If they continued to the right of the mounds they would reach the village in three days. If they followed the tree line to the left they would go where Hazeeta wished. After a long, nervous night Hazeeta made her decision.

"The path to the east would lead us directly to the village," she said. "But it is the farms along the river to the west that would be the most vulnerable. We will travel west for a time before heading to the village.

"Sister, is that a wise use of our time?" Sardah stepped forward, sincerity in her voice. "If the farms are isolated it is likely they no longer exist."

Hazeeta hid her feelings well. "That is true, but we have to be certain. The village would be less vulnerable because of its numbers. We'll trek west for a time, and then head east."

Asli looked at her but Hazeeta chose not to notice. She did not care what her friend or Nana Isabis thought. She had to know the fate of her child.

"We'll set up camp her for a time before advancing to the village. After we set up I need ten sisters to ride west with me."

Asli came forward, as did Sardah and others. Satisfied with the volunteers, Hazeeta dismounted and contributed in setting up camp. It was midday by the time they were finished. Asli pulled Hazeeta aside before she could go to her horse. "Where are you taking us?" she demanded.

"To the farm where I left my child," Hazeeta answered.

"You're risking the lives of villagers who might be alive for someone who is probably dead."

"I have to know," Hazeeta said. "If you have a problem then you don't have to go."

"This is wrong, Hazeeta. You know this."

Hazeeta didn't answer. She mounted her horse and stared at Asli. "Are you still coming?" she asked.

Asli stormed to her horse and mounted. The others followed suit. She rode up to Hazeeta, stopping just ahead of her. "This is not right."

Hazeeta reined her horse aside and galloped away. Her sisters followed, Asli eventually catching up to her. She remembered the way despite the dense growth, following the narrow path single file until it slowly gained width. The trail wound through the steep wooded hills, leading them to the riverbank. Hazeeta looked across the languid waterway and her heart sank. A ragged house barely rose over unkempt fields of sorghum. The barn was completely flattened, the grain huts crumbled. The silence reminded her of a graveyard and, for all she knew, that was what it had become. Hazeeta shook her head and guided her horse into the water.

"What are you doing?" Asli called out. "There is nothing here. We need to ride to the village!"

Hazeeta did not hear her. Once on the farmland, she kicked her mount into full gallop. She was halfway across the field when the first ginanga emerged from the wrecked farmhouse. Fury blinded Hazeeta as she freed her lance from its sheath. By the time she drew close, two more ginangas emerged from the house. The three creatures bounded toward her, running on hands and feet. She impaled the first to reach her with the lance, pinning it to the ground. The second ginanga leaped at her but her mount responded as it was trained, rising up on its hind legs and striking the beast with the sharpened hooves of its forelegs. Hazeeta did not anticipate her mount's reaction; she tumbled off the back of the horse, landing on her back.

The third ginanga wasted no time. It jumped on her, its maw plunging for her throat. Hazeeta punched the beast across the jaw with her left fist before its teeth met her flesh and shoved it away with her right hand. She was on her feet before it recovered, her sword in hand. The creature attacked again and she slipped to her right while slashing at its bowels. The beast collapsed on its own entrails.

She sprinted toward the house as other ginangas emerged, four more in all. Before she reached them, arrows thudded against their bodies, bringing them down. She glanced briefly over her shoulder and saw her sisters galloping to her, their bows loaded.

She ran by the bodies, over the collapsed carved door and into the house. The ginangas had been up to their foul habits. Human remains were strewn across the floor, dug up from their shallow graves. Hazeeta counted three bodies. She was still staring at the bodies when Asli and the others entered the house. Asli slipped her arm around Hazeeta's trembling shoulder.

Hazeeta ignored the curious stares of the other sisters as Asli led her from the house.

"Bury the bodies," Asli ordered. "We leave to meet the others at the village as soon as you're done."

They were a good distance away from the others when Asli spun her about. "What were you thinking?" Asli barked. "That was foolish."

Hazeeta said nothing, still stunned by the discovery of the bodies.

"This is what I was afraid of," Asli continued. "You are making bad decisions that could kill us all!"

"There were only three bodies," Hazeeta whispered.

Asli's eyes went wide. "What?"

Hazeeta finally focused on her friend. "There were only three bodies. The farmers had a son, which means there should have been four bodies."

Asli's face took on a hard look. "They probably took the other body."

Hazeeta shook her head. "No. Someone survived and buried the others."

"Hazeeta, stop it." Asli gripped Hazeeta's shoulders. "Your daughter is dead."

The words struck her hard but she did not flinch. She pulled away from Asli and walked to her horse.

"Hazeeta! Hazeeta!" Asli called after her.

Hazeeta closed her ears to her sister's calls and rode to the house. The other sisters crowded around the dead ginangas, collecting claws and teeth as talismans. They would not have time for a thorough harvesting, but they would claim what they could.

"Are we done here?" she asked as she reined in.

Her sisters stood. "Yes, sister, we are," one said.

She pushed past them to the graves. What was left of the bodies had been re-buried as Asli had directed. "Let's go," she said. "We ride to the village."

The sisters were mounted and ready by the time Asli caught up with them. "Hazeeta, maybe I should lead the sisters to the village."

Hazeeta fought back her embarrassment and anger. "No… sister. We ride as we always have."

The Shosa left the farm. Hazeeta whispered a silent prayer for them all, and a special prayer for her daughter. Despite what Asli said, she did not believe her child was dead. She would hold onto that belief until proven otherwise.

They retraced their trek and met up with the other Shosa at nightfall. Hazeeta suffered a sleepless night, her head filled with dreadful images of her daughter. When they rode out the next day she was exhausted, but dared not show it. She was their leader; she would not succumb to her weakness before them.

When the Shosa finally reached the valley, they couldn't believe what they saw. Farms thrived on both sides of the narrow road leading to a city that shouldn't exist. Women wrapped in colorful kangas weeded rows of sorghum while children wearing leather loincloths played and worked among them. A few of them stopped their chores briefly to smile at the strangers riding down their well-worn road. Boys strolled by driving herds of fat goats before them, the bells around the animals' necks playing a discordant tune. In the distance, Hazeeta spotted men draped in simple tunics and wearing wide conical hats sitting amidst a stand of broad acacias. The men chatted and smoked while keeping a lazy eye on the grazing cattle. It was a scene common to the warriors, but a scene that should not exist here.

Asli rode up beside her. "This is not right," she whispered.

"I know," Hazeeta replied. "This place should be a

graveyard." She looked left to the distant wooded hills. She could feel Karan's children through her talisman bracelets; she had no doubt they were there. For some reason they had not touched this land. Not only was the valley prospering but there was no sense of fear among these folk. That was the true mystery, for even in a city as protected as Wangara the people feared what came from the woods. She was determined to have an answer before she returned.

They came upon the village just before nightfall. Its walls were modest compared to those surrounding Wangara, but seemed massive given the circumstances. An adequate wooden gate secured it, the walls supported in intervals by tall wooden posts. Each post was crowned by some object Hazeeta couldn't make out in the dimming light.

Asli had no such problem. "Cha keep us!" she exclaimed.

"What?" Hazeeta responded.

"Those are ginanga heads on those posts!"

"Are you sure?"

"Yes, sister, I'm sure. Washakas, too."

"This is impossible!" Hazeeta blurted. "What is going on here?"

Two warriors emerged from the unguarded city gates. Both men were young and well-muscled; each holding thick spears with wide blades. The leather baldrics crossing their bare chests held short swords; war clubs rested in the sashes around their waists. They were impressive for village guards but nothing about them indicated they were capable of killing the nyokas whose heads decorated their walls. The taller of the two approached them and bowed.

"Welcome, sisters!" He spoke to them as if greeting long lost friends. "I am Teshome. Welcome to Wubet. I am to escort you to our woleab. Please follow me."

Hazeeta nodded and the Shosa followed the warriors into the village. Wubet was as complacent as the surrounding countryside. People trickled in from the farmlands, greeting each other with tranquil smiles. The marketplace in the village center was winding down, merchants storing their wares in battered carts for the short journey home. The woleab's compound lay just beyond the market, its boundary a ring of stone homes instead of a wall or gate. The woleab sat underneath a tall acacia on a simple stool, surrounded by elders and servants. He was young for a leader, the hair on his head and beard showing little gray. Like the warriors, his chest was bare. A richly woven cotton pange covered his legs. His toned body showed him to be a man of action. His welcoming smile did not disguise his curious eyes.

"You must leave your horses here," Teshome instructed.

Hazeeta and Asli dismounted; the other Shosa remained on their horses outside the domicile perimeter. The Shosa leaders followed Teshome to the woleab and mimicked his bow to the chief and the elders.

"Woleab, these are our sisters," Teshome announced. "I have brought them to you as you commanded."

"Thank you, Teshome," the woleab said.

Hazeeta bowed again. "Thank you for your warm welcome. Cha's grace touches all."

"It does," the woleab answered. Two male servants placed stools before the women and they sat. The women were offered drink and food which they both accepted eagerly. They were well provisioned before leaving Wangara, but nothing compared to fresh food and water.

"I am Ande Wubet. We are blessed by your visit but we are curious as to your purpose."

Hazeeta placed her food aside. "I am Hazeeta, leader of this patrol. I am happy to meet you, woleab, but I must admit this is not what I expected."

Ande's expression seemed puzzled. "I do not understand, sister Hazeeta. Is there something about our village that disturbs you?"

"No, woleab. What disturbs me is that it exists."

The elders' chatter was clearly unsettled. Woleab Ande's

expression changed from pleasant to stern. "I'm sorry if we have disappointed you," he snapped. "Our village is not as fine as Wangara but we are proud of it."

"I did not intend to insult you," Hazeeta corrected. "Karan's nyokas infect our land. They have destroyed the farms upriver. We assumed they would have struck here as well and without our protection you and your people would be wiped out. We do not doubt the spirit of your warriors, but we know that these creatures cannot be slain by weapons alone. Cha's blessing must grace a warrior for him or her to stand a chance against this evil."

Woleab Ande's smiled returned. "I understand. Your assumptions would probably be correct were it not for the woman of the woods."

Hazeeta's eyes widened. "Who is this woman of the woods? Is she a local priestess?"

"No. She is a nyoka hunter. Some say she is a witch. She roams the hills with her sisters. Together they hunt the nyokas. It is she who brings the heads upon our posts."

Silence fell on the woleab's courtyard. Hazeeta and Asli shared glances as well. An unbelievable notion appeared in her mind. Could it be? "It seems the only person who can answer our questions is the woman herself," Hazeeta finally said.

Ande frowned as his eyes drifted in Teshome's direction. "That will be difficult. She is rarely here. She spends most of her time in the hills. She comes occasionally to have her weapons repaired and for provisions."

"She will be here soon," Teshome said. Hazeeta gazed at his face and smiled. There was admiration in his eyes, and something more.

"Teshome!" Ande barked. "Know your place!"

The young warrior gave the woleab a sideways glance. "She always comes during the full moon."

"Can you take me to where she meets you?"

Teshome smiled. "Yes I can."

Hazeeta hid her joy. "Good."

She bowed to the woleab. "We thank you for your help, and we praise Cha for protecting you through the blessings bestowed on the woman of the woods."

Ande glared at the young warrior. "Surely you are not leaving? It is rare that we have visitors, especially those from great Wangara. I will summon a feast and we will celebrate your arrival."

"That won't be necessary, woleab." Hazeeta and Asli stood in unison. "We're warriors, not ambassadors. We came to scout this valley and possibly pray over you. But it seems our purpose has changed. I thank you for your graciousness but I think it is most important that we meet this woman of the woods. I only ask that you share some of your food and drink with the rest of my sisters."

Ande seemed disappointed. "Of course, sister. My servants will see to all of your needs. It's best you stay the night, however. The ride to the hills will take two days, three at the most."

Hazeeta hated to admit the woleab was right. It was near dark and despite her eagerness she knew her sisters were tired from the day's journey. Asli's pleading eyes confirmed her thoughts.

"We will stay, woleab," she agreed.

"Excellent!" Ande sprang to his feet. "We will see to your needs immediately!"

A feast ensued. The other Shosa were relieved of their beasts and led into the woleab's courtyard. Tables were set up and immediately filled with food and drink.

Hazeeta stared at her food, her mind swirling with hope and apprehension. Asli ate voraciously, occasionally looking at her friend. "It's her," Hazeeta finally said.

"That's impossible," Asli replied. "She was not trained, and she is alone."

"The woleab says she fights with her sisters," Hazeeta replied.

"You know we have no sisters here," Asli shot back.

"Who else could fight Karan's children?"

"Apparently this woman can." Asli pushed her plate aside. "Just because we are chosen does not mean someone else could not discover how to defeat the nyokas. This woman and her sisters are obviously powerful sorcerers. They may have discovered techniques we could benefit from. Of course we should invite them to become Shosa."

Hazeeta played with her food. "You are right, sister. Your explanation is more reasonable than mine."

Asli resumed eating. "You should be saying these words, Hazeeta."

"You won't have to remind me again, Asli," Hazeeta said. "I am certain of my daughter's fate now. Tomorrow, Teshome will take us to meet this woman of the woods."

Asli stared at her for a moment. "Don't put your hopes in this, sister. The disappointment may be worse than the loss."

Hazeeta scooped up a handful of the thick rice and goat meat meal. "Eat, sister," she said with a smile. "It has been a long day."

The Shosa were invited into the homes of the Wubetu for the night. Hazeeta and Asli were offered the home of the woleab's great wife which they reluctantly accepted. It was smaller than the space they occupied at the dormitory, but its small size made it easier to heat during the cold night. Hazeeta spent another fitful night, her mind racing with possibilities. When she finally fell asleep she was exhausted more from thinking than the journey.

They were awakened the next morning by Ande's servants and served a small but satisfying breakfast. Teshome awaited them as they emerged from the woleab's home.

"Are you well, sisters?" he asked.

"We are well," Hazeeta replied.

"Good. We leave immediately."

The Shosa followed Teshome through the village and out into the countryside. The journey was slow; Teshome walked before the Shosa, refusing to mount a horse with them. From morning to noon they traveled though farmland; after a brief rest they journeyed until they reached the fallow fields beyond the farmland. They camped in the shadow of the mounds, the Shosa posting guards to patrol the camp in shifts. They broke camp early next day and continued their march, reaching the river that separated the hills from the fields by late afternoon. Hazeeta and Teshome strolled to the river's edge, the two of them gazing at the verdant and ominous knolls.

"How long have you known the woman of the woods?" Hazeeta asked.

"Sadatina," he said.

"What?" Hazeeta's heart jumped. It was her! Her daughter was alive! She looked at Asli and her sister smiled.

Teshome looked at her and smiled. "Her name is Sadatina. I knew her before she became a hunter. I saw her one day when she and her mother came to Wubet. I met her when I worked on her baba's farm during the harvest season."

"How did she become a hunter?"

Teshome looked away. "You will have to ask her. If she wants you to know, she will tell you."

His reply angered her. "Does our presence bother you? You didn't have to lead us here."

Teshome squatted and pulled a blade of grass. "No, you are fine. I'm happy you have come. She needs help. I...we cannot fight the nyokas. We try, but they always kill more of us than we kill of them. If it weren't for Sadatina, you would have found what you expected."

Teshome stood and smiled at Hazeeta. "We will have to go slow, though. Sadatina only trusts her sisters and me."

"Since you won't tell me about Sadatina, can you at least tell of the other women?"

Teshome looked confused. "Other women?"

Hazeeta rolled her eyes. "Her sisters!"

Teshome smiled. "It is hard to explain. You will see." If Teshome knew anything else he was reluctant to provide it.

"When will she arrive?" Hazeeta asked.

Teshome stuck the grass blade between his teeth. "Soon."

Hazeeta and Teshome spent most of the day beside the

river, staring into the foliage. The sun began its descent behind the hills when the silence was broken by the faint roar of a shumba. Teshome suddenly stood. "She is coming," he whispered. He waded into the river, Hazeeta close behind. Asli ran to her side. Hazeeta turned and signaled for the other Shosa to stay back.

Teshome halted a few yards away from the forest edge. Hazeeta and Asli were approaching when he waved them back. "Wait. I will tell you when to come," he shouted.

Hazeeta heard the shumba roar again. It was coming closer. The foliage before Teshome jostled and Sadatina emerged.

It took everything in Hazeeta to keep from shouting for joy. There was no doubt in her mind that the woman emerging from the woods was her daughter. She was her father's daughter, from the intense eyes to the confident walk. The Wubetu nyoka hunter sauntered from the trees, a confident look on her young face. She was barely dressed, a leather top covering her breasts and a kanga resting low on her swaying hips. A sword hilt peeked over her shoulder; she carried a lance punctuated by an ornate broad leaf blade in her left hand. But what caught Hazeeta's attention was the ginanga head Sadatina held by its coarse hair in her right hand.

Another sight stunned the Shosa leader as well. Two female shumbas followed Sadatina, their snouts stained with nyoka blood. They trotted past her to Teshome, snuggling their heads against his legs and humming like docile pets.

Sadatina's tough demeanor fell away as she neared Teshome. A childlike smile graced her face as she dropped the lance and nyoka head carelessly and threw her arms around his neck. They kissed long and Hazeeta smiled. She couldn't remember the last time a man had kissed her that way.

Sadatina pulled away from Teshome and peered over his shoulder. Her smile faded. The shumbas took notice as well and their backs stiffened. Asli raised her lance.

"No," Hazeeta ordered. "No threatening moves. We'll let Teshome handle this."

Words passed between Teshome and the huntress. Sadatina marched up to them, the shumbas beside her. She stopped a lance thrust away. The shumbas kept their distance as they circled the duo.

"You are Shosa?" Sadatina asked. Her voice sounded as young as she looked. "Why have you come?"

Hazeeta wanted to reach out and hug Sadatina but she maintained her composure. Now was not the time. "We came to survey this valley and protect it if needed," Hazeeta answered.

"We need no protection," Sadatina replied.

"I see," Hazeeta agreed. "But we are curious about you."

"Why?"

"The ability to kill nyokas is not a common thing," Hazeeta answered. "We Shosa train years to acquire the skill and still we need talismans, gris-gris, Cha's strength and each other. Yet you hunt alone..."

Sadatina looked to the shumbas. "I have my sisters."

"Yes you do, which is another mystery. It is now obvious to me why Cha sent us here. He sent us here to find you."

"You have found me. Now you can go."

"Wait!" Hazeeta stepped toward Sadatina and the shumbas leaped between them. They crouched and roared. Asli rushed to Hazeeta's side, her lance leveled at the cats. The other Shosas advanced toward them, bows loaded and aimed. Sadatina turned her head and again Hazeeta was impressed. The young slayer was not intimidated by the Shosas' threat. If anything, she looked annoyed.

"Stand down!" Hazeeta shouted. Asli lowered her lance and raised an open hand, her signal reinforcing Hazeeta's words. Their sisters lowered their bows.

"Come, sisters," Sadatina said. The shumbas roared and trotted to Sadatina. She smirked at Hazeeta and returned to Teshome's side.

"She's fearless," Asli commented. "She is your daughter."

"Yes she is," Hazeeta replied. She patted Asli's shoulder.

"Come, let's leave those two alone. We'll set up camp a few yards away. I'll try to talk to her again tomorrow."

The Shosa set up camp. While her sisters tended to their needs, Hazeeta sat by her tent, watching Sadatina, Teshome and the shumbas. The child she had left behind thirteen years ago had followed in her footsteps despite not knowing anything about her. It was surely Cha's will she survived. Any lingering doubt of her decision to have her was washed away by the sight before her. Her daughter was meant to live.

It fascinated her at how completely the girl's hard countenance melted away when she was with the young man. The two of them cavorted as if the danger just across the river was nonexistent. The shumbas joined in the carousing, batting at the two of them like cubs rather than the fierce predators they were. It was a strange scene of innocence that went on most of the afternoon until Sadatina and Teshome went to the river. They stripped naked and plunged into the clear waters, no modesty between them as they bathed. They began to play again, but this time the play was more suggestive of things to come. As the sun settled behind the hills they retired to their tent. The shumbas moved before the entrance, their eyes and ears suddenly attentive.

"Hazeeta?"

Asli's voice startled her. She held a plate of food out to her. "Here, eat something."

Hazeeta accepted the plate and ate absently. "Did you see them?"

Asli rolled her eyes. "Who couldn't? Your child is not very modest."

"We're leaving her here," Hazeeta decided.

Asli stepped into Hazeeta's view, her shocked expression plain.

"We can't! She may be the one Cha has summoned."

"Then let Cha call her," Hazeeta retorted. "She is happy here, far happier than she would be if we took her back to Wangara."

"How long can she continue to fight the nyokas alone without Cha's guidance? You know what is coming. You know what Nana has seen."

"I know, but I cannot do this to her. If I were in her place I wouldn't want to go, either. Here she has companionship and love. In Wangara..."

Asli frowned. "You let your personal feelings get in the way of your duty."

Hazeeta dropped her plate. "Don't lecture me! I am in command here and if I say we leave her be then we leave her be. Do you understand?"

Asli looked more hurt than angry. "I understand."

She spun to walk away but Hazeeta grabbed her arm. "I'm sorry, my friend."

Asli grasped her hand. "I understand. I am your sister, remember? We will leave in the morning as you ordered. I will talk to the others. No one will speak of this upon our return."

"Thank you, sister."

Asli looked away from Hazeeta. "Nana will find out eventually."

Hazeeta nodded. "I know, but at least I'll have no guilt when she finally comes to Wangara. At least I can say it was not my doing."

Hazeeta slept easy that night, assured she'd made the right choice and happy that her sisters agreed. She knew she would have to deal with her choice in the future, but that was then. Her daughter was alive. Tonight she was at peace.

That peace was shattered with a familiar sick feeling in her stomach. The ground shook beneath her as she clambered from her cot, a strange rhythmic cadence that heralded a solitary approach. She donned her leather and chain mail and draped her gris-gris about herself. When she exited her tent, her sisters were in motion as well, mounting their horses and arming themselves. Hazeeta didn't look to them. Her attention went to the solitary tent closest to the river's edge. Sadatina stood with her sisters, their faces turned toward the wooded hills. Teshome stood behind them. She looked so vulnerable, her only protection her swords and her shumbas. Asli brought her horse. "What is this?" she asked. "This does not feel right."

"We'll find out soon," Hazeeta said grimly. "Come, we must hurry."

A garbled cry burst from the darkness, spooking the horses and sending a chill through Hazeeta. This was something different, she was sure; the confidence forged by her earlier experience against Karan's creations diminished with the realization. The Shosa gathered at the riverbank.

"Start a fire," Hazeeta ordered.

The sisters hurried to gather wood from the nearby forest and started a healthy blaze. Hazeeta did not need to give the next command. Her best archers went to the flames with arrows dipped in flammable oil, lighting the missiles in unison and loading their bows.

"Fire!" She commanded. Her sisters responded seconds later, blazing bolts streaking overhead like falling stars and peppering both sides of the bank. Another bellow shook the night and their adversary emerged from the woods. It was huge, much larger that the biggest washaka, a grotesque amalgamation of beasts built by malicious hands. Its massive body suggested the mountain primates but its stance was more human than beast. A jackal-like snout protruded from its face, its head crowned by a pair of thick, curved horns. Hazeeta had no idea about the meaning behind the beast's demeanor, but its size alone signaled caution. A volley of poison arrows followed by a gris lance charge would have been her command, but she had no time to call out the orders. Sadatina and her shumbas leaped through the flames no sooner than the arrows illuminated their way. The larger shumba leaped onto the beast's shoulder, digging in with teeth and claws. As the beast cried out and reached for her, the other shumba lunged at its left leg, biting into its hamstring. Sadatina ran at the beast and leaped into the air, her sword raised over her head.

But the beast was swifter that its size suggested. It grasped the shumba at its leg, ripped it free and threw it away like debris. The shumba crashed into Sadatina and they both tumbled into the river. It grasped the other feline with both hands and pulled it away, but before it could fling it free the shumba gripped the hand and bit into the wrist. A piercing howl caused Hazeeta and her sisters to cringe as they reached the flaming perimeter. The Shosa raised their bows ready to fire but Hazeeta stopped them.

Sadatina and the other shumba emerged from the river and renewed their attack. As her companion worried the beast's arms, the other climbed its torso. Sadatina worked her way behind it and hacked at its hamstrings like a woodsman, gritty determination warping her face. Again the creature managed to free itself. It twisted, throwing both shumbas from its body. Sadatina barely dodged a swipe from its clawed hand, jumping away to join her returning cohorts.

"Now!" Hazeeta shouted. A volley of bolts sprang from the Shosa bows. The beast crouched and they sailed over it, peppering the trees across the river.

"Reload!" she shouted. "Lancers advance!" The sisters split into two groups. Half replenished their bows and gathered behind Asli. The others slung their bows on their backs and freed their gris lances, the double tipped spears laced with gris-gris. They lined up behind Hazeeta. She raised her saber, preparing to signal the charge when a horrifying sight stopped her. Sadatina leaped before the creature again. She sliced at its neck but the creature ducked. It raised its head, slamming its crown into her. The girl warrior sailed backwards through the flame barrier, landing hard on her back.

Teshome ran toward her, a machete in his hand. "Sadatina!" he yelled as he approached the flame.

"Teshome, no!" Sadatina yelled back. "Get away!"

"Shossssa!" the creature hissed.

Hazeeta jerked with morbid shock. "It speaks?"

The creature charged through the fire on all fours. Teshome stood before it like a statue. Hazeeta had seen this scenario too many times before. A warrior too terrified to flee bolted in place by indecision.

The creature turned its head to the right and jerked it left. The left horn impaled Teshome's chest. For a brief moment he rode the horn until he slipped away and tumbled from the nyoka's path. Sadatina scrambled to her feet and ran to him. Hazeeta followed her with her eyes until she was clear. It was time for her sisters to act.

"Fire!" she yelled. Arrows swarmed the creature's face like bees, some penetrating into its head while others caromed off its horns. The creature collapsed, grabbing at the poison bolts protruding from its bleeding face.

"Second volley, fire!" Asli shouted. The second volley struck with such impact the nyoka staggered back, its arms flung wide. The second volley was no random fusillade; each sister aimed her shot at a point on the beast where the veins should be close, thus speeding the entry of the poison into its blood. The creature continued to stagger, though with the amount of poison coursing through its bulk it should have been dead.

Hazeeta said nothing to instigate the charge. She lifted her lance, spurred her horse and galloped forward, lowering the weapon as she neared the wounded beast. Her sisters spread out beside her, keeping pace as they neared the nyoka. It tottered, absently pulling at the projectiles in its flesh. The Shosa could have waited for the poison to take effect but Hazeeta would not let this thing die a peaceful death. She raised her lance to her shoulder and flung it with all her strength. The double edged projectile hit the nyoka full in its throat. It grabbed the lance's shaft and tugged at it weakly. Her sisters threw their lances as well, peppering the beast's body. The beast shuddered, falling onto its back.

Hazeeta veered away while her sisters drew their sabers and advanced on the dying beast. She searched the darkness and found what she was looking for. Sadatina knelt beside Teshome, cradling his head in her lap. She rocked back and forth, her sobbing loud in Hazeeta's ears. An old pain resurfaced in the Shosa's heart and her own eyes began to water. By the time she reined her horse and dismounted she was crying as well.

"Why, Teshome? Why?" Sadatina said between sobs.

Hazeeta approached slowly, wary of the shumbas which paced nervously, occasionally looking at Sadatina and the lifeless Teshome. When she reached Sadatina's side, she knelt beside her but said nothing.

"You always wanted to protect me," Sadatina said. "I didn't need your protection. All I needed was your love."

Hazeeta reached out and gingerly touched Sadatina's shoulder. When she was sure Sadatina wouldn't reject her she moved closer, holding her within her arms. This was not a time for words.

"Hazeeta?" Asli came up beside her, her face grim.

"Harvest the body for gris-gris and burn the rest," Hazeeta said automatically.

Asli lingered, glancing at Hazeeta and back to her sisters. Hazeeta looked at her again, her face stern.   "Go. I'll be here with Sadatina."

Hazeeta remained with Sadatina as the Shosa commenced their grim work. They butchered the slain nyoka, gathering as much of its blood as they could to use as the base for the poison that would kill its cohorts. They also stripped the skin from its carcass to keep it from spoiling before they returned to Wangara. There the priests would use their secrets to make it into armor stronger than the strongest metal. The process was essential to the Shosa's abilities and survival, so much so that none were excluded. But Hazeeta did not leave Sadatina. She knew what her daughter needed and she was determined to provide it. It was something she had been denied long ago.

Hazeeta did not remember falling asleep. When she awoke, the sun rested high over the hills. Sadatina lay against her, still cradling Teshome's body. Both shumbas stretched out before them, grooming each other and humming.

"I must bury him," Sadatina said.

"I'll help you," Hazeeta replied. "We can take him to the city today."

She felt Sadatina stiffen. "No. We will bury him here. This is our home."

Hazeeta stood first. Together they carried Teshome's body, Sadatina leading her to a thick ironwood tree near the riverbank. Hazeeta signaled some of her sisters and they came on foot, lending shovels and strength to the personal ceremony. The grave was dug deep to make sure wandering ginangas would not molest the body. They wrapped Teshome's body in leather and cloth and lowered it into the pit. Sadatina knelt by the grave as the Shosa paid respect to her fallen friend, each leaving a personal icon as was their tradition. Sadatina did not protest. She reached out for Hazeeta's arm and clenched it, her nails burrowing into the Shosa leader's skin until she bled. She was so strong. She was so young.

After each Shosa honored Teshome, the grave was sealed. Sadatina stood, still holding Hazeeta's arm. "Goodbye, Teshome. You were the last one. Now I am alone."

"You don't have to be," Hazeeta said.

Sadatina looked at her. Hazeeta saw the distrust rise above her grief as Sadatina let go of her arm. She gathered her weapons.

"You don't have to be alone, Sadatina," Hazeeta repeated. "You can come with us. You can become our sister."

"You are like the city folk," Sadatina snapped. "You care only about yourselves. You value what I do, not who I am."

"I will not lie to you. Your skills would be valuable to us," Hazeeta confessed. "But we are not like the city folk. We are warriors, like you. We have been chosen by Cha to defend our people from the nyokas you fight."

Sadatina let out a cynical laugh. "I care nothing for Cha. Where was Cha when the nyokas killed my parents? Where was Cha last night?"

"Last night he was with you through us," Hazeeta answered. "As for your family, I have no answer. If I understood Cha's ways I would be a priestess, not a warrior. What I do know is that we have a bond. It is a bond of skill and purpose. But you and I have a deeper bond. I have lost one I loved as well, but unlike you I could not mourn him."

Sadatina's look softened. "He cared for you like Teshome?"

Hazeeta nodded. "We Shosa have male counterparts in the mansa's army, the iSufu. We are matched with them upon our initiation as Shosa. We call them our brothers and we treat them as such. Embaye was different. He was handsome, kind and attentive. I knew when I first saw him we would be lovers." She pushed her musing aside. "Your pain will never go away, but you will find a way to handle it. You can deal with it better among sisters."

"I have my sisters." Sadatina smiled at her shumbas. "They will never leave me."

"I can only offer," Hazeeta said. "We are leaving soon. You can either join us or stay."

Hazeeta turned and walked away. She had done what she was sent to do but she had done it because her offer was sincere. Sadatina was many things, but she was not yet a leader. Time and Cha would make her so, but that was not Hazeeta's concern. Sadatina was still a child in many ways. She wanted to turn on her heels and sweep her up into her arms. But it was not time. Not yet.

"Wait," Sadatina called out. Hazeeta smiled before turning. Sadatina walked up to her.

"They must come, too," she said. The shumbas approached Hazeeta, circling her close and sniffing her. The smaller one purred and nudged her hand with its head; Hazeeta smiled and patted its head in response.

"Of course they will come," she answered. "They are your sisters, too."

Asli approached Hazeeta with her horse, a puzzled expression dominating her face. "We are ready, Hazeeta."

Hazeeta mounted her horse. She looked at Sadatina and extended her hand.

"Please come with us, sister," she said.

Sadatina gazed at Teshome's grave and looked over the river into the hills. She glanced toward the village and a frown creased her face. The she knelt and her sisters came to her, nuzzling her gently.

"Follow me," she whispered.

She stood, walked to Hazeeta's horse and took the Shosa leader's hand. Hazeeta lifted Sadatina onto the horse. Sadatina sat behind her, wrapping her arms around her waist and resting her head against Hazeeta's back.

"I am ready," she said.

Hazeeta beamed with pride. She knew well what was happening to her. She felt an intimacy between her and Sadatina, a connection that went beyond sisterhood. She was not gaining a sister; she was gaining a child.

She met Asli's approving look and smiled back. "Lead us home, sister," she said.

The Shosa had one more stop to make, at Wubet. When they returned to the village, the inhabitants looked at them with wonder, for Sadatina was with them. The woleab's men rushed to meet them, gawking at the young woman who ignored their stares. They were barely into the village when they were met by the woleab and his entourage. The young leader's face shone with sweat, his eyes wide and questioning.

"What is going on here?" he asked. "Why did you return? Why is the Woman of the Woods with you?"

"Teshome is dead," Sadatina said.

A wrenching wail rose from the gathered crowd. A young woman stumbled toward them, tears running down her cheeks. She fell on her knees before Hazeeta and Sadatina. The shumbas backed away from her nervously.

"Why do you mourn, Mizan?" Sadatina asked. "Teshome held no love for you."

The woman looked up at Sadatina, the hate clear in her wet eyes.

"Only one thing stood between us, and that was you. His death is on your hands!"

"His death means more to me than any of you!" Sadatina jumped from Hazeeta's horse. She stomped the few steps it took her to reach Mizan and push her on her back. A collective gasp rose from the onlookers as fear checked Mizan's voice.

"You are cowards, all of you! Not once did you fight against the nyokas! Not once did you come to my aid! Only Teshome tried. The rest of you hid behind your walls and prayed instead of lifting your swords and spears. Now the only one of you who had any strength is dead and you pretend to mourn him. Don't soil his memory with your hypocrisy." She strode away, her sisters following.

Hazeeta dismounted and approached the angry woleab. "Are you taking her with you?" he asked.

"Yes," Hazeeta replied.

The woleab spat. "Good. She is as much a curse as she is a blessing."

Hazeeta stopped herself from slapping the man. "Sadatina is right. You are ungrateful. It is because of her that any of you live. It is my duty to Cha to protect you. She had a choice."

The woleab looked away. The gathering shifted about, a tense silence settling over them.

"As I said, it is my duty to protect you," Hazeeta continued. "Half of my sisters will remain here. You will help them construct a fort near the river. They will remain until a permanent force can be established. Some of your daughters will be tested and trained."

The woleab's head jerked up, his eyes wide. "Our daughters?"

Hazeeta nodded. "It's time you protected yourselves."

Hazeeta strode away and remounted her horse. "Asli, pick your sisters," she ordered. "We should be back within the month."

"Travel well, sister, and take care," Asli said. "Don't let your feelings cloud your decisions."

"I won't," Hazeeta assured her.

"Things may not go well with Nana Isabis," Asli warned.

Hazeeta fought back a nervous pang in her stomach. "I know. But I also know I will not give up my daughter again."

"What do you mean?" Asli asked.

"If Nana Isabis does not accept her, she will be rejecting me as well."

"I don't think you'll have to worry about that. She's shown more talent untrained than anyone I've ever seen. Nana may have something in store for her far beyond our imaginings."

Hazeeta pondered Asli's words. What could be beyond their service? She shook her head. "I can't worry about that. I'll take her to Wangara. Everything else is in Cha's hands."

Hazeeta began to join her other sisters but Asli stopped her. "I'm glad you found her, Hazeeta. I'm glad she is alive."

The friends exchanged a warm smile.

"Thank you, Asli. Cha has given my daughter back to me for a reason. I'm sure we both will discover that reason soon."

-10-

A cloud-stained sky greeted the Shosa contingent as they emerged from the rugged hills surrounding the Wangaran plains. Sadatina's mind cleared at the odd sight; never had she seen such an open space. She felt vulnerable, as did her sisters. They shifted about at the edge of the forest, reluctant to step out into the miles of grass.

Hazeeta came to her side. "What is wrong?" she asked.

"My sisters," Sadatina answered. "I must tend to them."

She climbed down from the mare Hazeeta gave her then absently rubbed her backside. She'd yet to get used to riding the beast and preferred walking. Hazeeta insisted that she ride. Walking would slow them down, she explained. The Shosa leader was patient with her, explaining the ways of the Shosa as well as the customs of Wangara. Sadatina was thankful for her attention but not necessarily grateful. The further she traveled from the valley, the less certain she was of her decision. Although Hazeeta and the others thought she would become a Shosa, Sadatina had no such intentions. She sought only what the Shosa knew so she could kill nyokas more effectively. She knelt before her sisters and they crowded around her, humming loudly as they rubbed their heads against her. "Don't worry," she whispered. "We will be fine. As long as we stay together nothing can harm us." Her voice calmed them.

"Are they all right?"

Sadatina looked up to Hazeeta looming over them, concern on her face.

"No, they are not," Sadatina answered. "This is new to us. All of this. I will walk with them."

"It will slow us down," Hazeeta reminded her.

"I don't care," Sadatina snapped. "If you wish me to go any further, I will walk with them. Otherwise I'll go back to the valley."

Sadatina waited for an angry expression to form on Hazeeta's face but it did not. The Shosa leader smiled and nodded.

"I understand. I am asking much of you in a short time. If you wish to return home I will not stop you. This must be your decision; otherwise you will not see it through. You may do as you please."

Sadatina patted her sisters. "We will continue."

"Good," Hazeeta smiled.

They continued into the savannah. Hazeeta's reaction to her hesitancy made her think of the other reason she followed the Shosa to Wangara. Her parents told her that her mother was a warrior. Sadatina suspected she was a Shosa. She decided that when she arrived in Wangara she would reveal the story of her origin and ask for the woman who bore her to reveal herself. She knew she risked retaliation against her and her birth mother, but she had to know. It was important to her to know if she had family beyond her companions.

They camped on the savannah that night, the city still nowhere to be seen. The night sky was overwhelming, its view unobstructed by treetops, and the horizon seemed endless. The Shosa set up their tents and built fires to begin the evening meals. They were very adept at foraging in this land; the hunting parties returned with abundant game and wild flora for the cooking pots. Her sisters slipped away to do their own foraging; the night had become their favorite time to hunt. Sadatina sat alone by the fire when Hazeeta approached her with a steaming bowl of stew and a water gourd.

Hazeeta sat beside her. "Your sisters have gone?" she asked. Hazeeta extended the bowl to her.

"Yes. They are hunting," Sadatina said. "I'm not sure if they will be successful. They are not familiar with this land."

The stew was a welcome change from the road food they'd eaten during their journey. The freshness alone made it worth eating; whoever prepared it was a master of spices.

"They are hunters," Hazeeta said. "They will adapt. If they come back with nothing we have enough to share."

Sadatina downed another spoonful of the delicious stew. She sat the bowl down beside her and took a deep drink from the water gourd. It was time she asked her own questions.

"Why have you been so nice to me?" she said.

Hazeeta smiled. "It is our way. We Shosa extend our good will to all. It is from our good will that we protect ourselves from Karan's children. In unity there is strength."

"You repeat the words of your training," Sadatina replied. "I want to know why you, Hazeeta, have been so nice to me."

Hazeeta's smile faded. She looked away from Sadatina and out into the darkness.   "I sometimes imagine how my life would be if I was not called to serve Cha," she finally said. "I think I would have married and borne many children. I imagine my daughter would be like you."

Sadatina's eyes narrowed. "You don't know me."

Hazeeta nodded. "True. But what I do know of you makes me think so."

Sadatina's mind drifted to her family. The images of their bodies filled her head and she clenched her eyes in response. No matter how hard she tried, she could not see them beyond that moment. The image faded to blank fury. Her voice was tight when she finally spoke again. "Will your priestess teach me better ways to kill the nyokas?" she asked.

Hazeeta looked thoughtful. "I don't know. You have learned so much on your own. But I know Nana Isabis's knowledge is much deeper than what she reveals. She teaches us what we need to know. I believe she will have to dig deep to satisfy you."

"If she has nothing for me I will return home," Sadatina said. "There is no other reason for me to be here."

The next day the city of Wangara came into view. The horses sensed their home was near and their gait became lively. Sadatina strained her eyes to see the main city of the Shosa. It perched like a bird of prey in the verdant hills, jutting from the otherwise flat landscape. The moss-covered stone making up its walls blended well with the surrounding foliage. Tall spires rose high over the walls, giving those protecting the city a longer range of vision. As they came closer she made out a stone road winding up the hill to the city.

Hazeeta rode close to her. "We are home."

Sadatina noticed there was no emotion in Hazeeta's voice, no pride or happiness or any of the emotion expected from a person who had been long away.

"Wangara does not appear as I imagined it," she confessed. "I expected...more."

"What more could it be?" Hazeeta replied. "It is a well-built city with thick walls for protection and high towers to observe the surrounding savannah. Its wells are sweet and the streets wide. The farmers from the valley provide us with much sorghum and the grasses yield much game and nourishment for our cattle."

"It doesn't look like a city to me. It looks like a fortress... and a prison."

Sadatina braced herself for a harsh rebuttal but none came. Instead Hazeeta chuckled. "Yes, it would seem that way to some. But Cha is good to us. He has given us a safe place to live and a wise baba to lead us. Your opinion may change once we're inside."

"Will my sisters be allowed?"

"It may be best that they remain outside the walls until we can make arrangements for them. They will frighten many."

Sadatina agreed with the Shosa's logic, but it still made her nervous. This was a strange land to them. Her sisters might not handle the separation well. Neither, perhaps, would she. "I will stay outside with them until you make your arrangements," she said. "I can't leave them alone."

"I understand. It may take some time."

"We will wait."

The day was almost done when they reached the city walls. They were much higher than Sadatina imagined. She tried to hide her awe but the emotion filled her eyes. Never had she seen such a structure built by the hands of men. It was obvious Cha's Hand assisted the stonemasons who had constructed it. The continuous wall was split by a massive gate built from wide planks of ironwood joined by rusted iron clasps. The ramparts erupted in rapid drumming, whether a signal of warning or welcome she did not know. Her sisters roared in response and her horse neighed and jumped away. Sadatina steadied it before dismounting and went to her sisters. "This is not home, I know," she whispered. "We will stay here until they summon us."

Hazeeta rode up and took the reins of her horse. "It will take some time to clear the streets," she said.

Sadatina looked up at her. She really had no reason to trust this woman, yet she followed her to this strange city to present herself before another woman whose intentions she did not know. She thought back on her reasons and they suddenly seemed weak. Why was she here? Why was she doing this?

Hazeeta's expression changed. She dismounted and came to Sadatina, squatting beside her with her sisters. Her sisters did not move, instead they nuzzled against the Shosa, surprising both women. "I promise you will not be harmed," Hazeeta said. "If you wish to leave, I will take you back to the valley. This has to be your choice."

Sadatina looked into Hazeeta's eyes and a question entered her mind unexpectedly. "Are you my mother?" she blurted out.

Hazeeta's eyes went wide and she drew back. "What?"

Sadatina smiled as a warm sensation flowed through her. "You are," she said. "You are my mother."

Hazeeta reached out but quickly dropped her hand. "Clear that thought from your mind. Now is not the time for that question. We will speak after you meet with Nana Isabis."

"I will stay only for your answer," Sadatina said.

This time Hazeeta did not stop herself. She touched Sadatina's cheek and smiled in a way Sadatina had not seen since Mama died.

"I will be back for you. I promise."

She remounted as the city gates swung open. Sadatina watched Hazeeta as she led her sisters into the city amid drumming and anxious voices. Their eyes met and Sadatina needed no more words. She knew now why she would stay.

The gate remained open. A pair of plainly dressed women emerged with baskets and gourds. They froze when they saw the shumbas, dropped the baskets and gourds and ran back into the city before Sadatina could assure them that they would be safe near her sisters. One of the gourds shattered; the baskets fared better. Sadatina led her sisters to the baskets and they ate together. The tasty meals the sisters had prepared on their way to Wangara were nothing compared to the baskets' contents. If the Wangarans could not do anything else, they could at least cook. Sadatina shared the meat with her sisters and the three of them settled into patient waiting, her sisters falling asleep by her side.

After an hour Hazeeta and Asli passed through the gates. Hazeeta smiled, Asli frowned. "We are ready for you," Hazeeta announced.

Sadatina shook her sisters awake. The shumbas swatted at her playfully as they rolled about. "Not now, sisters," she scolded them. "We have things to do."

The shumbas calmed on her words. Together they followed the Shosa leaders into Wangara. The wide stone roads were lined on both sides by two- and three-story buildings built from the gray stone of the mountain but painted with vibrant colors. Green seemed to be the dominant hue, with some shades that were familiar to Sadatina and others that were a joy to her eyes. Shosa warriors stood at even intervals along the street, garbed in their charmed armor and armed with lances. The sight of the weapons took away from the otherwise peaceful reception.

"My sisters are not here for you," Hazeeta said without

looking back. "They are here to protect you from our people. It is rare that we get visitors to Wangara, especially ones like you."

Sadatina didn't reply. She pulled her sisters close to her as they continued through the city, following the winding road into the heart of Wangara. Soon they approached the city center. If it was constructed like the village, the Baba's house would occupy the center. The road merged into an even wider avenue that circled a cluster of bright blue buildings, each with tall columns rising into the sky and crowned with cones punctuated by red banners. One building stood prominent in the circle, sprawling before the avenue like an unmovable guardian.

Hazeeta turned to Sadatina. "This is our home, the Shosa hall. Nana Isabis waits for us there. Come."

The Shosa welcoming them at the hall entrance were not dressed in armor. They wore white dresses that bared their right shoulders, braided hair tipped with white beads covering their heads. They were older women, probably Shosas beyond the age needed to sustain the fight against the nyokas. Their faces were unemotional but their intense eyes followed Sadatina and the shumbas as they entered the hall. Unlike the streets, there was no armed gauntlet along the narrow halls. Apparently the bulk of the Shosa had turned out to guard her way to the temple.

Their journey through the hall ended at a pair of gilded doors, the only sign of opulence in the otherwise drab building. The women flanking the door stood behind djembes; they beat a rhythmic welcome and the doors opened inward. The room she entered was big and wide, surrounded by stone columns that reached to the building's ceiling. Various scenes were carved into the wall but Sadatina had scant time to look at them. Hazeeta and Asli led them forward to a trio of women waiting at the other end of the room. Two of the women stood holding tall golden staffs crowned with symbols Sadatina did not recognize. They were dressed as the women of the hall but they were much younger. The third woman sat between them on an expansive green silk pillow. She too wore white, but while the sisters' heads were adorned with braids and beads, the sitting woman's head was wrapped in a green turban held together by a jewel that pulsed with life. Sadatina did not need to guess who this woman was.

Hazeeta and Asli stopped a few feet before Nana Isabis. They fell to their knees, touching their foreheads to stone. "Nana, we have returned," Hazeeta said. "We bring unexpected good news."

"And an unexpected guest, I see," Isabis replied. She looked past Hazeeta and locked eyes with Sadatina. A strange sensation passed through Sadatina, a feeling that unnerved her. Growls emerged from her sisters' throats and the women flanking Isabis stepped forward, their staffs lowered. Isabis raised her hand.

"Come forward, girl," she said. "Sit beside your mother."

Sadatina's eyes went wide. Hazeeta sat upright, the same expression on her face.

"Asli, leave us," Isabis commanded.

Asli stood quickly. She glanced at Hazeeta and walked away. Her eyes met Sadatina's and she smiled briefly before leaving the room. Sadatina waited until Asli passed by before walking and moving to kneel beside Hazeeta. Her sisters lounged on her other side.

"How long did you expect to keep this from me?" Isabis said to Hazeeta. Her voice was stern.

"I brought her here to tell you," Hazeeta said.

Isabis sucked her teeth. "I doubt it. This child should never have been born. If born, she should be dead."

Sadatina's eyes betrayed her emotion. Who was this woman to say such things?

Isabis turned to her as if she heard her thoughts. "Every rule has a reason, child," she said. Isabis looked at her acolytes. "Kill her," she ordered.

The acolytes had barely lowered their staffs when Hazeeta leaped between them and Sadatina. Sadatina was on her feet, her sisters standing as well. Nana Isabis raised her hand and the acolytes returned to their peaceful stance, unmoved by Hazeeta's actions.

Isabis smiled. "Nothing and no one can come between a Shosa and her duty to Cha."

Hazeeta bowed to Isabis's wisdom and sat. It took Sadatina a moment to settle her sisters. Nana Isabis, apparently, was a woman who preferred demonstrations to lectures.

"Yet you bring me a child whose blessings are obvious," she said. "Don't be alarmed. No harm will come to either of you. It is not my place to judge; that right belongs to Cha. But some decisions must be made." Isabis focused her penetrating eyes on Sadatina. "Why did you come here, child?"

"To find my mother and to learn how to kill more nyokas," Sadatina answered.

Isabis frowned. "Emotion rules your decisions. A leader can jeopardize the lives of those who follow her making such decisions." Her eyes drifted to Hazeeta.

"I'm no leader. I fight for myself," Sadatina replied.

"And how long will that anger last? When will you weary? The nyokas will keep coming, child. They have for hundreds of years."

"Then I will keep killing them until they kill me." Sadatina's voice did not waver. She felt in her heart the words she spoke.

Isabis nodded. "I believe you would, but that may not be necessary."

Sadatina's eyes narrowed. "What do you mean?"

Isabis smiled. "That's enough discussion for now. We must concern ourselves with immediate matters." She stood and her acolytes moved closer to her. "Hazeeta, you have violated our laws, yet you have given us a blessing. It is obvious Cha's Hand is at work here, for no child should grow with such strength and prowess without our guidance. This is a dilemma that I alone cannot judge." She stood silent for a moment for her words to take effect. "Tonight you will stay with us, Sadatina," she continued. "Tomorrow I will send a messenger to the mansa asking him to decide on this situation."

A look of dread crossed Hazeeta's face. Sadatina looked

at her mother but felt no fear in Nana Isabis's word. "I have no interest in your baba's words," Sadatina said.

The acolytes' eyes widened. Hazeeta gave her a scolding glance. Isabis smiled.

"I will stay the night for I and my sisters are tired. Tomorrow I will go home." She stood and walked away. Her sisters lingered for a moment, the feisty one releasing a roar that echoed in the chamber. They trotted to join her.

Sadatina was out of the chamber and leaving the hall when her mother finally caught up to her.   "Where are you going?"

"Outside of the city," Sadatina replied. Her disappointment was growing with every second.

"You can stay in the hall with us," Hazeeta offered.

"No. My sisters need to be outside."

The two walked in silence through the hall and out into the streets. The Shosa were still stationed along the wide roads but the Wangarans were no longer huddled in their homes. They stared wide eyed and gawking at Sadatina and her sisters, and her sisters stared back. Then Nokofa became agitated; she let out a roar and people scattered.

"Stop that," Sadatina scolded. "They mean us no harm." Pausa roared soon afterward, sending another crowd into flight. Sadatina smirked. "This is no game, sister. These people fear us. Now be quiet before you get your sister started again."

Asli blocked the open gate when they arrived. She approached Sadatina, a thick wool blanket resting on her shoulder. She handed it to Sadatina.

"The mountains are cold at night. A person from the valley won't be used to it. This will keep you warm," she said as she handed it to the young woman.

"I thank you, aunt," Sadatina said. Asli's gesture surprised her; she was not sure what Hazeeta's friend thought of her.

"I wish you would stay," she said.

"This is not for me," Sadatina replied. "There is much I must do and I do not need what you have to do it."

Hazeeta touched her shoulder and she turned to face her birth mother. "I'm so glad I had the chance to meet you," she said, her eyes glistening. "I thought about you every day."

Sadatina felt uncomfortable watching Hazeeta act in such a way. Although they had formed a bond of friendship during their journey to Wangara, her feelings for this proud woman were not as deep as those she received. "Cha bless you," she finally said.

"And you, daughter." Hazeeta moved toward her, the stopped. She reached out and touched her cheek, smiled, and walked away. Sadatina watched her for a moment and then headed down the trail leading into the valley. She had no wish to sleep on cold stone, preferring the warm soft grasses of the savannah. They reached the valley floor at sunset. There was little rustling about from the three of them for they were exhausted from the descent and quickly fell asleep. The muted sun woke them the next day. Sadatina shared her provisions with Nokofa and Pausa. She didn't want to waste time hunting.

As they traversed the wide acacia-studded grasslands, she kept glancing back at the fading visage of Wangara. Had she made the right choice? At the village she would resume her role as reluctant protector, hunting the nyokas and slaying them until the day they killed her. She had no family in the valley, only the memories of loved ones long dead and people who did not appreciate what she did for them.

But what of Wangara? Her life wouldn't be that much different. She would still fight nyokas, yet she would not be alone. She looked at her shumba sisters strolling beside her. They were companions, but she did miss the company of her own kind. Teshome's face slid into her thoughts; she pushed it away as tears came to her. Images of her family soon followed, drifting before her like smoke from a dying fire. No, she would not join them. She had enough pain to deal with; why should she allow more to enter her heart? Her life would stay as it was. She needed no more pain.

Her sisters left her side to hunt while she made camp for the night. They returned with a young impala and she took a portion for herself. She made a meal of it, trying her hand at the spices Hazeeta had included in her pack. The result was not as good as that of the Wangarans, but it was satisfying. They spent another night under the clear sky, Sadatina drifting to sleep with much on her mind.

They woke late and set on their way. At their pace Sadatina figured they were at least three more days from the forest and another week from the valley. She was thinking of the village when Nokofa nudged her leg. "What is it, sister?"

Nokofa turned to look behind them. Sadatina looked back while Pausa lay down then licked her paws. It was a few moments before Sadatina saw what Nokofa sensed. They were being followed, and the followers were Shosa. Anger flared inside her as she took her muder from its sheath.

"Come, sisters," she snarled. "We have work to do."

Nokofa roared in response.

The three strode toward the Shosa. Sadatina caught sight of two things that slowed her pace. The Shosa seemed to be in no hurry, and their weapons were stowed for traveling. She recognized the lead rider immediately; Hazeeta and Asli rode side by side. But it was the sight behind the Shosa vanguard that drew her attention and made her nervous. It was a large procession led by bare-chested young men wearing golden necklaces. A man with a bright red tobe rode a beautiful black horse adorned with red fabrics trimmed in cowries. Two servants walked beside him, one carrying a large red flag, the other a beautifully embroidered parasol. Riding to his right with her acolytes was Nana Isabis. More riders accompanied them, men covered in kapok from head to foot, their horses protected in the same manner. Sadatina's anger waned, replaced by wonderment. This processional was meant for her. By the time her mother and the other Shosa reached her she had regained some of her composure.

"I thought you told me I was free to leave," Sadatina said.

"I did not lie to you," Hazeeta replied. Sadatina could tell by her mother's smile that she was happy to see her. Sadatina's feelings were still mixed. "Baba Sekou insisted on seeing you himself," Hazeeta explained. "He was not happy when he heard you were gone. So he came to see you."

Baba Sekou's entourage surrounded them. The mansa of Wangara was younger than Sadatina imagined. He smiled as his trained horse knelt and he climbed down to stand on the woven blanket spread before him. One of his warriors, a man covered in leather armor and wearing an iron cap, handed Baba Sekou a wide sword covered in an intricately crafted leather sheath. Nokofa growled and Sadatina patted her head.

"No, sister. I don't think they mean us harm. But if they do, we will be ready."

Nokofa growled her doubts, but sat. Pausa seemed oblivious to the entire situation, but Sadatina knew better. One roar from her sister and Pausa would strike with deadly intent.

Baba Sekou sauntered toward her with his guards, a generous smile on his face. Nana Isabis joined him, leaning close and whispering in his ear. The mansa chuckled and whispered back. Isabis grinned.

The Shosa fell to their knees before Sekou, sprinkling their heads with dirt. Sadatina was about to imitate their gesture, but Sekou waved her off. "Please, do not bow," he said, his voice deep and smooth like a steep valley. "If what Nana Isabis tells me is true, it may be I who should honor you."

"I am not sure what you mean," Sadatina replied. "But I'm sure I am not a person to be honored."

Sekou looked at Isabis. "Only Cha would have the wisdom to send us one so powerful yet so humble. Once again we are blessed."

Now Sadatina was completely confused. A few days ago Nana Isabis was struggling to figure out what to do with her. Now she was a blessing? "I don't know what you mean, Baba," she finally said. "Your ways are confusing to someone as simple as me. I came to Wangara to find out who my birth mother was and if the Shosa could teach me how to kill nyokas better. I succeeded in one and failed in the other. All I wish now is to go home... with your permission."

Baba Sekou let out a loud laugh and his guards grinned. "There is nothing we can teach you, daughter," he replied. "You have all you need. I have come to give you one last gift from Cha, one which has been in my trust and those before me. It was meant for you, or someone like you." He approached her, the weapon resting on the palms of his outstretched hands.

Sadatina took the weapon by its jeweled hilt. It felt light, almost too light to be a weapon that could inflict much damage on another man let alone a nyoka. She unsheathed the weapon from its covering and was surprised by its appearance. The blade widened quickly from the hilt, ending in a sharp curve. She'd never seen anything like it. "I'm sorry, Baba, but I don't know how to use this sword," she said as she sheathed it and tried to give it back.

Sekou refused it. "It is yours," he insisted. "You will discover its use soon enough. As for me, I have fulfilled my obligation." He turned and took the few steps needed to mount his horse and neatly took his seat there. "I hope you are all the prophecy says that you are. Only Cha would send our deliverer to us as a woman who never should have been born. Once again, Cha proves his power." He raised his hand and his entourage began its procession back to Wangara.

Sadatina studied the strange blade, slipped a hand's width from its sheath.

"I hope you will change your mind and come back to us one day," her mother said.

Sadatina looked into her pleading eyes but said nothing.

"I must go, daughter. May Cha bless you."

Sadatina watched her ride away with her sisters, trying to summon an emotion for her birth mother without success. Maybe one day she would have some feeling for her, but not now. She sheathed Cha's gift and hung the baldric across her shoulders.

"Come sisters," she said. "There is much for us to do in the valley."

The three warriors trotted toward the eastern horizon.

Book III

The Face In The Temple

-1-

Gumel scrambled up the boulder-strewn hill under a lead gray sky, driven by the cries of his dying friends. There was nothing he could do for them; their fates were in the hands of Cha. Jakada, the medicine-priest, gave him the idol once they knew the ginanga was on their trail. Gumel was the strongest; he had the best chance of reaching the caves. He looked up into the disconsolate sky as his battered hands found a flat surface. Gumel dragged himself up over the ledge, grunting with effort. As he climbed to his feet fatigue struck violently and his vision blurred as a wave of nausea hit him. He fell, his knees slamming into jagged rock. Gumel retched; the pain cleared his head. He scrambled back to his feet and continued to run.

Gumel didn't notice when the voices of his friends faded, replaced by the low grunts of the ginanga. He dared to look back and met the fiery eyes of the nyoka as it charged after him, its snout and horns smeared with his companions' blood. Gumel turned away and ran faster. There was no reason to cry out; no one would hear him. His only salvation lay in the caves ahead.

The hill steepened as he neared the caverns. Three openings beckoned; he had no idea which one held his refuge. The ginanga howled, closer than Gumel expected. He could run no faster; his energy seeped from him like blood from his abraded knees. Then he noticed the cave to his left emitted a blackness that seemed to steal the light surrounding it. "Cha help me," he whispered.

Gumel felt the ginanga's claws tear his flesh as he dove into darkness, the blow knocking him deep into the abyss. He smashed into roughened earth, his outstretched hands barely breaking his fall. The idol tumbled away, disappearing into the dark. Gumel rolled onto his back, expecting to see the beast in his final moments. Instead, the nyoka paced back and forth outside the cave, peering at him and howling in obvious fury. It took Gumel a moment to realize the nyoka could not see him. Whatever lurked in this cave was hiding him.

Gumel's back burned with the ginanga's poison. He was dying. He felt about and found the idol, a small gold statue molded to the likeness of a praying woman, her hands hiding her face. He fumbled with the precious object with weakening hands, standing it upright in the rubble. He knelt before it and covered his face with trembling hands.

He was about to recite Jakada's prayer when something cold brushed his back.

He uncovered his face and saw darkness shifting about him, slithering along the walls, weaving through the stalagmites and stalactites and exposing gray stone in its wake. The darkness formed a mass before him, pulsing with a rhythm matching his failing heart. Then it condensed, forming a thick column looming a full two feet above him. The column mutated further, its shape finally complete. A man stood before Gumel, a man with skin as black as the darkness that formed him. His muscular body seemed as strong as the cave stone. His face was an Adamu face; a broad nose and full lips common among Gumel's people. Then the figure opened his eyes, revealing white orbs that burned like the ginanga's. Tendrils emerged from his head, white like his eyes.

Gumel watched the man-thing reach down with his massive hands and pick up the idol, the object insignificant in his grip. He looked past Gumel's trembling form to the ginanga pacing outside and grinned. "So, Karan, you have found me at last." His voice rumbled like thunder.

Gumel could stand no longer. He eased down to his knees, his breathing shallow.

The man looked at him. "You are dying," he said. "Why have you come here?"

"Jakada said you could save us," Gumel answered. "He said you could kill the ginanga and free us from his terror."

"I cannot save you," the man answered. "But I will kill the ginanga." The man placed his hand gently against Gumel's back and the burning faded. Gumel closed his eyes and let death claim him.

Rashadu eased the dead man to the ground and tossed the idol away. His eyes focused on the ginanga and he grinned again. The stupid beast didn't realize its vision was obscured by a spell, a spell that sparked Rashadu's self-imposed exile. He strode to the opening, breaking the spell with a wave of his hand. The ginanga's head jerked toward him; Rashadu struck the beast in the throat with his left hand and lifted it into the air, his iron grip stifling the creature's protests. He threw the beast into the boulders fifty feet away, the sound of breaking bones reverberating off the granite cliffs. The ginanga struggled to stand, its legs snapped by the impact. Confusion flashed in its feral eyes as they focused on the rapidly approaching Rashadu.

An expression resembling a smile came to the ginanga's face. "Rashadu!" it growled. The ginanga managed to lunge at its enemy despite its injuries.

Rashadu caught the beast's horns, twisted his body and slammed the beast to the ground. He stood over the creature, his foot on its chest.

"Karan sees what I see," the ginanga whispered hoarsely. "He knows."

"Then he will see this," Rashadu replied. He gripped one of the ginanga's horns and ripped it from its head. He rammed the horn in its eye before it could cry out, driving it through the back of its head and pinning it to the ground. Rashadu kept his foot on the beast until it ceased thrashing. Years ago, he would have celebrated his kill and taken the head as a trophy. But he no longer felt any pleasure in the deed.

He shuddered unexpectedly, an image he hoped had been banished by time re-emerging in his thoughts. It burned inside his head, raising fear in a place it was never meant to exist. This time he would control it. He would not go mad again. Rashadu strode from his cave with determination. His mountain refuge was rich in the minerals he would need to make weapons. Once he was armed, he would set out to find this object of his fear and destroy it. No one, not even Karan, would stop him.

-2-

Wangara brooded under a misty, cold night sky. Situated close to the Old Men, the city knew more wet days than dry, the clouds from the Basa Sea releasing their contents on the verdant slopes at the end of their languorous journey. Though the high walls of the city resembled the clouds in color, the homes of the inhabitants protested the constant gloom by decorating the rectangular buildings with white-washed walls and colorful geometric patterns. Still, the dark weather weakened the will of the most optimistic, planting a seed of cynicism for which the inhabitants, the Adamu, were well known. Once a city that symbolized hope and blessing, Wangara now loomed as a bastion of a people under siege.

Three figures walked purposefully through the wet streets, their forms obscured by their rain cloaks. Two carried pikes, flanking a third person who seemed weaponless. They followed the spiraling roadway to the lowest level of the city until the middle figure raised her head. Her armed companions halted, shifting their pikes to guard position.

Sadatina, First Shosa of Wangara, removed her hood. Mist settled on her curls and eyelashes as she looked about with intense brown eyes, her brow wrinkled in concentration. It had been twenty seasons since she had returned to the city and there were still times she regretted the decision. This night was once of those times.

"There," she said, her golden bracelets jangling as she pointed to a faded house before them. Firelight flickered through the ragged shudders, smoke struggling to rise from the chimney. At least they wouldn't have to wake them, Sadatina thought. Not that it would make what she came to do any easier.

The guard to her left banged on the weak door with the blunt end of her spear. The portal creaked open, revealing an old man with an expectant look on his face.

"Make way for the Nana," the guard announced. The old man sighed, opening the door wider. The guards enter first; Sadatina followed, her eyes and senses probing the shadows of the small house. Her attention finally rested on the man. "What is your name?"

The old man bowed. "Yassoungo, Nana."

"You know why we are here."

The old man nodded. "Follow me." He led them to a crowded room at the rear of the house. A young woman lay in a small bed in the center of the room, cradling a newborn in her weak arms. Two older women sat on either side of her, the grandmother and the midwife, Sadatina suspected. The mother clutched the baby to her chest, her eyes wide with terror.

Sadatina approached her and the others moved away, hate clear in their hard expressions. Sadatina ignored them as she knelt beside the mother, her stern face transforming into to a sympathetic countenance. "What is your name?" she asked.

"Fara," the mother replied. "Nana, please don't take her! She is my first!"

Sadatina hesitated. Twenty seasons and still she was moved by a mother's plea. She knew what awaited those who were chosen. At least this little one would know its true mother. "This is not my decision, Fara. Cha chooses those he wishes."

Fara closed her eyes and held out the child. It was a girl, as Cha demanded. Sadatina placed her hand on the child's head and chanted Cha's calling. Suddenly she opened her eyes.

"She is not the one."

The guards did well hiding their surprise. Sadatina did not.

Fara slumped with relief. The other women looked away

from Sadatina, their faces tense. Something was wrong.

The eldest woman cleared her throat and dared to look into the Nana's eyes. "Great Mother, forgive us for our relief. We understand Cha's Blessing and its responsibility, but we all know families whose daughters were chosen. We know the price they pay."

Sadatina ignored her words. She signaled her guards. "Search the house and the compound," she ordered. "Bring everyone you find to the courtyard."

Sadatina left the guards to their duties and went back into the courtyard to wait under the outstretched branches of the meeting tree. Her acolytes forced the family into the rain, lining them before her. Sadatina walked along the line, an empty feeling growing inside as her suspicion became certainty. She stopped before a young girl who looked up at her with defiant eyes. Sadatina noticed her strong frame, rare for her young age. She wore clothing common to the poorer families of the outer wall, a simple kanga with a speckled family pattern. She was about to move on until the girl's necklace caught her eye, a small piece of amber dangling from a thin leather cord. She admonished herself for not noticing it sooner. She touched the petrified stone and felt the nyama it contained. There wasn't much, only enough to distract a Nana too arrogant to believe the people of Wangara would deliberately avoid their duty.

She grasped the necklace and yanked it from the girl's slender neck. Her status was obvious; she was Chosen. The girl's arrogant stare faded as she saw the truth in Sadatina's eyes. She cradled her face in her hands and began to cry.

Sadatina summoned her acolytes and showed them the necklace. "Check the other girls. If they are younger than one season, take them to the temple."

"What about the others?" an acolyte asked.

"They are not ours to take. They still may be of use, but they are too old to train."

Sadatina returned to the house and found Fara. The new

mother screamed and clutched her child, the elder women rising to their feet with resolved faces.

"You are foolish if you think you can stand against me," Sadatina warned. She opened her robe, revealing her leather armor and her sword hanging from her belt, the gilded hilt glistening in the flickering firelight. The old women sat again, but Sadatina was not done with them.

"I will ask you a question, but take care before you answer. You have committed an unforgivable crime against Cha and Baba Sekou. Your lives should be forfeit for such a transgression. Cha can forgive, but Baba Sekou cannot." She waited for her grim words to take effect.

The women's eyes shifted back and forth, their defiant fire replaced by the emptiness of defeat and despair.

"Baba Sekou need not know what has happened this night," she continued. "All I ask for is the source of these necklaces. Where and who will be sufficient."

"They came from the countryside," the eldest woman said. "The farmers bring them when they come to market. They don't have them all the time, for they are difficult to obtain. They are very expensive."

"Which farmers?"

"Those from beyond the river."

The farmers close to the Tuji, the closest to nyoka infested lands. These talismans were created by Mosele. "Thank you for your honesty," Sadatina said. Before she went through the doorway, she paused. "Keep your daughter, Fara. I hope she lives to see a better day for the Adamu."

"Take her," Fara said.

"Fara, no!" her mother exclaimed.

Fara pushed her mother's hand away. "You are right, Nana," Fara said. "I am selfish, but it is a mother's right to be. I know how important my daughter is to all of us. You will raise her to be a Shosa. She will be your daughter, too"

"Yes, she will," Sadatina agreed.

Fara removed the amber necklace from the baby's neck and extended the child to the priestess. "She will need feeding soon," she whispered.

Sadatina cradled the girl in her arms, gazing into her questioning eyes. Long ago, when she was another person, she imagined holding her own child, Teshome peering over her shoulder with pride. She imagined her birth mother, Hazeeta, giving her away to the parents who raised her. Time and Karan had killed those dreams. She handed the child back to her mother. "Cha can do without one."

Sadatina hurried out of the house, ignoring Fara's joyful crying. She signaled her acolytes and left the compound, trudging up the winding road to the temple. The temple doors opened as they approached, torchlight spilling into the damp darkness. Sadatina dropped her soaked robe at the door, barely acknowledging her daughters as she stormed to the altar room. The dim hallway gave way to the expansive sanctuary. At the far end of the room the stood Cha's altar, a wide platform built of granite and plated with gold. A cord of sorghum filled the altar. Incense fires burned left and right of the pedestal; beside the pedestal stood golden lamps in the shape of a woman, elbows against her sides and arms angled outward. Her extended hands held tiny flames dancing in each palm. Other lamps circled the chamber unlit.

Sadatina approached the altar with reverence and apprehension. Cha's Voice had once filled her head so much it pained her. Now it came in whispers hard to hear, let alone interpret. She refused to speculate on the meaning; her faith or lack of it was to blame. She knelt and scooped incense into each hand which she tossed into the flames. The sweet pungent aroma enveloped her and she closed her eyes, savoring Cha's Breath. She didn't notice how the smoke gathered over the altar until she opened her eyes.

This was not random. The smoke, the soul of Cha, was preparing to speak to her. Sadatina fell to her knees abruptly, hurting herself. The world was changing again. An image emerged from the gray, a face that she'd never seen but found oddly familiar.

The name escaped her lips before she realized it. "Rashadu."

She stared into his white eyes, his wild pale hair writhing about his head. This was no image of the past but a visage of the present. Sadatina covered her face, praying for guidance. As a young woman she had no room in her heart for Cha's words. As the First Shona, it was Cha's strength that kept her sane. She listened for Cha's voice, clearing her mind of any thoughts while grasping for a divine whisper of clarity. The image of a magnificent city surrounded by bountiful farmland formed in her mind. Spires rose from behind its bleached walls, their domed tips flying triangular golden banners. A single tower loomed over the others, broad and shimmering with spiritual power. Her vision brought the structure closer, to a window near the tower's pinnacle. A man stood before the window, a deep green turban wrapped around his head, his strong body covered by priestly robes. Her mind-sight drew closer; the priest's body was easily discernible, but her last vision startled her. The priest had no face.

Sadatina fell away from the pedestal, striking her head on the floor. Her attendants were immediately at her side.

"Mother, are you well?" they chimed.

Sadatina pulled away from their grip and stood. "I am fine," she lied. "Send a messenger to the Mansa. Tell him I must see him immediately."

She fled the sanctuary for her private chamber, changing to a more formal robe and adorning herself with jewels befitting her station. When she emerged her escort was waiting. She donned her rain cloak and they set out for the Mansa's palace. The massive compound rested on the crest of the hill on which Wangara stood, surrounded by an imposing granite wall. Sadatina knew her request would not be refused; she sent a messenger only because of the odd time. The palace gates swung open and they entered. Sadatina ascended the palace stairs alone. She was greeted by the Mansa's gesere, Joloki.

"Greetings, Mother." Joloki bowed deeply and waved his arm towards the gilded palace entrance. "The Mansa will be delayed," he said. "The hour is late. He had to be awakened."

"I apologize for the intrusion," she replied. "The information I must share with Baba Sekou is more important than protocol."

Joloki nodded slightly." Follow me."

He led her down the long corridor to the Mansa's scroll room. Baba Toure sat at a small desk, his fingers laced before his mouth, his eyes still bleary. He was the youngest mansa ever to sit on the stool, born the same year Sadatina returned to Wangara. Everyone knew him as a gloomy, pessimistic boy. That part of his personality had not changed through the years. But Sekou was also intelligent and caring. Baba Toure believed the final war between Wangara and the Mosele would occur during his lifetime, so he spent hours and hours developing weapons and strategies to defend the city and reclaim lands lost once the Mosele were defeated.

His eyes finally cleared and he gifted her with a smile. It was a rare expression for him but one he shared with her freely. "What brings you so late, Sadatina?"

Sadatina's smiled faded. "Rashadu has returned."

Toure closed his eyes and breathed deeply. "So it begins. If Rashadu has risen, Karan and the Mosele are not far behind."

"I'm not so sure," Sadatina replied. "Rashadu's image came to me in the smoke. I didn't sense evil in him toward us. I sensed... confusion." Toure's face bunched with skepticism. "What does a jinn have to be confused about? He serves Karan. His intentions should be clear."

"He seeks a temple in a great city, served by a priest with no face."

"You speak in riddles," he said. "Speak clearly."

"This is all Cha granted me."

Toure rubbed his chin. "We are still in danger if Rashadu has returned. We both know the Dausa. We know what he did to Djenna." He stood and folded his arms behind his back. "The Shosa must find him and kill him. Is this in your power to do?"

Toure's directness disturbed her. He was too certain of the

jinn's intent. "It is in our power. But it will require all the Shosa to confront him. The city will be unprotected."

"The city will be safe," Toure replied. "I have planned for this day since I took the stool. Our male army may not possess your spiritual prowess, but we have skills of our own. Call up the Shosa. Once you have dealt with Rashadu, you can join us to defeat the nyoka as well."

Sadatina bowed and exited the chamber. Toure's anger closed his mind to any further discussion. He had given his order: the Shosa were to find Rashadu and kill him. They would find him. Sadatina wasn't sure what would happen afterward.

She walked the wet city streets to the Shosa dormitory. The plain square building sat behind the temple, an undistinguished structure except for the golden disc mounted over the entryway. Sadatina approached the side gate, banging on the wooden door with her fist. The door jerked open, revealing the stern face of a burly Shosa.

"Mother!" she blurted. "We were not expecting you."

"Is Adande awake?"

"Yes, Mother. She is in your sisters' chamber."

Concern gripped Sadatina. "What is she doing there?"

"Your sisters have been restless. They attacked their feeder."

Sadatina stormed through the door and the dormitory. She scrambled down the stairwell to the lower floor which held her sisters' chamber. Adande stood inside flanked by two senior Shosas bearing lances. Her sisters crouched before them, teeth and claws bared.

"Get away from them!" she shouted.

Adande and the Shosa spun about, shocked at Sadatina's presence. They fell to their knees. "Mother," Adande said, fear evident in her voice, "I was going to send for you, but I thought I could handle them."

Sadatina shoved her aside. Nokofa and Pausa paced back and forth, their ears flat on their heads. They roared as they approached her. There was no threat in their movement, only acknowledgment and aggravation. She knelt and they came to her, nuzzling against her. The two female shumbas were her only link to her past, her only family. She would not tolerate any mistreatment of them.

Sadatina petted and hugged them, sensing their discomfort. "Cha has spoken to you, too?" The sisters hummed in response. "It's been a long time," she whispered to them. "But it ends soon. We will hunt soon."

The shumbas tensed. Sadatina turned to see Adande approaching.

"I'm sorry, Mother. I was trying to calm them."

"Gather my daughters in the courtyard," Sadatina commanded. "We have matters to discuss."

Adande bowed and hurried from the chamber, the other Shosas close behind. Sadatina lingered a moment longer, savoring the security she felt with her sisters. They would never let anyone or anything harm her. Their intentions were honest and direct, not colored by the murky designs of gods and men. Why had she come back? Twenty years past and she still asked that question. Those who she cared for were gone now; Hazeeta, Asli, even Nana Isabis. With each passing her heart grew as heavy as her responsibilities.

"Come, sisters, we have much work to do."

The trio bounded up the stairs to the main level. Shosas preceded her to the meeting hall in plain sleeveless sleeping gowns that covered their firm bodies like sacks. They were indistinguishable under the dim torchlight, resembling true sisters as they staggered into the massive room. She waited, giving them time to settle down before entering.

Adande's voice resonated throughout the hall. "Daughters of Cha, children of Baba Toure, our Mother requests your attention."

Sadatina entered the room flanked by her sisters. An excited murmur coursed through the hall. The presence of the sisters meant only one thing: a hunt was imminent.

"Praise to Cha!" Sadatina shouted. Her daughters fell silent immediately, their hands covering their faces. Sadatina looked at them solemnly. She wanted to remember every face, study each expression. This would be the last moment of peace for many of them; for those who survived, their lives would be forever altered. Sadatina observed them for a moment longer.

"My daughters, servants of Cha, protectors of the Adamu, tonight I come to you with auspicious words. Cha has spoken words of truth to me. For many seasons we have used our blessing to protect our people, our families and our way of life. Many of us have died knowing that in our sacrifice our loved ones live.

"Cha has come to me this night, daughters. Tonight, our duty changes. No longer will we defend. From this night forth we attack. We will strike the Mosele, the ginangas and the washakas until vultures grow fat on their putrid flesh. We will take our fight to the mountains to where their god resides, cleansing our land of his stench once and for all. We begin by finding the one who led these creatures to our gates long ago, Rashadu the betrayer, the destroyer of Djenna."

Sadatina felt the uneasiness ripple among her daughters, a stream moving over rocks in a dry riverbed.

"I know you fear, daughters. It is an honest feeling. But we are Shosa. We will rise above our fear, find Rashadu and slay him. We are Cha's chosen. We are the blessed few!" She jabbed her arms into the air and her sisters roared in reply. Her daughters responded, their voices crowding the chamber as they shouted words of assent. Sadatina let her face show her pride in her daughters. In her heart, she prayed her words would be proven true.

-3-

Luanda cried out as the fire of resurrection coursed through his stiff limbs. For decades he slept in a sliver of space carved into the surrounding granite by inhuman hands, his freedom stolen and replaced with a cold crypt. He kicked the sealing membrane instinctively, shattering the barrier that preserved his flesh. Light seeped into his tomb; he could see the serrated ceiling inches away from his eyes. As the burning subsided, he slid from his tomb into the main chamber. His feet touched the ground and he collapsed, sis legs too weak to support his weight.

Someone grasped his head and bent it back. A gourd touched his lips and he sipped instinctively. Heat and energy surged through him, filling his feeble body with strength. By the time his eyes cleared, the woman who gave him the elixir had moved on to the next vault. She was dressed simply, a single piece robe that flowed from her narrow shoulders to the top of her gray feet. She glanced his way and Luanda saw his life played out before him in her wide black eyes. A feeling of melancholy seeped from those eyes, conveying a message of despair. Luanda wondered how long she had served Karan, if her people had also been misled. The look on her face said he would find no answers here. He examined his gaunt body, his once sepia skin gray like the surrounding rock. He attempted to be angry but despair proved the stronger emotion. As much as he wished, he could not blame Karan for his condition.

He had asked, no, begged for Karan's help. They all had.

A ginanga crept up to him, its foul face distorted by a smile. "Karan summons you," it rasped.

Luanda nodded. He stood on wobbly legs then followed the beast through the labyrinth to Karan's chamber. Nothing had changed. The lair of the Stone God was as sparse as Luanda's crypt. Karan sat in a crudely carved throne, his massive stone body an exaggeration of every human feature except for his nearly featureless face. The body was merely a shell, a container providing focus for the creatures that served him. His true form manifested in his molten eyes, the simmering heat rising from his head in visible waves.

The ginanga bowed in the presence of its master; Luanda did not.

"The years have not cooled your anger, I see," Karan spoke, his voice an avalanche of sound.

"It's been a century and my people still wither away in stone graves," Luanda countered. "We pledged ourselves to you in return for our land and revenge, but the Adamu still trample our ancestors' graves."

"What is a century to me?" Karan said. "My promise is to the Mosele as a people, not to Luanda the warrior. Feel blessed that you stand before me to experience the fulfillment of your desire."

"Has something changed?" Luanda asked.

Karan shifted, his sparse mouth forming a thin smile. "Rashadu has returned."

Any anger Luanda harbored towards Karan dispersed at the mention of the Betrayer. "Where is he?

Karan's smile faded. "I do not know. A ginanga discovered him in the Wada Mountains. I'm sending washakas after him. I thought you might wish to accompany them."

"Why?" Luanda asked.

"You know why. The washaka are easily distracted. They need guidance."

"And how are we to stop a nyoka that destroyed half an army before he disappeared?"

"He is weak now," Karan answered. "He must feed to regain his strength. The longer you wait, the stronger he becomes. Do this for me and your lands will be returned."

Luanda did not believe Karan but he had no other option.

He reluctantly bowed his head, descending to one knee.

"As you wish," he said.

Karan placed his hand on Luanda's head and energy coursed through him. His skin became brown and full again, muscles bulging underneath. He felt stronger than ever; a rank taken away long ago had been restored. He was a mjibwe again.

"I will not fail you," he decreed.

Karan smiled. "I know."

-4-

When the people of Mahari saw Rashadu descending the hills, they knew their messengers had failed. Although the nyoka that terrorized them earlier had disappeared, this new strangeness approaching them stirred terror far beyond the previous menace. The villagers exploded in activity. The women gathered the children and livestock and fled to the forests. The men submerged their fear then armed themselves. They gathered at the village entrance draped in gris-gris, mouthing pleas to the ancestors to stop the man-like nyoka advancing on their home.

Rashadu pushed through their feeble defense, shattering their weapons and sweeping their nyama aside with a simple gesture. He glared at the hapless pile of men and was disappointed to see most were still alive. He still hadn't recovered his full strength, then. The reason for his intrusion into the village beckoned: a herd of zebu shifted nervously behind a frail thorn bush fence. Rashadu strode to the barricade, tore opened the gate then dragged the nearest bovine out by its oversized horns. He slammed his fist into the animal's skull, killing it instantly. He ate the cow, sparing nothing. For the rest of the day he repeated his slaughter and consumption ritual, the villagers looking on pitifully as he devoured their wealth.

A crescent moon rode high in the sky when Rashadu ceased his depredations. The village women wailed for the destruction of their herd; the men sat silent, glaring at the unstoppable evil before them. Their anger transformed to dread as Rashadu approached them.

"Which of you are blacksmiths?"

The men did not answer.

"The smiths will step forward or I will kill the rest of you."

The men shouted and jostled about, pushing three of their own forward. The three fought to remain hidden but were soon alone before Rashadu. They fell to their knees, their faces in the dirt.

"Gather your tools and come with me," he commanded. He strode back toward the mountains, feeling stronger after consuming the zebu. A mjibwe would have eaten the villagers as well, but Rashadu had no desire for human flesh. Why this was so, he did not know.

He found the place where he'd seen ore deposits earlier. The smiths seemed familiar with the area, for they set about gathering stones as soon as they arrived. Their arms full, they looked at Rashadu furtively, unsure despite the imminent threat to their lives.

Rashadu sensed their indecision and knew its source. "You must ask yourselves what is more important, your secrets or your lives?"

The smiths' shoulders sagged and, as a group, they led him to their sacred furnace. Rashadu knew the men would not be able to produce what he needed alone, so he manned the bellows. It was his turn to share a secret. "Your tools are weak," Rashadu said. "We must start at the beginning."

The smiths watched intently as Rashadu took the blooms they had created, handling the process in a way that produced a metal unknown to their experienced eyes. The tools the nyoka-man forged were of such great weight the iron mages could barely handle them. Rashadu wielded them with ease.

For days they toiled over the anvil, Rashadu pushing the mortals beyond normal endurance. As the sun rose over the mountains on the seventh day, Rashadu's labor bore fruit. He held two daggers in his hands, blades that shone like gold despite their true composition. He strode to a nearby boulder then struck the rock with his new weapons and grinned as the rock split in half.

He turned and gazed into the astonished faces of the exhausted smiths. "You have done well. For this I will spare your village."

He left the men where they stood, ascending the nearby hills to their highest peak. Grasslands extended before him and beyond, the savannah separating the grasses from the distant forest. Somewhere beyond his sight waited the answer to his madness. He hoped he could find it before Karan found him.

-5-

Sadatina led the Shosa from Wangara on a rare sunny day, but there was no joy in their departure. Shosa on the march meant danger beyond the walls, and fear was evident on the Adamubu faces. Sadatina had no idea where to find Rashadu; she was totally dependent on her sisters and Cha to locate the nyoka. There was one destination to reach before they set out on their journey: the village of Tuji. It was a week's ride from Wangara, a land of fertile farmland bordering the river. It was also the closest land to the frontier and the source of the tainted necklaces supplied to the Wangarabu to hide their daughters from Cha's selection.

The nyoka hunters worked their way down the winding road in silence, a somber mood among them. Though skilled in battle and imbued with the blessing of Cha, many had never been blooded and most had never fought a ginanga, let alone something as powerful as Rashadu. Their confidence was in Sadatina.

They camped at the base of the hills for the first night. A huge bonfire was built and Adande led the women in a martial dance to lift their spirits. Sadatina joined in, continuing a tradition begun by Hazeeta, her birth mother. The others fell away one by one to watch her, enthralled by her perfectly timed movements and blend of speed, power and grace. She reached out and Adande tossed her two sabers. She caught the blades in time and continued to dance. The daughters understood. They picked up their sabers and formed a line. One by one they stepped into the circle, sparring with Sadatina until nicked by her blurring blades. The sparring became more intense as the group leaders came forward.

Sadatina defeated them as well; thought she was very impressed by their skills. These were by far the best group of Shosa she could remember. Their mastery of Cha's Eye was impressive.

Then there was Adande. Sadatina had chosen the woman as her second because of her strength and ferocity. She did not disappoint in her sparring. Where Sadatina's style was graceful and patient, Adande's manner was forceful and direct. Such a style was usually easy to defeat, but Adande possessed a natural quickness that helped her recover from her mistakes. The sisters cheered as the two danced before the fire, their match the longest by far. But eventually Adande felt Sadatina's blade, the tip touching her cheek and leaving a small red welt. Sadatina dropped her guard but Adande did not cease. She lunged at Sadatina, her eyes filled with rage. Sadatina stepped aside and swept Adande's legs from under her. Adande's quickness kept her from crashing face first into the ground; her swords flew from her hands as she threw her hands out and caught herself. She attempted to rise but felt Sadatina's blade on the back of her neck.

"Enough," Sadatina said. The drumming ceased and the Shosa dispersed. Adande attempted to rise again but Sadatina did not move her sword. "You were very determined tonight, my daughter."

"I always am, Mother."

"More so tonight. Is there something I should know?"

Adande raised her head slightly. "No, Mother. I have nothing to say."

"My position among the Shosa cannot be fought over or earned, Adande. Cha chooses. There is no other way. If Cha decides to withhold blessings from me and bestow them upon you, I would gladly step aside and honor you as my Mother. Believe me, what seems a blessing from a distance shows its flaws upon closer inspection." She lifted her saber, allowing Adande to stand.

"I'm sorry, Mother,"

"We are on the march, daughter. I need discipline, not emotion. Can I trust you?"

Adande went to her knees. "Yes, Mother."

"Gather the group leaders."

Adande jumped to her feet and moved to obey. They met Sadatina before the fire, assembled in a large circle so that all could hear.

"Tomorrow we ride on Tuji;" Sadatina announced. "There will be Mosele and ginangas present. There will possibly be washakas. This city has been corrupted by Karan. You can trust no one. You will kill anyone or anything that approaches you. This is not a rescue. This is a cleansing."

Sadatina had no true friends among the Shosa. She had arrived skilled from birth and experience, then chosen by Cha to lead. She was more than Adamu in her sisters' eyes, the reason why they kept their distance, she believed. She did not regret it, but sometimes she longed for human closeness, not just the companionship of Nokofa and Pausa.

One of the group leaders stepped forward. Sadatina recognized the tall graceful woman as Beyla. Her young face expressed her concern. "Mother, must we kill everyone? The Tujibu are also Adamu."

"Not anymore," Sadatina said sternly. "They produce the necklaces that block Cha's Will. If the Mosele are there, those who opposed them are dead."

Beyla sat, her face despondent.

"We will divide into two groups," Sadatina continued. "Adande's group will circle the city and block the south road. My group will enter the city from the north. We will sweep the streets with lances, and then we will dismount and search each house for survivors. Anyone fleeing will be intercepted by Adande's group."

"How do we know Mosele from Adamu?" a daughter asked.

"Remember your teaching," Sadatina scolded. "Karan is a

being of stone. Those who have accepted his ways are gray as stone. Eventually they become stone, making formidable fighters."

"Not to us, though," Beyla said.

Sadatina smiled at her. "Not to us. Our lances can shatter the hardest stone and our sabers can slice diamond. Faith is our strength!"

"Cha is our armor!" her daughters responded.

Sadatina was satisfied. "Go to your units and share my words. We ride tomorrow."

Tuji was a cluster of round homes crowned with conical grass roofs, hugging the banks of the Kasa River. The surrounding lands were inundated with farms in every direction. The gentle spring floods made the land perfect for farming, leaving behind abundant minerals in the soil. Many such towns existed along the river's winding path, but Tuji was special. Its land was the most fruitful, its people the most prosperous. If any city along the river would draw the attention of Karan, it would be Tuji.

Sadatina looked at the city from an acacia grove with concern. The distance between the trees and the city was greater than she expected. A slow advance was impossible; no cover grew between the grove and the village. They could not attack during the night, for it would be difficult to distinguish between the remaining Adamu and those converted. She was certain Adande and the others were in position. They had journeyed north of the city and crossed the river though the woods along the banks. They lurked in the trees at the base of the hills, ready to slay anyone attempting to escape. Everyone was in readiness; they waited on her decision.

Though the attack would be a challenge, the obstacles were not the reason for her delay. She had chosen the best riders with the strongest mounts for her group. The charge would strain them, but it was doable. The real reason rested within her. She could not feel Cha's presence as she had in the temple. She had her vision as her only sign. She would have to trust her instincts.

She turned and saw all her daughters' eyes directed to her. It was time.

"Now!" she shouted.

The Shosa burst from their hiding places and were in full gallop in seconds, descending on Tuji like a rolling storm. The drumming of hundreds of hooves filled the air like thunder, the sun flashing off their chain mail in bolts of lightning. The Mosele charged out to meet them, proving the Shosa attack was not as covert as Sadatina thought. The gray men of Karan lumbered forward, led by a vanguard bristling with heavy pikes meant to deter the Shosa's assault.

Sadatina raised her hand high in response, clenched her fist and pumped it twice above her head to signal to the group leaders. Shouts carried her orders to the lancers, who reined back their mounts and let the archers ride between them. In seconds, scores of arrows tore through the Mosele's leather armor and thin wooden shields, the pike men falling in piles. By the second volley the Mosele were in full flight, headed for the safety of the village. As the gray men disappeared among the homes, the monsters of the stone god emerged. Hoards of ginangas swarmed the road, their shrieks echoing off the distance hills. Washakas seethed among them, huge hunchbacked jackal-faced creatures trudging among their frantic brethren. There were too many of them to be a coincidence; Karan's minions must have been aware of the Shosas' approach. Sadatina could not dwell on the villagers' obvious betrayal. She had nyokas to kill.

The Shosa swept into the ginanga horde with lances and sabers ready, their charge a planned strategy. Ginangas attempted to bring down the horses and expose the riders to the waiting washaka. A Shosa rider went down and a washaka attacked. Sadatina charged the beast, impaling it in the throat and lifting it from her daughter. The Shosa rolled away and into the clutches of another nyoka. The beast plunged its teeth into her throat and ripped it apart. Its victory was short-lived as a lance sliced into its back, tearing through its chest and pinning it to the blood-soaked ground. The lancer was followed by another Shosa whose flashing saber sliced the washaka's head from its thick neck.

Sadatina charged into the midst of the ginangas, slashing creatures with the practiced precision. She pushed her way through them to the washakas, taking on the more powerful creatures with her skill and speed. Nokofa and Pausa ran rampant among the nyokas, their fierce presence stirring a special fear among the horde.

Shosa discipline overcame nyoka fierceness; the Shosa herded the creatures back into Tuji. They broke and fled through the streets, running down the south road into the waiting ranks of Adande's group. The sisters finished the slaughter Sadatina's group had begun.

The Shosa were all bloodied. Sadatina rode among her daughters as they walked among the dead ginanga, dragging the beasts away. The washaka carcasses were separated into a special pile; they were not done with them yet. The sisters trained to harvest gris-gris worked their way to the pile and loaded the bodies onto donkeys brought to the battlefield by another group of Shosa.

"Take them to the trees," Sadatina commanded. "Make sure to collect all the blood. Burn everything else and collect the ashes."

She led the others into Tuji. Her hand shook as she dismounted; she reached behind her back and extracted Judgment from its sheath baldric. She knew a nyoka horde this large did not operate on its own. A sinister being controlled it, one that could only be slain by the fetish sword gripped in her sure hands.

"Sisters, to me!" she called out. Her feline companions flanked her, their snouts and claws stained with nyoka blood. They sniffed the air, their twitching ears attuned to senses invisible to all but them and their human sibling. Sadatina turned to her Shosa daughters. "Stay behind me," she warned. "Do not enter the city until I summon you."

She crept forward with her eyes closed. She did not need to

see to find what she sought. It would easily fool the tangible senses, but it could not avoid Cha's sight. Her attention was eventually steered to the center of the village, where the chief's home stood. A vain one, she thought with a smile. Creatures such as this should be beyond emotion. A blacksmith's hut would have been a much better hiding place, but this one wasn't hiding. It was probably young, no more than a century. An older spirit would have sensed the weapon she gripped in her right hand and fled. This one had other plans.

The chief's hut exploded. Stone and dust showered Sadatina but did not blind her. She sidestepped and the mjibwe's massive fist slammed into the packed mud. Sadatina swung her sword, cutting through the creature's stone-like muscles as if they were mere thin branches. A deafening howl blasted the lingering dust away, revealing the monstrosity in full form. Molten rock poured from the severed limb, the mjibwe's red eyes glaring in pain.

"Cha's bitch!" it rumbled.

Sadatina said nothing; the mjibwe words meant it was unsure. She kept its attention while her four-footed sisters maneuvered around it, their ears flat against their heads.

"The others said you were dead, but I see they were wrong." The mjibwe's stone lips curved up on one side, eliciting a nerve-jangling squeal. "They were wrong about Rashadu as well."

The mention of the man-thing's name broke her attention. The mjibwe pounced, striking her chest with its smoldering stump. Searing heat and pain forced a scream from her throat as she tumbled across the ground, the sword still gripped in her fingers.

She rolled to her knees to see her sisters' attack. Nokofa rose like an eagle over the mjibwe, falling onto its shoulders. Her front limbs and massive paws wrapped around the nyoka's neck as she sank her teeth into its flesh and raked her hind claws across its back. The creature howled and halted in its advance on Sadatina, attempting to turn its head to see this unexpected foe.

Pausa moved in, tearing at the back of the mjibwe's legs,

hamstringing the beast and bringing it to its knees. Sadatina followed, Cha's Judgment held high over her head. She leaped, coming face to face with the beast as she brought the blade down and cleaved the mjibwe's head down to its faint lips. She hung onto the sword as the dying mjibwe fell back onto its legs, its dying spirit absorbed into the ancient iron of the sword. The priestess jerked the sword free and climbed down from the carcass. Molten rock flowed from the crevice, hardening as it cooled in an expanding black pool about the mjibwe's head. Sadatina and her sisters lingered a moment, making sure the thing was dead.

The Shosa came forward, each one in awe of the coordinated attack they had just witnessed.

Sadatina exhaled, letting the full brunt of her pain finally emerge. She took off her chain mail, revealing a hideous burn covering one breast. The healer pushed her way to her immediately.

Sadatina gave thanks for the soothing salves but stopped the healer's hands.

"Send word to the camp that I need the skins of the washaka," she ordered.

She sank to her knees then, her breath coming in painful gasps. Nokofa and Pausa came to her, nuzzling her and licking her with their rough tongues. They watched as the body of the mjibwe erupted, consumed by molten rock that once flowed through its veins. An acrid smell burned their nostrils as Karan claimed its own. Sadatina noticed the warmth of Judgment in her sword hand and managed to smile. The blade would be stronger now, the next confrontation easier.

The healer returned with the skins, looking at the priestess with questioning eyes.

"Spread the salve on the smooth side," she instructed.

Once the healer was done, Sadatina took the skin and pressed it against her wound. The effect was immediate and welcomed, the pain dispersing as the washaka's poisons deadened her exposed nerves while the salve healed her burned skin. The healer wrapped Sadatina's torso with herb-soaked cloth before gently replacing her breastplate.

Adande came and stood before her as she came to her feet. Sadatina checker her anger as the woman bowed. "Mother, the ginangas and the washaka are all dead."

"What about the Mosele?"

Adande looked up nervously. "We have...detained them."

Sadatina could taste her own anger. "Detained? They were to be killed."

Adande looked away before meeting Sadatina's eyes. "I know what you said Mother, but these people are not true Mosele. They were converted."

"They accepted a false god," Sadatina retorted. "They sacrificed their children to him. They sent tainted talismans to Wangara to mask Cha's Chosen and weakened us. If they are not Mosele, then what are they?"

"Mother, I..."

"Silence! Take me to them." Sadatina glared at Adande's back as they trudged through Tuji. The Mosele captives lined the edge of the road on their knees, their hands tied behind their backs. Sadatina looked into their blank, feral eyes and automatically knew they were lost. They would eventually degenerate into ginangas. Some would become washakas.

Adande opened her mouth to speak but Sadatina silenced her with a raised hand. She brushed by her second-in-command then marched to the nearest Mosele. In a sudden motion she struck off his head. She turned to Adande. "You will execute the rest." She ignored the protest within Adande's eyes. "You will kill them or join them," she said.

Adande walked slowly past Sadatina and took up her saber. She marched to the next Mosele and cut his head free in a single powerful stroke. She moved down the line quickly and returned to Sadatina, her chest heaving, her eyes burning.

"Dispose of the bodies," Sadatina ordered, unmoved by Adande's anger. "Once you're done here your unit will gather our dead and return with them to Wangara."

Anger fled Adande's eyes, replaced with shock. "Mother, I have done what you asked! Surely..."

"I don't have time to repeat my commands!" Sadatina shouted. "Your arrogance is a weakness. Return to the city and remain there until we return."

Adande bowed. "As you wish, Mother."

"Beyla!" Sadatina shouted.

The young Shosa ran up to Sadatina and knelt before her. "Yes, Mother?"

"You will take Adande's place as my second."

Beyla's head jerked up, a broad smile on her face. "Thank you mother. I am most honored."

Sadatina gave her a sad smile. "You may not feel that way when this is over."

The feline sisters loped to Beyla, sniffing her and pushing their heads against her. Beyla stood still, her joy evident on her face. Nokofa and Pausa finished their ritual and returned to Sadatina's side.

"I need a head count of healthy, wounded and killed," she ordered, absently scratching her companions' smoothly furred heads. "I also need to know if there are any truly untainted villagers alive. Set a perimeter along the forest edge. Some nyokas may not have been present during our assault and may return."

Beyla was visibly nervous. "Do you think more mjibwe may come, Mother?"

"No," Sadatina assured her. "They are not so common. We are safe from them for now."

Beyla bowed and sprinted off to her tasks, careful to avoid Adande and the Mosele disposal detail. Sadatina watched the young Shosa briefly before settling her gaze on Adande. Her instincts had failed her once again. Watching her former second bully the disposal detail made it obvious she was a bad choice. Sadatina could not blame her. She had given Adande responsibilities which she was not prepared for, with little guidance. Her preoccupation with Cha's previous silence led her to neglect her duty among her daughters. Her birth mother only had to focus on her martial duties. When Nana Isabis died she passed her spiritual duties to Sadatina as well. Destiny demanded it, the dying Nana said. In Sadatina's mind destiny had not been kind to her.

Beyla interrupted her thoughts. "Mother, people are emerging from the woods. They seem to be Tujibu. Many of them say they fled when the washaka arrived. They have lived in the woods since."

Sadatina stood and winced, the pain in her chest still evident, though reduced in its intensity.

"Share what we can. Send a rider to the city for provisions. What are our numbers?"

A solemn shadow passed over Beyla's face. "Thirty wounded, ten dead."

Sadatina managed to keep a stoic expression despite her shock. "We will remain here until the wounded have time to heal. Set up camp along the river; and make sure the refugees are well treated."

Sadatina grimaced as she knelt before her sisters. She closed her eyes, summoning the image of Rashadu in her mind, the dark face and glowing white eyes unsettling. Her uncertainty returned and she opened her eyes.

"Cha help me," she whispered as she closed her eyes again. The nyoka's image returned, the clarity such that it seemed he stood before her. This was no dream image; it was real. She was looking at Rashadu in real time.

"Nokofa, come," she said. Her sister sauntered to her. Their heads touched as Sadatina transferred the image to her sister. Pausa came when bidden, her uncertainty a mirror of Sadatina's feelings. "Come, sister, it is safe. Nokofa will be with you."

Pausa bumped her head against her human sister's. Sadatina passed the image to Pausa and the shumba knew playtime was done. She sulked away, letting out a roar to express her disappointment.

Sadatina opened her eyes. "Find him," she said.

Nokofa strode away, certainty in each step. Pausa roared once more and followed, her usual playful pouncing set aside for the serious events to come. Sadatina watched them fade into the distance, wishing she was with them. There was work to do in Tuji, however, and she needed time to heal.

The Shosa lingered in Tuji for two weeks. They helped the villagers resettle and repair. The days were not entirely peaceful; as Sadatina had predicted, not all nyokas were in the village on the day of the battle. Ginangas straggled into the land and even a few washakas appeared along the wooded perimeter. The Shosa dealt with them quickly and unmercifully, gaining confidence and skills with every encounter.

Sadatina was meeting with her senior daughters when another unexpected arrival occurred. A young guard charged into the tent, bowing deeply. "Forgive me, Mother. Baba Toure is here."

Sadatina's eyes narrowed. "Go to your units," she ordered her seniors. "Make sure your sisters are ready for display. Beyla, come with me."

The women filed out of the tent behind Sadatina and Beyla, who headed for the town center. They reached the market place as Toure's forces entered the town. Bodyguards preceded the young mansa; one hundred kapok-covered cavalrymen rode armed with double-headed lances and curved sabers, their horses protected with kapok as well. Toure followed, the monarch astride a magnificent black stallion draped in golden patterned tassels. Toure wore layers of tobes, the topmost an exotic weave of blue, white and gold threads. A gilded talisman pouch hung from his neck. Sadatina was familiar with the procession marching into the city; it was the last rank of warriors who sparked her curiosity. The horses and men were covered in black chain mail, the riders carrying crossbows slung over their shoulders and holding short lances similar to those of the Shosa. Bouncing off the flanks of each horse was a leather sheath holding a weapon she did not recognize.

The bodyguards made way as Sadatina and Beyla approached. Tradition ranked the Shosa higher than male warriors, for they were considered Baba Toure's wives. Beyla prostrated before him, touching her head on the ground. Sadatina folded her arms carefully across her chest. In the city she answered to Toure, but in the field she was his equal.

"Why have you come here?" she asked.

Toure waited as a servant brought him a stool. He waved his gesere away as he stepped down before her. "I wished to see what the nyoka did to my village," he said.

"I also came to bring assistance." He gestured with his fly whisk at the armored men.

"If you wished to see the aftermath of the battle, you would have come a week ago," Sadatina said, her voice heavy with displeasure. "As far as your help, the Shosa have never needed the army's help, nor can we accept it."

"Adande said you suffered significant losses."

"Adande speaks out of turn," Sadatina snapped. "Our losses are manageable." She walked around Sekou to the ranks of warriors. "You know we cannot accept them," she told him over her shoulder. "Cha will not allow it."

"You are not the only one who speaks to Cha," Toure replied. "I know men failed Cha long ago. That is why Cha's Blessing is only bestowed upon women. But I also know this coming storm cannot be weathered by the Shosa alone."

"How can you help us, Baba?" Sadatina's question was sincere. She was weary of the solitary burden and disturbed by Cha's recent distance from her mind.

"Cha only blesses our women with the strength to confront Karan's nyoka, but shares wisdom with all. I have put the gris-gris you sent to good use." Toure signaled for one of his new warriors to approach. The man moved to obey, the weight of his armor obvious in his stride.

"Strike him with you saber," Sekou said.

Sadatina obliged by whipping out her saber and aiming to cleave the man's shoulder. Her blade bounced away before it could strike the armor.

Sekou grinned. "The effect is temporary," he explained. "It gives the warrior a moderate advantage."

"Will it stop a washaka's claws?"

"We will see, won't we?" Toure said. "Warrior, bring me your Voice."

The warrior went to her horse and untied an object from the saddle, a long metal tube decorated with gris-gris and bearing a small hole on its closed end. There was also a metal support on which the tube was mounted. The warrior walked a distance from the group and planted the weapon in the ground.

"I call it Cha's Voice," Toure said to Sadatina.

"Why?"

Toure smiled. "You'll see."

The Mansa nodded and the warrior loaded the weapon. He pointed it at an acacia tree, stepped back and pulled the trigger. The weapon boomed like thunder and emitted a cloud of smoke. Moments later, the projectile smashed the acacia, knocking away a huge piece of the tree. People ran from the village, fleeing to the woods. Sadatina stared at the stump that was once a tree, her heart thumping against her chest.

"We mixed the mjibwe's ashes with the flash powder of the medicine priest. As you can see, it makes a potent weapon."

Sadatina couldn't hide her interest. "This could be useful."

Toure nodded. "Then you will accept my unit?"

Sadatina's expression hardened. "They will answer only to me. I will accept no dissent."

"Of course," Toure agreed.

"They will stay separate from my daughters. The Shosa are warriors, but they are still women."

Toure grinned. "As you wish, although I believe companionship would make the rigors of the road less arduous."

Sadatina glared at Toure. "Baba?"

The mansa backed away while raising his hands in mock defense. "They are yours. I know you will use them well. When do you set out?"

"As soon as my sisters return."

"Then I will depart. I will send aid to Tuji. Cha's blessing to you."

"And to you," Sadatina replied.

Toure spoke to one of his men and he dismounted. He was a tall, narrow-shouldered man who carried his armor lightly despite its weight. He strode to Sadatina and bowed. "I am Dogo Ba, commander of Cha's Hammer."

Sadatina studied the young man's face and was impressed. "I know your family. You have a sister among us."

Dogo hesitated, his eyes gleaming. "Yes I do. Her name is Oafe."

Sadatina smiled. "She is a good daughter."

"We are proud of her."

Sadatina touched his shoulder. "Your voice betrays you. Your worry is no different than that of other families who have given their own to Cha's work. But you'll feel better now that you are here to protect her."

Dogo smiled. "Yes, Mother, I will."

The word "mother" caught Sadatina off guard. In all her years, she had never heard a man say her title in such a way, full of respect and deference.

"I have sons and daughters now," she mused.

Dogo stood. "Yes you do, mother."

Beyla joined them unexpectedly. Sadatina looked into the eyes of the two young leaders and saw the instant attraction, the one situation that would jeopardize this new union.

"Dogo Ba, this is my second, Beyla. You will defer to her in all matters. She is mother to you in my absence."

Both Beyla and Dogo looked disappointed.

"The men and women will camp separately," Sadatina continued. "Beyla, you will select the best among your sisters to

learn how to use Cha's Voice. We must be prepared for difficulties."
She looked at the two one last time, hoping her serious expression
would make an impression on her young commanders.

The men set up camp while Beyla returned to her duties. The
tension between the female and male warriors increased during the
week, some of it sexual, some competitive. Sadatina worried about
controlling the growing pressure until a familiar and welcomed
sensation entered her heart. Her sisters had returned.

The shumbas loped over the distant hills together, carrying
an object between them, tugging at it as they came closer. Sadatina
shielded her eyes from the noonday sun, attempting to discern
what they held. A chill dampened the joy of their arrival. Her
sisters were bringing her a ginanga carcass. They came up to her
and dropped the foul body at her feet.

Beyla and Dogo were the first to reach her. Dogo's eyes
betrayed his shock; Beyla smiled confidently at the mauled nyoka.

"Gather the warriors," Sadatina announced. "My sisters
have found them."

-6-

Five thousand Tomba warriors followed their priests into the bare fields separating their city from the mountains. They were the elite, warriors selected for their bravery, prowess and nyama. Their brethren watched from behind the city walls, proud yet relieved they had not been selected. The priests chanted loudly, spreading gris-gris before them as they called on the ancestors to strengthen them against the impending attack. For months rumors had come, stories of a beast ravaging the villages and towns beyond the Lukungu River, slaying men and consuming entire cattle herds. At first the Tomba elders laughed at the stories, especially when the gesere claimed this beast was a creation of the Afa, an insignificant people who had once been slaves of the Tomba. But the tribute from the outskirts of their domain dwindled as the rumors became warnings. A search party was dispatched and never returned; a larger force was sent weeks later and suffered the same fate. The kabaka, ruler of the Tomba, summoned his elders and nobles to discuss this mysterious threat to their lands. The priests consulted the ancestors and confirmed what the stories described. A great evil was approaching, a creature older than the ancestors themselves. It would take strong nyama and powerful warriors to defeat it. Many would die, but the Tomba would survive. They would be victorious.

Rashadu watched the Tomba ritual from far beyond the sight of the keenest human eye. At last he'd found a people worthy of his attention. He sensed their power; a strength reminding him of the humans he fought long ago. The old memory brought the bright pain and he willed it away as he stood. He waved his hand, dispersing the spell concealing him. He saw the Tomba priests react, raising their heads in unison in his direction. No fear came to their faces, only acknowledgment. Rashadu grinned wider. The Tomba were worthy opponents indeed.

He glanced at the anxious Atabu horde lurking nervously behind him, brandishing assegais and swords forged from his special metal. They had become his scavengers, picking over the remains of the villages and towns he destroyed like jackals. They grew wealthy from his remnants. He smirked; they would be dead if he had been at full strength when he emerged from his self-imposed exile. Their luck was that they were the first he encountered. The Tomba had no such fortune.

Rashadu strolled toward the waiting Tomba army. The priests responded, raising their arms as they summoned the nyama of their ancestors. The invisible power struck him like a gale. He stumbled back briefly, then continued to advance, although much slower than before. The priests continued their summoning and the power swelled. Rashadu could no longer move forward; he was forced still, struggling to stay on his feet. The priests strode forward and the army advanced behind them. They shared confident glances with each other and raised their voices. Rashadu collapsed onto one knee, then the other. The priests' voices grew even louder and Rashadu bent over, his hands pressed against the dirt. The Tomba army surrounded him, the priests hovering over him with sweaty brows. Their arms trembled as they tapped the spiritual power of their tribe, heaping the sacred energy on him. It was all there, pressing down on Rashadu's broad back, crushing him into oblivion. Or so they thought.

Rashadu raised his head, the veins in his neck showing his exertion. A bright grin came to his face. The priests had made a terrible mistake. He rose up, arms outstretched, his hair and eyes glowing white as he absorbed the power into his hungry body. The priests chanted frantically but they were too weak. The energy of their ancestors quenched Rashadu's hunger deeper than any feast of cattle. The life force of the priests was trapped in the mystic maelstrom. They fell one by one, their emaciated bodies shattering like glass at Rashadu's feet. The last priest quaked, his mouth working frantically as he glared at Rashadu. His face went slack and he collapsed.

The Tomba warriors displayed no emotion toward the death of their priests. They had expected them to give their lives to stop the nyoka and they had. The commanders emerged from the ranks and raised their ornate orinkas. The warriors responded by locking their shields and lowering their assegais. The commanders lowered their war clubs and the warriors advanced.

Rashadu crouched and drew his blades. The nyama of the ancestors had restored him to full strength, but the warriors' nyama was welcomed. The Tomba surrounded him in a spear-edged ring, creeping toward him with determined faces. Rashadu reared his head and released a deafening howl. The Tomba attacked.

Throwing spears shattered against Rashadu's skin like chaff against stone. He whirled with his blades, cutting through men and metal with equal ease. Tomba warriors climbed over their dead and continued attacking, their faces set in resignation to their fate. Rashadu saw they would fight to the last man so that at least one man could deliver a fatal blow. That was not to be. As Rashadu sliced the last warrior in two, the gates of the city swung wide and the bulk of the Tomba army attacked. Rashadu responded, leaping high with his new power and landing in their midst whirling and slashing. The pressure of their assault subsided sooner than expected. The Atabu had judged the time right for their intervention. They flanked the Tomba, their prize the undefended folk of the city. Rashadu ignored them as he continued his slaughter. When he was done he walked away. Fifteen thousand Tomba warriors lay dead in the grass while their city suffered the ravages of the Atabu. Rashadu did not hunger; he was as strong as he could be in such an isolated place. He set out for the old world, determined to discover the source of the debilitating images in his mind.

-7-

Luanda bounded over the rocky landscape, his minions struggling to keep pace. The feeling of power was intoxicating. He leaped over a massive boulder, scanning the drab landscape below as he descended. He landed on a smaller boulder, crushing the rock with his bulk. He waited for the ginangas and washakas to catch up with him. They surrounded him, panting as they glared at their human leader. A washaka crept up to him, its ears folded back in submission.

"We run in circles!" it growled. "Rashadu is not here."

Luanda cut his eyes at the creature. "Then where is he? Tell me and we shall kill him now!"

The washaka snapped at him. "Karan told you to find him, if you are capable."

Luanda kicked the washaka and shattered its chest. The beast fell dead at his feet. The others took a quick look at their fallen comrade and moved away. Luanda was angry because the washaka's words were too close to the truth. He had no idea where to find Rashadu. The trail had gone cold and the ginangas he dispatched did not return. Returning to Karan without Rashadu was not an option.

Another washaka dared to approach him. "We cannot wander forever," it rasped. "We must feed."

Luanda nodded. He reached out with his senses, scanning the miles for sign of his ancient adversary. With nothing before him he decided to choose at random.

"We will travel east toward Wangara. I'm sure we'll find nourishment there."

The washaka bared its teeth and ran down the hill to its cohorts. Together they loped east, Luanda following instead of leading. He did not have the same needs as the lesser nyoka. His strength came directly from Karan.

They traveled for miles before coming upon a village resting on the banks of a small lake at the base of a cluster of low hills. The beasts attacked immediately, ginangas charging into the streets driving the terrified villagers into the open where the washakas waited. Luanda had witnessed the tactic thousands of times. In the beginning, the thought of people devoured by nyokas sickened him. The years had hardened his heart. As long as they were not Mosele he didn't care.

He strode through the village. The ginangas had been thorough; not one person remained, nor had anyone been killed within the gates. The carnage took place outside the walls. The creatures left nothing.

A satisfied washaka came to him. "We have something for you," it said.

"You know I don't feed this way," he snapped.

"Even if it's an Adamu priest?"

Luanda's eyebrows rose. "Show me."

The beast led him to the pasture that served as the killing fields. The horde moved aside, revealing a lone man in ragged and bloody clothing surrounded by dead ginangas and washakas. He was tall, his short cropped hair speckled with gray. A bloody, rune-etched sword occupied his right hand, a thick wooden staff in his left. The washaka was correct. Luanda was happy to see him.

The man's blank face did not change as Luanda approached him. "You're a long way from home, Adamu," Luanda snarled.

"And you are far from what you used to be, Mosele," the priest spat back.

Luanda circled the priest, anger rising with his blood. He would kill this man, but he would have to be cautious. He wanted more than just his death.

Luanda lunged and the priest dodged to the left, raising his staff. Luanda grabbed the staff and felt searing pain near his ribs. The priest had stabbed him. It was a simple and deadly technique executed by a man who had obviously slain many ginangas and washakas during his sojourns. But Luanda was no weak beast. The blade passed no further than his skin. The burning pain was generated by the nyama-infused blade. Luanda wrenched the staff from the priest's stunned hand and hit him across the sword arm. The crack of the old man's arm made him smile; the man crumpled to the ground. But the priest was not done yet. He reached into his cloak with his good hand, extracting a fistful of a gray substance. With Cha's words on his lips, he threw the dust into Luanda's face. Luanda succumbed momentarily, his body stiffening. He fell to his knees as the pain bored into his core. He saw the priest smile with his fading eyes as he fell backwards. His fury fought the poison and his eyes cleared. The pain dissipated and Luanda stood. He grabbed the priest by the throat.

"Your tricks won't save you today, Adamu," Luanda said.

The priest's face remained calm. "It was not my place to take your soul. Cha has chosen another."

The priest grasped Luanda's wrists with both good and crippled hand. An image exploded in the Mosele's mind, a vision of Rashadu striding across a featureless desert, his powers fully restored. The image was ripped away, replaced by another vision of scores of mounted warriors led by a priestess glowing with Cha's Blessing. The vision faded and the priest went limp in Luanda's hands, a smile on his face.

Luanda yelled and tossed the body to the ginangas.

"Leave him be," he said. "He has given me what I needed."

The washakas and ginangas looked at him in confusion as he smiled.

"I know where to find Rashadu," he announced.

-8-

Adande stormed down a temple corridor to Cha's Chamber, her acolytes barely keeping pace. The word of Baba Toure's visit had come moments ago, sending the Shosa compound into a frenzy of preparation. The anger she felt from Sadatina's dismissal spilled onto the unfortunate sisters left behind.

"Why is he coming here?" Adande moaned.

"I don't know, First Sister," an acolyte answered.

"Shut up!" Adande snapped. "Make sure there is enough food prepared in case he wishes a meal. I will meet him in the main chamber."

Adande wore Sadatina's robe. The clothing fit snugly; she was huskier than the Nana, more handsome than beautiful. She didn't know how long Sadatina would be on the field but she knew her position was not permanent. The only way she could become Nana was if Sadatina died. It was a situation Adande had mixed feelings about. To lose her would be an unfathomable blow to their war against the Mosele. On the other hand, Sadatina's death would mean another Mother would be selected. Or would it? The Mother had been born gifted. Cha had only enhanced her powers. Would Cha select a new priestess?

She sat on the plain stool and waited, flanked by her attendants. Baba Toure entered moments later accompanied by a small entourage of guards and servants. His gesere, Tekie, the linguist and historian of the Royal Stool stepped forward.

"Baba Toure thanks you for accepting his visit on such short notice," Tekie announced.

Adande prostrated before Toure, to everyone's

astonishment, and then returned to her stool. "I am not the priestess although I serve in her stead. I hope Baba Toure accepts me as one of his children."

Toure signaled Tekie. The linguist raised his hand and the entourage left the chamber.

"Have you word from the Nana?" Toure asked her directly.

"No," Adande replied. "I don't expect to hear from her." Toure smiled. "I understand. She is not one to ask for help. Besides, she has Cha."

"It was kind of you to send warriors to our aid," Adande said.

Toure nodded. "It was Cha's will. This new threat is not like that of old. With Rashadu revived everything changes."

Adande's curiosity showed through her eyes. "What is so special about Rashadu?"

"Nana has not told you?"

Adande lowered her eyes. "Nana does not share all her visions. Sometimes she is selfish with her blessings." Adande admonished herself for her last words. She had let her emotions creep into her conversation.

Baba Toure studied her before responding. "The old books say Rashadu was Karan's first, for the lack of a better word. He was the one who turned the tide in the war between Adamu and Mosele. He possessed the intelligence of a man and the cruelty of a mjibwe. It is also written that his power was second only to Karan."

Adande's forehead furrowed. "How did the ancestors defeat him?"

Toure looked worried. "They didn't. Karan's army beat the Adamu back into Wangara. As Rashadu led them on their final assault he went mad. The books say Cha chose to save us at the last moment. Rashadu turned on Karan and the Mosele, slaying half of his army before fleeing. The Adamu charged from the city and completed the slaughter, but the damage was done. The Djennebu fled their city in fear; some hid in the surrounding hills and grasslands but others came here to establish Wangara."

"So you think Rashadu's return means an attack on Wangara?"

Toure smiled. "Possibly, if Sadatina fails. I doubt that will happen, especially with my warriors assisting her."

"She does not intend to kill him," Adande said.

"What do you mean?"

Adande sat straight in her stool. "Nana is not sure Rashadu means us harm. Cha's vision has not been clear to her on his fate."

Toure rubbed his chin. "It's the same with my visions. Cha does not give me an answer on this."

Adande leaned toward Toure, her face eager. "Maybe it is because we have the answer. Rashadu led the Mosele against us once. He will do so again. His resurrection is a sign that the Adamu and Mosele will fight again. Can we hope that Rashadu will fail again?"

"Rashadu is an unknown," he finally said. "It seems his actions are masked even to Cha. Such a variable must be eliminated. Sadatina must kill him when she finds him."

Adande pushed her advantage. "Sadatina must be informed of your decision."

"That is true. This is a task for you."

Adande lowered her eyes. "I understand, Baba, but Sadatina placed our sisters in my hands."

"I'm sure you can find someone else to administer while you're away. Besides, I sense you are anxious to be with the hunt. I will send a message with you explaining to Sadatina my insistence."

"Are you sure, Baba?"

Toure stood. "How soon can you be ready to leave?"

Adande bowed. "By sunrise, Baba."

"Good. It is time we ended this Rashadu threat once and for all."

-9-

Rashadu reached the forest lands with the rainy season. His trek across the desert and savannah was unopposed, which surprised him. An attack from Karan was inevitable; he defied him and deserved no less. Still he wondered why his former master held back. Maybe he knew of the temple and waited for Rashadu to discover it. The bright pain emerged at the edge of his mind, driving him from thoughts of his destination. He had to concentrate on the moment, distracting himself by observing the flora and fauna of the region. An unexpected sensation emerged; a feeling of pleasure at the sight of green hills, and sparse trees, roaming herds of wildebeests, zebras and giraffes scattering from his presence. He came within sight of a few man villages, the alarm drums rumbling over the distance calling the inhabitants away from the malevolent spirit striding across their lands. He ignored them. With his spiritual appetite sated he had no need to approach the small settlements.

Evening drew near when the sensation he anticipated jarred his reverie. He stopped, closed his eyes and raised the spectral image in his mind. The group was smaller than he expected. Karan must have thought him weak from his solitude and sent a small force to deal with him. He sensed two hundred total, divided evenly between ginangas and washakas.

They stopped and Rashadu sensed something else. A smile formed on his face: there was a mjibwe with them, a very powerful one.

The washaka stood still as the ginangas spread out through the acacias. Rashadu drew his knives and continued on; he could not avoid or escape them. There would be death this day, his most likely, but he cared little. He had no desire to go back into hiding and death would be preferable to the mental torture lingering at the edge of his consciousness.

The sensation struck Sadatina with a force that stole her breath and made her dizzy. Her sisters stumbled, broken from their powerful lopes as the overwhelming wave of malicious spirit covered them. The felines recovered first, both cats standing rigid, their eyes focused on the east, their ears flat on their skulls. Sadatina's confusion cleared to a foreboding vision. They had found Rashadu and his pursuers.

Beyla raised her lance, halting their advance. She rode up to Sadatina, accompanied by Dapo. "Nana?" she asked.

"Our target is near, but so are those who pursue him," Sadatina said, trance-like.

"I thought we were only after Rashadu," Dapo said, worry evident in his voice.

Sadatina smiled grimly. "There are others who hunt him, those who once considered him an ally."

"Maybe he seeks to join them again," Beyla pondered.

"No. They intend to kill him. They are so focused on him they have not sensed us."

"Then they will do our job for us," Dapo concluded.

"No," Sadatina answered. "We will do our job." She turned to Beyla. "Call your sisters. We don't have much time."

-10-

Luanda watched from a distance as the ginanga forced Rashadu toward a small rise overlooking the grasslands. The nonchalant look on his rival's face angered the Mosele; Karan's favorite pet had returned as he had left, overconfident and unaffected. Rashadu had to be aware of his situation, but he proceeded up the sparse slope as if a long life lay before him. Luanda thought of ending it quickly, leaping over his minions and confronting Rashadu immediately. Once Rashadu stopped walking Luanda was glad he waited. The ginanga pounced on him from all sides. Rashadu responded just as suddenly, whipping out two gold-colored blades then slicing through the ginanga with blurring speed. A spray of blood and body parts filled the air at the hill's summit. The dull-witted ginangas charge into the carnage, but the washakas refused. They milled about, waiting while their lesser brethren were torn apart by the being they were sent to subdue.

Luanda had not expected the knives. Rashadu was more resourceful than he remembered. He picked up his pace as the washakas inched up the hill to the battle. Luanda was confident they would attack; they would be more cautious, observing their prey's movements before attacking. They wouldn't win but they would wear him down, preparing Rashadu for Luanda's killing blows. He picked up his pace, his expression grim. He would exact his revenge.

Sadatina and her daughters watched the battle from the cover of the trees beyond the river. Rashadu's power was obvious as he meted out death easily among the ginanga assaulting him. The washaka advanced warily as was their way. But it was the Mosele mjibwe slowly striding to the fray who caught Sadatina's attention. Agitated growls rumbled from her feline sisters as they watched the mjibwe move toward Rashadu.

She turned to her commanders. Beyla's face was stern, her eyes focused on Sadatina. Dapo rubbed his sweating hands together.

"We must wait until the washaka and mjibwe join the battle before we attack. Once they are engaged, we'll cross the river. Dapo, you will position your weapons around the base of the hill. Your primary target will be the washakas. Beyla, you will keep your sisters behind Dapo's forces until they draw the washakas. I assume both of you can execute your duties?"

"Yes, Mother," they answered.

"Good. I and my sisters will deal with the mjibwe."

Beyla looked concerned. "Mother, what if Rashadu attacks you?"

"Let us pray that does not happen until we are ready," Sadatina answered. She smiled at them both. "Whatever happens, do not attack Rashadu or the mjibwe. Return to Wangara if I should fail."

"Yes, Mother," they replied. Sadatina read the concern on their faces and knew the question haunting their minds. What if she failed? What would be the outcome? What would be the fate of the Adamu? Sadatina had posed that same question many times before Cha and received no answer. She could only believe that she would not fail.

Rashadu had no respite between the death of the final ginanga and the washaka assault. Packs of the stronger beasts surrounded him and darted in and out, wary of Rashadu's gleaming blades that had decimated their lesser brethren. Their strategy was to confuse him, to spin him about and wear him down for the kill. Rashadu focused on the washakas before him while tracking the others with his senses. He waited until the pack behind him was in full attack before he spun to face them. He jumped among them, decapitating the first creature while punching the second with the hilt of his blade. He ducked and the third beast sailed over his head. A dull pain rose in his left calf; he looked down to a washaka gnawing his leg. He stomped the beast's head and crushed it. The wound was superficial and advantageous. The smell of his blood would cause the washaka to lose their composure and attack instinctively. If that occurred, they would be short work. He let it bleed and the washakas went wild.

Luanda frowned as the washakas' coordinated attack degenerated into blood frenzy. Rashadu slaughtered them like the ginangas even though the washakas managed to cause more wounds. The time had come for him to enter the battle. He crouched and leapt over the advancing washakas and landed beside Rashadu. The nyoka looked at Luanda casually, his knives dripping blood.

"You finally decided to fight, eh Mosele?" Rashadu sneered. "It seems there is some bravery left in your kind."

Luanda charged Rashadu and blacked out. When he awoke his nose bled. Rashadu's back was to him as he battled another group of washakas, slicing the beasts apart with his blurring blades. The other washakas milled about the mjibwe, their puzzled expressions angering him. He cursed; Rashadu had played his emotions. Luanda approached cautiously. Rashadu turned toward him as he advanced, flinging away a dead washaka. Luanda barely dodged a slash aimed at his throat and blocked a vicious kick toward his abdomen. He punched at Rashadu's face and missed; his follow-up kick grazed the nyoka-man's leg, knocking him off balance. Washakas pounced immediately, dragging Rashadu to his knees. Their victory was brief; Rashadu hacked himself free in moments and regained his feet.

Luanda's third attack was interrupted by a thunderous roar. He jerked his head to the sound and saw black-clad warriors surrounding the base of the hill with strange objects mounted on stands. Hundreds of mounted riders waited behind them, their lances and sabers enveloped in gris-gris. One warrior stood apart, a woman who radiated so brightly with spiritual power it was hard to look at her directly. A priestess, he assumed. His distraction was ended by a blow to the head. Luanda spun and grabbed Rashadu's hand, stopping the blade meant for his neck. He caught the other blade with his other hand, its destination his gut. The two stood locked like massive ebony statues.

Sound erupted again and an object struck Luanda with a force that tumbled him head over feet. He lay on his back dazed, his eyes open but seeing nothing. This was a new power unknown to him. The sky slowly came into view and he struggled to his feet. His left side was numb but he could still move. He expected to see Rashadu standing before him but, to his amazement, the nyoka-man lay sprawled at his feet. He was about to savor his good fortune when searing pain pierced his leg. He looked down to see a shumba pulling at his leg, her strength more potent than any washaka. He balled his fist to strike the beast when a similar pain burst forth on his shoulder and raked across his chest. Another shumba had pounced on him, biting with vicious fury. The first shumba leapt out of his reach as he swung at her; the other jumped away before could grab her. He realized the diversion too late. Luanda spun as the priestess soared toward him, her hands gripping a weapon so filled with nyama it burned like the sun in her hands. He leaned away desperately then howled as the blade tore through his shoulder. He fell away as his arm dropped to the ground. Fear commanded him; he grabbed his arm and fled, his strength waning with every drop of blood spilled. In seconds he disappeared into the woods beyond the river, leaving his horde and Rashadu to the Adamu warriors.

Sadatina watched the Mosele mjibwe flee across the river with a mix of astonishment and amusement. Never before had she witnessed such a thing. Karan's creatures fought to the death, for death was their eventual fate if they failed. The novelty of the mjibwe's retreat was quickly swept away by the reality at her feet. The being of her visions lay sprawled before her, the slight rise and fall of his chest the only indication of life. She gripped Judgment tighter as she edged closer, her sisters taking position opposite her. He was handsome, the opposite of any of Karan's creations she'd encountered. Part of his torture, she suspected. Sending a creature with physical perfection to destroy those he mimicked. She raised her sword and stepped closer. Kill him and be done with it, she thought. It was what she should do. But Cha did not confirm or deny. She was alone again at a crucial moment, abandoned to take the future of the Adamu in her hands.

Her daughters and sons struggled up the hill. Many lay among the dead and dying washaka and ginanga, but not as many as had died in Tuji. There was no confusion on their faces as they looked down on Rashadu's body.

"He is dead. Good!" Beyla spat. "We shall burn his body here and claim his ashes for gris-gris."

"Cha's Voice has triumphed!" Dapo shouted. He faced Sadatina with a wide smile. "Karan's demise is assured!"

A cheer exploded among the victorious Adamu, hugs and kisses betraying the failure of Sadatina's celibacy rule. The priestess showed no joy, her expression quickly tempering the celebration. "We will not kill him," she stated.

"What?" Dapo exclaimed. "Baba Toure wishes him dead!"

"Baba Toure is not here," Sadatina replied. "Cha is not certain of the being. Until I know Cha's will, we will do nothing."

Dapo stepped toward Sadatina. "This is not acceptable!"

Sadatina didn't realize her sword was at Dapo's throat until she heard her sisters' roar. Shosas surrounded the sofas, their hands gripping their saber hilts, their bows loaded and drawn. Beyla looked back and forth at the priestess and Dapo, her expression concerned but her loyalty unfaltering. Her saber was drawn and pointed at Dapo's chest.

"Baba Toure sent you to support and obey me," Sadatina began. "I say we will not kill Rashadu this day."

Dapo cleared his throat. "Yes, Nana."

"If you have a problem with my decision, ride away now. Tell Baba Toure what happened here and be a witness against us when we arrive. Otherwise, stay here and do what you are told."

"We will stay," Dapo answered.

Sadatina lowered her blade. "Beyla, gather rope from your sisters and treat it with gris-gris. Hurry!"

Beyla ran off shouting orders. Dapo approached Sadatina and bowed. "Forgive me, Mother. I am in no position to question your decision. We will do as you ask. How can we assist?"

"You will tie the ropes around Rashadu." Sadatina extended her sword to Dapo. "Place this on his chest before securing him. Make sure it is firmly placed."

Dapo bowed. "I will, Nana."

Sadatina watched as the warriors trussed Rashadu, securing Judgment on his chest. Her daughters brought an empty supply wagon and they loaded the nyoka man in with great difficulty. He was huge, twice as tall as the tallest Aduma and heavier than a small tembo. The wagon groaned under his load; two extra mules were added to the team to pull the nefarious cargo. Sadatina and her sisters rode with the wagon while the others kept pace before and behind them. Nervousness worked through the group, tension of the confrontation still high, the unspoken fear of their powerful prisoner heavy on their minds. Sadatina was not immune to the emotions. Her eyes were locked on the unconscious giant while her mind begged Cha for some indication of what she should do. Her sisters reflected her confusion, their behavior agitated at best. They fought each other and lunged at any Shosa or sofa that ventured too close.

Two days on the march did nothing to allay the mood. They camped on the banks of a narrow river, taking advantage of the water to bathe. Shosa and sofas openly flirted and teased each other, their way to ease the constant tension. Sadatina ignored them. She continued to gaze on Rashadu. She wanted to be prepared when he regained consciousness.

Night came unnoticed to her. Beyla quietly prepared a fire

for her and slipped away, Dapo waiting in the distance. Sadatina ignored the food set before her, her lips moving as she silently prayed to Cha.

"You should eat, priestess," a deep voice rumbled.

Sadatina sprang to her feet, her saber in her hands. Her sisters were up as well, their eyes glowing with firelight. Rashadu looked at them and smiled.

"Eat. I am not going anywhere."

Sadatina kept her weapon raised. "Why have you returned?"

"To find the answer," Rashadu replied.

His voice was soothing, almost hypnotic. She realized what was happening and shut herself away. "You seek a tower," she said.

Rashadu winced. "Be careful, priestess. That image is a curse to me. I must keep it from my mind to keep control."

"Are you sure?" Sadatina leaned closer to the bound nyoka. "Maybe something else keeps you from seeing the image. Maybe your truth lies through the pain."

Rashadu looked thoughtful for a moment and grinned. "You would have me kill myself? You are skillful, but not that skillful."

"Have you come back to fight us?" she asked.

"Your master has not told you?" Rashadu laughed, a sound that was as menacing as it as joyful. "It seems even Cha does not know what to do with me."

Sadatina felt anger rising in her throat like bile. "You didn't answer my question, nyoka."

"I have no desire to harm the Adamu unless you interfere in my journey. I only wish to find the tower."

"Why? What does this tower mean to you?"

Rashadu's face twisted. "I believe if I see the tower the madness will cease."

"If so, then what will you do?" Sadatina's suspicions usurped her anger.

"I don't know."

Sadatina stood, her mind resolved. "Then I cannot allow you to find it."

"That too is beyond your power." The nyoka-man sat up Judgment falling to the ground as he snapped the charmed ropes like thread. He reached down and Judgment rose from the ground into his right hand.

Sadatina stood stunned. Only she could possess Judgment. At least that was what she was told the day Cha placed it in her possession. Her feline sisters attacked, abandoning their staggered assault and leaping at Rashadu simultaneously. He slapped them both with the flat of the blade and they crumpled to the ground.

"Do not call your companions," Rashadu warned. "If you do, I will kill them all."

Sadatina backed away. She was sure now that Cha had abandoned her. Rashadu held her most powerful weapon like a toy and her sisters lay unconscious at his feet. Yet he made no threatening moves toward her.

"Where is the tower?" he asked.

Sadatina swallowed hard. "I do not know."

"I believe you do."

Sadatina tried to show confidence. "I don't!"

"Then what use are you to me?" Rashadu inched closer.

"Don't threaten me with death," she said, defiance plain in her voice. "Cha's bosom awaits me."

"What about your daughters and sons? Does Cha's paradise await them as well? They will die as surely as you if you don't tell me what I desire."

Sadatina's shoulders sagged. "There is no tower in Wangara, at least not the one you seek."

"Then where is it?"

Sadatina closed her eyes and reached back into her memory for her priestess teachings. She revived her lessons, the memorized passages scrolling through her mind. Then she saw it. The way to Djenna appeared as clear as Rashadu's face. Sadatina was shocked at first; why would Cha reveal this to her after letting Rashadu possess Judgment? The answer came just as quickly: Cha wished him to find the city. The towers had almost destroyed him before. This time the destruction would be complete. She held her joy inside, her face frozen in solemn defeat. Cha had summoned Rashadu to his doom.

"Djenna, the fourth incarnation of Wangara," she said, "the Gleaming City, the city of towers."

Rashadu grimaced. "So you do know where it is," he managed to say.

"Yes and no," she confessed. "The directions to Djenna are clear in the legend, but it is a legend."

"But there must be some truth to this legend," Rashadu said, his voice anxious.

Rashadu's desperation gave her hope.

"The legend will lead us to the city. Come, we must go now." Sadatina gazed at her shumbas. "What of my sisters?"

Rashadu glanced at them. "They will find us." He extended Judgment to her. Sadatina hesitated, and then grasped the hilt. Cha's power still pulsed strong inside it. Then Rashadu grabbed her, cradling her in his massive arms like a child. Instead of feeling fear, she felt safer than she'd ever felt in her life.

"We will make better time if I carry you. Your daughters will not be able to sense me."

Sadatina looked into Rashadu's fiery eyes. "You are not a nyoka yet you are not a man. What sort of thing are you?"

"I don't know," he replied. "The towers will tell me."

-11-

Luanda jumped into the river, hoping to quench the searing pain emanating from where his arm used to be. The limb had rotted away hours after it was severed by the priestess's infernal sword. Luanda attempted to clear his mind of pain and make sense of the past few days. The ginangas and washakas were dead, killed either by Rashadu or the Adamubu warriors. Rashadu might be dead but not by his hands. The new Adamu weapon felled both of them, but he had regained consciousness before the priestess and her beasts attacked him. The pain flared again and his thoughts scattered. He doused his wound in the river once more. Karan would kill him if he returned to the mountains. Failure was not an option and he was no use to the stone god if he could not carry out his commands. He was man and mjibwe, but he was less than a ginanga. The stupid beasts fought to the death from instinct. The wary washakas fought to the death for they knew what awaited them if they failed. It was the human in him that made him weak, driving him to flee the priestess and her ferocious companions.

Luanda dragged out of the river and lay on his back. The pain subsided, the priestess's gris-gris diluted by the river's magic. He dared to touch the wound and felt the beginning of a new limb emerging from his torn flesh. He breathed deeply to calm himself and concentrated his remaining power to locate Rashadu. He found the nyoka-man traveling west, his aura much brighter than when they had confronted each other on the hill. Another revelation caught him by surprise. The priestess traveled with him. Had she deliberately spared him for her own purpose or had

Rashadu somehow won her over? Luanda came to his feet. The reason did not matter. He could not go back to Karan without victory. He set out after the duo. His body would eventually heal and his strength would return. He would kill them both. He had no other choice.

-12-

Adande had no idea where to find Sadatina and the others. Baba Toure met them in Tuji and departed before knowing in which direction they headed. The Tujibu were somewhat helpful; they were able to point them in a direction at least, which was better than nothing. They followed the trail, picking up signs of the Adamu corps as they plunged deeper into unknown territory. They finally emerged into a morbid sight. A field littered with dead ginangas and washakas, writhing with scores of buzzards and carrion crows feasting on the nefarious remains. There were no Shosa or Adamu warriors among the dead. The bodies surrounded a low hill capped with burned grass and broken earth.

"It must have been a terrible battle," one of the Shosa spoke.

Adande twisted in her saddle to glare at the woman, angry that she had not been present for what was obviously a glorious victory. The signs on the mound suggested a powerful struggle. Had Sadatina and her sisters confronted Rashadu here? There was no body, which raised many questions. The dead ginangas and washakas had not been processed like the ones in Tuji. Maybe there was no time or maybe too few Shosa survived the battle. Had Sadatina slain Rashadu or did he escape? There was only one way to know for sure.

"Spread out and look for sign of our sisters," she ordered. Shosa dismounted then scanned the ground carefully for sign as well. After a few minutes they found it. The group had headed back by a different route, taking the main highway rather than the narrow trails. The signs indicated they were only a few days ahead.

The Shosa rode hard over the next few days, taking advantage of the unusually dry weather. On the fourth day they crested a steep hill adjacent to the Kamba River and discovered the Adamu camp. It was apparent to Adande that something was terribly wrong. Her mood darkened further when she was greeted by Beyla and Dapo. Beyla was obviously shocked to see her while Dapo's expression was as grim as her own.

"Where is Sadatina?" Adande snapped. Beyla froze, looking at Dapo with sympathetic eyes. Adande grasped Beyla's chin, turning her face to hers.

"Look at me! Where is Sadatina?"

Beyla snatched Adande's hand from her chin. "I don't know."

"And she chose you as her second?"

"You don't understand," Beyla responded. "Sadatina is gone."

"She is gone with Rashadu," Dapo spat.

Adande's mind blanked. She stared at Beyla and Dapo, trying to form a thought. "Nana? Gone with the nyoka? What are you talking about?"

"We captured Rashadu," Beyla explained. "Cha's Voice brought him down and wounded the mjibwe he fought. We surrounded Rashadu but Nana would not kill him. She ordered us to bind him and load him into a supply wagon. We were to bring him back to Wangara. Three days later they both disappeared."

"No guards saw them leave?"

Beyla shook her head. "None."

"The nyoka is stronger than Sadatina imagined," Adande concluded. "Cha has abandoned her."

Adande saw protest in Beyla's eyes despite her silence. Sadatina was gone; she was the senior Shosa now. "We will return to Wangara," she said.

"I hoped we would search for Nana," Beyla countered.

"And where would we start? We don't know where the nyoka took her. She could be cowering before Karan."

"I will notify my sisters we are departing," Beyla stormed away.

"I wanted to kill him," Dapo confessed. "Nana would not allow it. She seemed confused."

"It is of no matter now. We must return to the city and prepare. With Sadatina gone, Karan is sure to attack. We must be ready."

-13-

Anyone gazing upon the figure bounding across the teeming grassland would consider themselves mad. The sight of a large muscular man with glowing eyes and stark white hair carrying a woman in his massive arms seemed of myth, yet it was real. Rashadu had run since the day Sadatina shared her knowledge with him, stopping only for the priestess to tend to her personal needs. Rashadu needed no such respite; he ran throughout the day and night, moving so rapidly Sadatina had to keep her face turned away. Strangely, she felt no fear in his arms. An eerie contentment overtook her across the miles and days, gradually morphing into unexpected sympathy for her captor. She knew Rashadu was hurrying to his death. Cha would clam his life as soon as he glimpsed the Djenna's towers. It was a fate he deserved yet she found no joy in it. Somewhere in this creature was a man, a soul who had given himself to Karan for some unknown reason. Did he know his decision would result in this? It was a new sensation for her to doubt the truth of the One she worshiped so she fought against it. She would think of it no more. Cha had chosen her as an instrument of his judgment and she would obey whether it made sense to her or not.

They entered a land unknown to her, a cold flat land of endless grasses. Gray clouds dominated the sky, grudgingly parting to reveal glimpses of blue sky and anemic sunlight. Sadatina shivered, her thin garments useless in such a cold climate. Rashadu veered from his course. After a few miles she sensed why. There was a village nearby. A new fear rose in her, a fear of what Rashadu would do to these folks.

He slowed his pace until he could stop running then set her down.

"You are cold," he said. "We will seek clothing."

Sadatina looked at the village, still a good distance away. "You will not take me there?"

"The villagers will find me disturbing. I have no need for distractions."

"Since when does Karan's minion care for the feelings of men?"

Rashadu's eyes brightened. "I am no longer Karan's servant and I care nothing for human feelings. Their fear of me would force me to kill them. I must save my strength for more important confrontations. Now go."

Sadatina began to leave, and then stopped. "You trust that I will return?"

Rashadu grinned. "You will, for the sake of your daughters and the villagers."

The village consisted of a cluster of homes constructed with black sod cut from the ground. Smoke wafted from the irregular stone chimneys to form a gray cloud over the settlement. A ragged wooden fence surrounded a small herd of large horned cattle while goats and sheep grazed unattended on the perimeter.

Women dressed in thick woolen dresses and headscarves sat before the homes in groups, preparing food and tending children who fluttered around them like birds. Sadatina saw no men, though she knew they were close by. A wail rose from the village and she knew she'd been seen. The women grabbed the young ones and fled into their homes. Men mounted on small sturdy horses appeared, charging her with long thick lances.

Sadatina did not panic. She stood still, stretching out her arms in the Adamu stance of submission. The horsemen galloped toward her, reined in their mounts and dismounted. They resembled the Adamu; it was obvious they were descended from the same folk. Their stern faces melted into astonishment.

One man rode closer, his wrinkled and bearded russet face signifying him as an elder. His scrutinizing eyes widened as he neared.

"Priestess?" he gasped.

Sadatina let out a sigh, thankful they recognized her status. The men dropped to their knees in unison, covering their faces. Their language was close enough to her own that she understood them, another sign of a common ancestry.

"I seek clothing and food," she stated. The elder lifted his head and nodded. He ran to his horse and offered it to her. She climbed on; the others mounted their horses then they took her to the village.

Farmers peeked from behind their doors as she was led to the central home. Then elder assisted her off the horse then opened the central house's door, bowing as Sadatina entered. A woman stood before the fire, her long braided hair decorated with various gris-gris. Sadatina recognized the woman as the village shaman. She looked at Sadatina as if she expected her.

"Why have you come here, priestess?" she asked, her voice clear and resonant.

Sadatina sat at the table and the elder brought her a hot bowl of fragrant stew. Her stomach grumbled; it had been a long time since she'd eaten and the stew smelled delicious.

"We don't need your suspicions, Tisha," the man said. "It's obvious she is a priestess. She seeks clothing and food. It is all we need to know."

"How can you be so certain?" the shaman argued. "I sense a nyoka about. It could be her."

Sadatina was impressed. The shaman's vision was not clear, but she knew something was amiss. "I am no nyoka, but your sense is true. There is a creature nearby but he will not harm you."

"How can you be sure?"

"He is under my control," she lied.

She felt the Tisha's astonishment. The shaman removed the blanket from her shoulders.. She held it out to Sadatina.

"I have others," she said.

Sadatina took the coat. She warmed rapidly, impressed by the quality of the garment. The stew sped her recovery, tasting as delicious as it smelled. She stood up from the table as soon as she was done. "I must leave. I thank you for your kindness."

"Wait," Tisha said.

Sadatina turned. "What is it?"

"That sword on your back. Where did you get it?"

Sadatina's eyes narrowed. "It was given to me...by Cha."

The shaman covered her face. "Then you are truly sent by him. That same blade was given to another a long time ago."

The shaman's words struck Sadatina hard. "Are you sure it was this sword?"

The shaman nodded. "I was a girl then, a student at the temple. Our High Priest, Ihecha, received a calling to fight the Mosele and their new god, Karan. Cha gave him the sword you carry, or one like it."

It was like seeing the words of history come to life. If what this woman said was true, she was very old. Impossibly old.

"When the nyokas appeared at our walls, we knew our warriors had failed," Tisha continued. " Still, we prepared to fight them. They were led by a nyoka we'd never seen before, a creature who was even more terrible because he resembled a man. But strangely enough at the peak of battle he turned on his own and destroyed them. No sooner had he done so did he flee. But we were too afraid to stay in the city. Most of us escaped. A few like me, stayed as long as we could but eventually we had to leave. And so we live in our villages now, and the nyokas have not returned."

Tisha stood. "So I ask you again, priestess, why are you here?"

"I travel to Djenna. There is a duty I must perform."

"And the creature you travel with," Tisha said. "He is not under your control."

Sadatina dropped her head. "No. He is not."

"So you travel with a nyoka to do his will, yet you carry a

weapon that can slay him easily. This I don't understand."

"Neither do I," Sadatina said. "But I'm sure this is the way Cha wishes it to be."

Tisha stood and walked toward the door. "Let us both be sure."

Sadatina followed her outside. They mounted two short horses and rode swiftly to where she had departed from Rashadu, spotting the nyoka-man as they crested the hill overlooking the river. Tisha reined her horse to a stop as did Sadatina.

"He feels familiar," Tisha said. She closed her eyes for a moment, and then they flew open. "He is the one! The one who led the nyokas against Djenna!"

"I believe he is," Sadatina said.

"I know he is," Tisha replied.

This was the first time in many years Sadatina had met the insight of someone with more wisdom than herself. "Tisha, what should I do?"

"What Cha wills you to do," Tisha replied. "You have his sword and you have his vision. Whatever happens is his will."

Sadatina dismounted and handed the reins of her frightened horse to Tisha. "Thank you for your gifts and your wisdom."

"Thank you for taking up the sword," Tisha answered. "Be well, sister, and be safe." The shaman briefly covered her face in farewell and rode away.

Sadatina strolled down the hill to Rashadu. He stood as he came close.

"Why did you bring a shaman?" he asked.

"I didn't bring her, she followed."

He looked at her garments and nodded. "You are comfortable now?"

"Yes. Why does it matter to you?"

"It doesn't. I need you to find the temple. The cold can kill and I don't want you to die. At least not yet."

He swept her into his arms then leaped over the river,

continuing their run to the city. Sadatina cringed at the touch of his skin now, his last statement swirling in her mind. Did he intend to kill her once they found the city? She could not stop him if he tried. Or could she? Maybe Cha had not abandoned her completely. If this was part of his plan, she still had hope. If only she knew for certain. So much was not as it should be. Cha continued his silence, leaving her to her own assumptions. Whatever the outcome, she was only sure of her uncertainty.

That night they camped in a patch of riverwood trees which provided protection from the flatland's bitter wind. The villagers had provided Sadatina with provisions, including a thick blanket for sleeping. She wrapped herself and sat close to the dying fire, the fading light subdued by the glow in Rashadu's eyes. Sadatina stared at him, her confusion overriding her apprehension.

"Who are you?" she asked.

"I am what Karan made me," was the nyoka's reply.

"Karan can transform but he cannot create. Only Cha can do so," she corrected. 'Every creature that serves the stone god was something or someone else before. So I ask again, who are you?"

Rashadu clenched his eyes in obvious pain. "I remember Karan's face. I remember being relieved to see him. I was ready to do anything he asked because..." His eyes narrowed. His face tightened and his fingers curled into massive fists. Sadatina eased to her feet and backed away.

"I...will...not...hurt...you," he stammered. "To...to speak of certain things causes me pain."

Sadatina stepped toward him. "Why?"

Rashadu looked at her, his eyes wide with confusion.

Sadatina saw the humanity in him for the first time. "I don't know," he whispered.

His respite was brief. The fire flared in his eyes again. Whatever had emerged dissipated quickly. "The temple will tell me."

Sadatina could not continue to hide Cha's plan. "The temple may kill you."

Rashadu shrugged. "I will find either answers or death. Maybe I will experience both. It doesn't matter. Whatever happens, the pain will be gone and I'll be at peace."

As the first hint of sunlight trickled over the horizon and began diffusing into the cold blue sky, Sadatina heard a low, rumbling voice.

"We must go."

Rashadu swept her up then ran before she had her eyes open far enough to see. Something was different; his pace seemed frantic, almost desperate. Sadatina clutched him tight, fearing she might be thrown free. The land flowed by in an undulating blur so disconcerting she had to close her eyes. Darkness was no respite; the jostling made her dizzy and queasy. Then Cha touched her and Rashadu stumbled. She hit the ground hard, the unyielding frozen soil battering her as she rolled with the momentum of Rashadu's pace. She stopped flat on her back, her body bruised and the taste of blood in her mouth. Struggling to her feet she looked for Rashadu. She found him strides beyond her. He crouched, his hands clamped against his head as his body jerked spasmodically.

"Not again," he hissed. "Not again!"

Sadatina slowly turned away. Djenna hunched over the horizon like a broken mountain, a dying monument of stone and memories. Hundreds of towers reached toward the sky like spectral fingers, their once smooth sides gouged by wind and time. A large temple rose from the city center, its damage masked by Cha's light.

Sadatina felt Cha's power stronger than ever as she turned back to face Rashadu. He came to his feet, his hair dancing about his head like malevolent flames, his eyes black with rage.

Cha's command formed in her head.

"Run."

Sadatina obeyed. She ran toward the city. Rashadu

followed, his voice ripping the silence apart. His cries grew louder as they neared the crumbling walls, but Sadatina's power increased as well as the city came closer, so much that she feared she could not contain it. She burned, her skin glowing white hot.

"Stop."

Sadatina halted and swung about. Rashadu charged at her like a mad bull, his handsome face mutilated by blind rage. She reached behind her, taking Judgment from its leather sheath. He arms quaked as she lifted her arms. The heat became unbearable; her skin and hair burned. She stabbed the blade skyward then screamed as Cha's Blessing burst from her, slamming into Rashadu and lifting him into the sky. The heat fled, replaced by constant warmth.

"Heal."

Sadatina collapsed on her knees and fell over to one side like a dropped sack of yams. She curled her wrecked body into a tight ball, sighed, and slept.

-14-

Luanda watched from a distance as the priestess released her pent-up power on Rashadu. The nyoka-man rose into the sky as the priestess collapsed, her body charred and smoking. Rashadu crashed into the ground with an impact that trembled under Luanda's feet. He lay still in a crater of his own making, the priestess' burned body before him.

Cha's work, he was sure. Who else would kill his enemy and his servant? He was no different than Karan, creating and destroying at will for his own reasons and leaving humans to suffer his whims. Luanda's disappointment with himself for not slaying Rashadu was tempered by the fact that his adversary's body remained. He could still claim his trophy, two trophies in fact. The heads of both Rashadu and the priestess would soon swing from his waist. He was halfway to his victims when Rashadu climbed from his self-made grave. Rashadu was clearly weakened. He stumbled to the burnt priestess and knelt beside her. Luanda expected him to tear off her head; instead he lifted her gently and cradled her in his arms. Luanda's face split with a wide grin. The priestess had not killed him; she transformed him. Karan's disciple was no more. He was a normal man, a worthless Adamu.

Rashadu knew he was being followed as he walked with the priestess in his arms. He ambled for a few more steps, and then laid her down. He turned to face Luanda. He'd felt the mjibwe's presence just before Sadatina's attack. "So, you are still alive."

"Yes," Luanda grinned. "Face your death, Adamu!"

Rashadu raised his hand. "No Luanda, wait."

Luanda lunged and Rashadu dodged sideways, delivering a blow to the back of the mjibwe's head that sent him sprawling face first into the grass. Luanda sprang up, angry he'd underestimated the Adamu again. Apparently Cha's energy was wasted; Rashadu was still a dangerous foe. He approached him cautiously, his hands raised, his feet poised.

"Leave now and live," Rashadu warned.

Luanda laughed. "If I leave without your head I'll surely die. If I fight you, I have a chance."

"Walk away from me and Karan," Rashadu suggested. "Don't go back. The longer you stay away, the sooner his power will fade."

"Without his power I cannot kill you. Only with Karan will the Adamu pay!" He rushed Rashadu. The nyoka-man did not move. Their bodies met with a palpable thump; their arms locked, muscles bulging as they each strained for advantage. Their feet shifted, seeking a firm stance for a position to throw one another.

Luanda summoned all his energy, unnerved by Rashadu's calm countenance.

"Why do you persist?" Rashadu asked calmly. "What purpose does my death serve for you?"

Luanda pushed harder but Rashadu did not move.

"We had them!" he shouted. "We were only a step away from claiming our land back and you took it away. You turned on us!"

"If it was meant to be yours alone you would not have lost it," Rashadu answered.

Luanda's fury overrode Rashadu's grip, He broke free and lunged again, his target now Rashadu's legs. His arms wrapped around Rashadu's thighs and he lifted him high, triumph on his face. He threw the betrayer with all his might and Rashadu sailed away to hit the ground, digging a deep, long furrow before his momentum was checked by the mound of dirt building before him. He was regaining his feet when Luanda slammed into him with his shoulder, knocking him over the mound and into the river. He rose from the river to see Luanda plunging down on him like a raptor.

"Enough of this," he whispered. Rashadu jumped and met Luanda in mid-air, wrapped his arms around him and plummeted into the river. A plume of water sprang up where they entered. Rashadu straddled Luanda, holding the mjibwe under the water. Luanda struggled violently but Rashadu pressed him deeper.

"Damn you, Karan," he hissed.

He held the Mosele underwater until he ceased struggling and released him to the currents. Luanda's body drifted away, another life wasted by Karan's ambitions. Rashadu climbed onto the bank and trudged to Sadatina. Her body was ravaged, her skin charred and her hair burned away. But she was still alive, her chest barely moved by her shallow breathing. Lifting her carefully, he carried her to the river and immersed her in the cold current that moments ago had taken Luanda's life. He submerged her completely except for her face, his huge hand bracing the back of her head. He closed his eyes and raised his free hand over her. Rashadu's hair lifted from his head, waving with the rhythm of the current. His eyes glowed behind his eyelids as the power he summoned passed from his head into his hands. He waved his hand slowly over the water, outlining Sadatina's body. Countless small fish appeared, attracted by the luminescence. They nibbled away Sadatina's burned skin, leaving behind a layer of pink. Rashadu continued to wave his hand. Brown specks emerged on her skin, spreading and expanding until she attained her original umber hue. Her hair was another matter. It would have to grow back on its own if it returned at all. The hair was an extension of Cha's spirit. He would have to raise it.

Rashadu strained to lift Sadatina from the water. His actions had weakened him; the thought of what he had to do to replenish his strength sickened him.

Go to your temple. Learn who you are.

Cha's voice startled him. Rashadu held Sadatina in his arms, his eyes on the huge temple within the Djenna's crumbling walls. The pain emerged in his mind but he steadied himself. He clutched her close to him and set off for the temple.

-15-

Adande awoke as the morning sun seeped through her curtains and touched her eyelids. She pushed away her covers, stumbled to the chest across the sparse room and retrieved her robe. She shivered, not from the cold mountain chill but from the uncertainty haunting her since returning to the city. A sister met her at her door and she shoved her away before marching to Cha's Chamber. The closer she came to the chamber, the more her anxiety increased. Her sisters took furtive glances at her, annoying her even further. She knew they disapproved of her actions; Sadatina's body had not been found so the possibility remained she could still be alive. Adande disagreed, which made what she wished to do more urgent.

She entered the chamber and stood before Cha's Eye. She approached reverently as she had done for months, chanting the litany she had overheard Sadatina recite when asking for Cha's Sight. She knelt before the dais and cleared her mind. Cha's Voice was the only step remaining to transform her status from Shosa to Nana. Sadatina's weakness would not exist in her; she would be decisive, a sharp and eager weapon for Cha to wield. She'd kill Rashadu and the Adamu army would march to Karan's mountain with Baba Sekou's new weapons to eliminate the Mosele threat once and for all. Most of all, she would use her power to destroy Karan and remove his blight from the world. She would finally secure Cha's birthright to his children. The land beyond the mountains would be Adamu land without dispute.

She chanted louder. Surely Cha heard her words, felt her sincerity, and sensed her strength. Why did he not answer? Why did he refuse to choose her?

She shouted the chant, her voice reverberating throughout the temple. Sisters gathered at the chamber entrance, their expressions a mixture of wonder, sympathy and amusement. Adande felt their eyes on her and ceased chanting. Cha would not answer her this day.

"What are you staring at?" she hissed. She stood and faced her sisters, her fury rising with every breath.

"We heard your pleas and came to help." Beyla emerged from the throng and stood before her. Adande's anger subsided. At lease she had put this one in her place. Beyla's eyes revealed her feelings. Adande had watched them change from respect to disappointment to hate. She would eventually have to kill her. Her loyalty to Sadatina would not wane even if Sadatina's death was confirmed. Her heart would open to Karan in her despair, just as Sadatina had succumbed to Rashadu.

"I don't need your concern." Adande pushed past Beyla as she exited Cha's chamber. "All I need from you are reports from the field."

"Ginanga encounters have increased, as have washaka incidents," Beyla barked. "We are evaluating the villages and setting up temporary camps outside the walls."

"I know that," Adande snapped. "What about the outriders? Any word from them?"

Beyla looked away. "No reports as of yet."

"Rashadu will come, I'm sure of it," Adande mused. "Our only hope is that he doesn't arrive at the same time as Karan and his horde."

"Maybe he is dead," Beyla guessed. "Maybe Nana killed him."

"Sadatina had her chance and apparently failed. You would do well to face reality. Despite my personal feelings you are an excellent warrior. What exists between you and I is Sadatina's fault. I need you to focus on what is happening now. Otherwise I'll have to replace you."

Beyla's expression was respectful but her eyes betrayed her anger. It was obvious to Adande that Beyla would not give up on Sadatina until she saw her body.

"I must visit Baba Toure," she said. "You will accompany me."

"There is much for me to do here, sister," Beyla argued.

"It can wait." Sadatina ignored Beyla's expression and returned to her room.

The city was mobilized for war and Baba Toure ordered the Shosa to wear full armor at all times. Adande changed to her uniform and made her way to the compound atrium. Beyla waited with four other Shosa. Adande mandated no Shosa would travel alone during such times. Although no ginangas, washakas, or mjibwes had breached the city, the possibilities increased with every day. Six Shosa were more than enough to handle a handful of skittish ginangas and clever washakas. The mjibwes were her greater concern and fear. No one but Sadatina had faced these powerful nyokas and she was armed with Judgment and aided by her sisters. Cha's Voice was effective against them but the weapons were few and cumbersome. She hoped six Shosa would be enough for the beasts but she wouldn't know until an encounter occurred. Together they rode uphill to the palace. The guards opened the gate immediately and they continued to the central palace. They dismounted before the gilded doors where servants gathered their mounts and led them away.

They were greeted by Baba Toure's gesere. "Welcome, daughters. Baba Toure apologizes for the delay. His meeting with the elders is almost complete. Will you please follow me?"

The gesere took them to six stools surrounding a circular ebony wood table. Gourds of water sat beside a bowl of figs and kola nuts. Beyla smiled generously as she grabbed a fig and stuffed it in her mouth. Adande was more reserved. She took an orange from the bowl and cut it neatly with her dagger, a frown on her face as she watched Beyla and the others. The gesere watched also, smiling pleasantly as always. Adande frowned at him, too. He was recording everything, composing the words that would become part of Baba Toure's song, his history to be passed down through the ages. Their visit was mere footnote.

A boy in a white kilt with a golden necklace appeared as they finished the fruit. "Baba Toure will see you now," he announced.

The Shosa followed the gesere and the boy into the mansa's sanctuary. They passed the elders, old men draped in thick tobes and walking with staffs carved with their family totems. They gave the Shosa a respectful nod and the women returned the gesture.

Baba Toure waited for them in his meeting hall, a large sparse room containing the Mansa's simple stool surrounded by large patterned pillows. He was dressed plainly as was his way when in his abode, a simple blue tobe with a single talisman hanging from his neck. He smiled and gestured for the women to sit. Adande took the center pillow with the other sisters sitting on either side. The gesere took his place beside the mansa.

"The elders are concerned," he began. "They think that by moving everyone into the city. We are falling into a Mosele trap. We have ceded land to them. They foresee their villages flooded with Mosele and nyokas."

"We will not let that happen," Adande assured him.

"You speak of defeating Karan as if we can. No one has personally confronted him."

Adande was about to answer but Toure held up his hand.

"We are not here to discuss possibilities. Cha tells me that Sadatina is still alive."

Adande could not hide her disappointment. If Toure noticed her sour expression he did not respond. Beyla's feelings were just as transparent. She sighed and smiled.

"So she managed to slay Rashadu?" Beyla asked.

Baba Toure's face turned grim. "No. Rashadu is still alive."

"Aren't they together?" Adande asked. Her heart beat anxiously as she awaited the mansa's answer.

"I don't know," he confessed. "Cha's message is unclear. If

they are that may be a good sign, for a time."

"How can this be good for us?" Adande asked

"Sadatina will not fight against us," Toure surmised. "She would die before betraying Cha. She would go against Karan. So if she is still alive and with Rashadu that means they are going after Karan."

"Rashadu is Karan's servant," Adande argued. "He wouldn't defy him."

"He already has." Baba Toure stood and paced. "Rashadu was under attack when Sadatina and the Shosa discovered him. Karan wants him dead. Rashadu may have stopped running and enlisted Sadatina to help him. Together they could possibly kill Karan if they could get through his minions. The question is if they kill him, then what?"

"We should march out to aid them," Beyla blurted.

Baba Toure smiled at the young Shosa. "If I was as sure of my thoughts as you are of yours, we would, daughter. But Cha does not answer me on this. He will reveal his purpose when it is our time to play a part. We must wait and prepare just in case Karan leads his army to us."

"So nothing has changed." Adande concluded. "Why did you summon us?"

"To see if you had any information to add."

Adande glared at Beyla. "We do not."

Baba Toure sat on his stool. "Then we will continue to prepare for an attack. How far are our scouts riding?"

"Fifty miles from city center," Adande replied.

"Increase the distance to one hundred miles. Maintain the flag and relay system for any urgent messages. How many are out on patrol?"

"Six."

"Shosa?"

"Yes."

"Split the teams, three Shosa, three sofas. We can't afford to lose any more daughters and the men need the experience. Each team will have one Voice with them just in case they encounter a mjibwe."

Adande smiled, impressed with the mansa. His intelligence was obvious and he was greatly favored by Cha.

"Adande, do you agree with my plans?"

His question startled her. "Yes...yes, Baba."

"Good. Let the words be recorded." The gesere nodded, the episode now sealed in his memory. The sisters rose to leave.

"Adande," the mansa called out. "A word please."

Adande took a moment to compose herself and moved closer Toure.

"Has Cha spoken to you?"

Adande lowered her head. "No, Baba."

"I assumed so. Cha does not always share the same message among his chosen. There are things I mentioned you would have known if Cha had spoken to you."

"I don't know why he hasn't!" she blurted. "I go to his chamber every day and recite the prayers. I ask him..."

"Cha is to be listened for," Toure advised. "When we ask, we listen for the answer we wish to hear. Cha knows what we seek before we pray."

Toure gestured and they both sat. "You seek him for the wrong reasons, Adande. Cha's blessing is not a badge of honor. It is a responsibility. To be Chosen is to wield power to create or destroy. It is not meant for the selfish or the petty."

Adande bristled at the mansa's words. "I wish only the best for the Adamu. I could best help fulfill his destiny for our people."

"You know our destiny? Please, share it with me."

"This land was given to us. I believe it is Cha's will that we possess it once and for all. That can only be accomplished by the defeat of Karan and the annihilation of the Mosele."

"That is what our ancestors believed, but still the land is not ours."

Adande shifted uncomfortably. "What are you saying,

Baba?"

"When Cha led our forefathers to this land he didn't tell us of the Mosele. He also did not tell us they were our enemies and that it was our duty to drive them from this land. The geseres say nothing of this." He stood and paced again. "You have seen the land. It is truly blessed, so much so that our people cannot begin to fill it. I don't believe Cha meant for us to conquer this land. I believe we are meant to share it and extend Cha's blessing to the Mosele.

We chose to be masters instead and Karan is the punishment for our decision."

Adande looked at her mansa skeptically. "What about Rashadu?"

"I'm not sure," Toure admitted. "Once I thought he was our enemy. Sadatina wasn't sure, now nor am I. It's probably why she travels with him now, to learn the truth. It may be that Rashadu is our key to winning this war."

Baba Toure smiled. "I'm rambling." He stood and Adande stood as well. "When you go to Cha's chamber, pray and listen," he advised. "Cha will reveal your purpose. You will not replace Sadatina. After her, there will be no more."

Adande bowed to the mansa. "I understand."

"I hope you do," he said.

There was nothing else to say. Adande bowed again and departed Toure's chamber to join Beyla.

"He lies."

Adande stopped and fell to her knees as though she were boneless. She covered her face. "Cha?"

"The nyoka Rashadu has corrupted their souls. They are his tools."

Adande's body shook with joy. Cha spoke to her! "What must I do?"

"You must kill the one who leads you."

"Sadatina?"

"Yes. Rashadu is my concern, as is Toure."

"I understand."

"Do not fail me like the others…Adande."

Adande uncovered her face, her expression sure.

"I will not."

-16-

Sadatina awoke naked on a bed of fresh straw. Bleached white walls surrounded her, their pitted surfaces illuminated by firelight and a soft white glow. The smell of cooking meat intoxicated her with hunger. She sat up to see Rashadu hunched over a spit and flame, juices dripping from some unlucky animal over the fire. The mjibwe looked at her and smiled. "You are better," he rumbled. "Soon you'll be completely healed."

Sadatina remembered Cha's touch and immediately began to inspect her body. Her skin was splotchy, dark and light brown patterns scattered over pink healing flesh. She touched her head and felt stubble where thick black hair used to reside. She plucked a hair, looked at it and gasped. It was white.

"A consequence of Cha's touch," Rashadu commented. "It may change back, but I wouldn't wait for it."

He took the spit from the fire and extended it to her. "I'm not sure if it's properly prepared," he said.

Sadatina bit into the meat too eagerly. It was bland but done. She studied Rashadu as she chewed. "Your pain is gone?"

Rashadu glanced down. "Yes."

"Why?"

Rashadu looked about. "This was his tower. This was his room. He lived and worshiped here."

"Who is he?"

"The man in my mind," Rashadu answered. "The face in the temple. Now that I am with him, he is content."

Sadatina stopped eating despite her hunger. "What did he do?"

"He was a high priest of Cha. He was a good man and well respected. He was a man of peace. But one day Cha spoke to him and told him of Karan. He instructed this man of peace to raise an army to defeat the Stone God. The priest reluctantly obeyed, converting his disciples to warriors and leading them across the desert to face Karan. His army fought ginangas, washakas and Mosele but was defeated. Karan was weakened. It was a hundred years before Karan could attack Wangara."

Sadatina's eyes narrowed. "And you led that attack."

Rashadu nodded. "And once again the priest protected his city. It was he who drove me mad and turned me against my own army. If not for him you would be dust."

Sadatina nodded. "You sit here free of his madness. What will you do now?"

"You don't understand. I am free because I am where he wants me to be. His tower is my prison. The pain will never return as long as I remain here."

"How do you know this?"

Rashadu grinned. "Cha speaks to whomever he wishes."

Cha's touch came upon her suddenly, stronger than she had experienced in years. "There is another way."

Rashadu's eyes sparkled with interest. "How?"

"You can fight against Karan...with the Adamu."

"And if I agreed, would you trust me?"

Sadatina's face became solemn. She was filled with Cha's presence and sure of her words.

"You can lie to me but you cannot lie to Cha. You know this."

Rashadu's laugh reverberated through the small chamber. "It seems the only way I can have peace is to take sides." He stood, his head almost touching the room's roof. "What must I do priestess?"

Sadatina didn't answer, stunned by the mjibwe's easy conversion. There was no reason for her to fear; if he lied his spiritual tormentor would not release him from his new prison. Cha was in him now. Anything he did to defy him would be punished.

"We will travel to Wangara," she said. "We need the Shosa and Baba Toure's help."

"We must go to the village first," Rashadu said. "You need clothes."

Rashadu's eyes focused on her nude body. Strangely she held no fear of his attention. Cha was changing him; if seeing her as a woman was part of that change, she was happy for the interest.

She finished her meal and they left the tower, descending the wooden stairs to the decrepit doors. She watched Rashadu as they passed through the portal and into the ruins. He seemed unaltered, striding purposely to the city gates. His demeanor remained the same once through them.

"How do you feel?" she asked.

"I feel...free."

He turned to her and opened his arms. He meant to carry her again but Sadatina hesitated. She recalled the look in his eye as he scanned her body. Looking was one thing; touching was another.

Rashadu disarmed her reluctance with a warm smile. "Cha has not changed me that much. You are safe, priestess."

She approached him and wrapped her arms around his neck. He cradled her in his arms, his hard muscles pressing into her pliant flesh. He was so warm, so calming. It would be a difficult journey to the village if she had to walk herself.

The site of the village sobered her. Luanda had destroyed it. Not one building stood. If there were bodies the scavengers had long since carried them away.

"Damn him!" Sadatina shouted.

"I was too easy on the Mosele," Rashadu growled. "I killed him too quick."

Sadatina touched his shoulder. "I will pray for them."

Rashadu waited as Sadatina performed a mourning ritual.

She secretly hoped the mjibwe would join her, but she was too optimistic. After the prayer she picked among the debris, eventually finding a mix of suitable garments. Rashadu watched stoically, but she could sense his anger. It was the first time she felt any emotion emanating from him.

When she was done he took her up into his arms. "Which way to Wangara?" he asked.

"That way," she replied, pointing to the northwest.

"Will your people accept me? Will they accept us?"

"Cha is with us," Sadatina said. "They will have no choice."

-17-

The Wangaran patrol had traveled for nine days, one day short of their destination. Their journey had been relatively uneventful. They spotted two ginangas that fled too fast for them to follow and one lone washaka that was killed from a distance by Cha's Voice. The Shosa and sofas were setting up camp for a chilly night when they spied a strange sight emerged over the horizon. A figure approached, running faster than any man should. It slowed and his visage became clear; it was the mjibwe Rashadu. Nana Sadatina was slumped in his arms.

Shosa and sofas mounted in seconds, sabers drawn and lances lowered. The mjibwe halted and Nana raised her head. Slight relief swept the patrol; at least she was alive.

Rashadu placed Sadatina down, his eyes fixed on the approaching force.

"We've been seen," he said.

"I'll go to them." Sadatina took a step and Rashadu raised an eyebrow.

"Is that wise? You are with me and you are not dead. Your hair is white like mine. Your eyes, too."

Sadatina reached for her face. "My eyes are white?"
Rashadu nodded. "They will think I converted you."

"My daughters will know better. It's Toure's sofas that worry me."

"I should kill them then," Rashadu concluded.

"No!" Sadatina shouted. "Go back a ways. I will speak with them alone."

Sadatina was well aware of Rashadu's speed but she was

still amazed at how rapidly he retreated. He was hundreds of yards away in seconds, standing with his arms folded across his chest, his white hair waving in the still air. He was prepared to fight if necessary. She would make sure it would not be.

Her daughters rode up to her but the sofas kept their distance. The smiles on their faces were tempered by uncertainty as their eyes focused on her hair. Sadatina opened her arms.

"Embrace me, daughters," she said.

Nsomi was the first to dismount and come to her, which wasn't surprising. Nsomi was always bold, fearless and loyal. If she asked Nsomi to follow Karan she would without hesitation. Luam was not far behind. She was calm, soft spoken and just as loyal.

Both hugged her tightly.

Meria was more cautious than her sisters. She looked to see if the sofas had set up Cha's Voice and approached slowly with an unsure expression on her cherubic face. She was obviously in command. Her hug was perfunctory.

"Nana," she said. "We are happy to have found you. Baba Toure will be pleased. Is the mjibwe your servant now?"

"No," Sadatina admitted.

Worry flashed in Meria's eyes. She glanced at the sofas.

"But we saw him carrying you before you sent him away," Nsomi said.

"Rashadu is not my servant. He serves Cha now."

"So why is it that you resemble him?" Meria asked.

"One cannot be touched by Cha and not be transformed," Sadatina answered.

Nsomi and Luam's expressions were filled with awe. Meria remained skeptical.

"Baba Toure ordered us to send word if we found you. We are to keep you here until we hear otherwise."

Meria was a bad liar. She was forming a plan as she talked. They had been told what to do if they found Rashadu or her. No one expected to find them both together.

"Nsomi, you and Luam will ride back to Wangara."

Meria continued. "The sofa and I will stay here with Nana and Rashadu."

Both women nodded to Meria, and hugged Sadatina again.

"It is good to have you back," Nsomi said. "Things have been different since you've been gone."

She shot a mean glance at Meria before walking to her horse and returning with her pack. "Here is my tent. You'll need this."

"What about you?"

"I'll share with Luam. She's not so big."

Sadatina accepted the bundle and touched Nsomi's cheek.

"Ride fast, daughters. There's not much time."

Nsomi's eyes narrowed and she nodded. She ran to her horse, Luam on her heels. The two galloped away.

Meria approached Sadatina, her anger wrinkling her brow.

"What did you say to her?"

Sadatina smiled. "I told her to ride fast. We don't have much time."

"I am in command of this patrol!" Meria snapped. "Until we hear from Baba Toure, you are not permitted to give orders."

Sadatina closed her eyes and sighed. Never in her years as Nana had a daughter spoken to her in such a way. When she looked up, Meria's hand sat on the hilt of her saber.

"I will do you no harm, daughter. We will wait for the Mansa. His decision will prevail."

The wait was shorter than expected. Sadatina sat before her borrowed tent five days later, enjoying a simple afternoon meal when riders appeared over the horizon. Nsomi and Luam appeared first. They stopped and gestured, pointing towards the camp. Shosa and sofas swarmed past them, riding hard to Sadatina and her overseers. Sadatina looked beyond the riders to the entourage of Baba Toure. As they approached, Rashadu appeared at her side.

"Go, please," she urged, "it is best I meet them alone."

"I feel Karan's presence," he revealed. "He has influence among them."

"Nonsense. The mansa is closest to Cha and cannot be swayed. My daughters are loyal to me."

"There is one among them who smells of stone," Rashadu insisted. His persistence raised doubts in her mind. Could a daughter have turned? And if so, who? An answer came to her as quick as the question. "Go, Rashadu. I will deal with her."

Rashadu frowned. "If she kills you, I will kill them."

In an instant he was gone. Sadatina stood alone as her daughters surrounded her. She sensed their emotions and was sad for them. Joy, anger disbelief ran through them like pestilence. The uncertainty had been encouraged by the betrayer, the woman who rode beside Baba Toure, a triumphant smile on her face.

The mansa's entourage halted before the priestess. Baba Toure dismounted and approached followed by his warriors, his gesere and Adande. Sadatina bowed but did not prostrate before them as was custom. Adande sneered.

"You are not dead," Toure said.

"I'm not," she replied.

"'The question now is who do you live for? Who do you serve?"

"Look into my heart for the answer, Baba," she replied.
Toure was about to reply when Adande kicked her mount and rode between them.

"You will see a lie!" she shouted. "Look at her. Her hair is white like a mjibwe as are her eyes. The creature lurks beyond our sight, ready to pounce on her word. Cha has spoken to me and tells me she must die!"

Sadatina's hand instinctively reached Judgment then stopped. Adande leapt from her mount, jerking her saber free as her boots touched the ground. She attacked and Sadatina defended, avoiding Adande's ferocious assault, the saber licking at her like a viper's tongue. Sadatina moved like a dancer, ducking and dodging and leaping the tempered steel wielded by a daughter possessed. Baba Toure gestured to his men but Sadatina shook her head slightly until he nodded once. This was her punishment to receive and administer. Adande had always been a difficult one, but Sadatina considered her a challenge to her faith. She had failed to see her daughter's weakness. Ambition and power were not a virtue among the Shosa. In the past Sadatina had been quick to release such women from her charge, sending them back to their families with provisions and status to make amends for the lost years. But so few were born with the gift that she was forced to make exceptions.

She ducked a vicious slice at her head and took the kick to her stomach. Adande's triumphant smile was brief as she realized Sadatina's intention. She tried to jerk her trapped foot free but the priestess's grip was unwavering. Sadatina anticipated the sword stroke, grabbing the Shosa's sword arm at the wrist as she swept her supporting leg. Sadatina added her weight to Adande's, driving her into the ground. The sword flew out of her hand; Adande yelped as her head struck the ground. Sadatina pinned Adande with a death grip on her throat.

"Karan is in you, daughter," she whispered. "I can free you but you must help me. Give up this power he gives you. Renounce it."

"I...cannot," Adande said. "If I renounce him, I will die."

"Rashadu did and he still stands. You must trust Cha."

Adande's eyes narrowed. "Kill me."

"No." Sadatina struck Adande's temple and knocked her unconscious. She stepped away from her daughter. Baba Toure hurried to them.

"Cha still dwells in you," he confirmed. He looked to the distance. "You say Cha has changed him. Can we truly trust him?"

"I don't know," Sadatina confessed. "He may not be with us but I'm sure he's against Karan. He will help us until Karan is finished."

"We will return to the city," Baba Toure decided. "We must prepare for Karan." The mansa turned to his men. "Bind her," he said, pointing at Adande's unconscious form. The mansa turned his attention back to Sadatina. "Your daughters have been compromised by Adande's delusions. You must unite them before Karan comes. You have a lot of work to do in a short time."

"Look!" a Shosa shouted.

Two feline figures streaked toward them from the south, two shumbas that disappeared from Sadatina's side the moment Rashadu intruded. The women parted and the sisters ran to her. They halted, pacing about confused by her altered appearance. She knelt before them and opened her arms. They sniffed her fingertips and licked them, hesitant at first but with greater vigor once they had identified her to their satisfaction. With a sudden surge they pounced, nuzzling her so hard she tumbled over. She laughed, her joy genuine. Everything was in place now. It was time to face Karan.

-18-

A year had passed since Sadatina last set eyes upon Wangara. As she approached the city by the South Road she experienced a mix of pleasure and sadness. It was good to see the high walls and towers, the sturdy gate holding the heart of the Adamu behind its massive bulk. But she also realized she gazed upon a desperate refuge, the final stand of her people against their enemies. All her life she fought to keep their foes at bay. Though Cha's voice was with her again, she couldn't help but doubt his message. Their final hope rested in the hands of a man-beast that once sought their demise, a creature that now sought Karan's death for its own reasons.

A horn echoed across the hills, announcing their return. Sadatina reached out instinctively and her sisters nuzzled her hands. It was good to be with them again. The big cats were the only creatures sharing her history. They accepted Rashadu's presence with indifference, displaying no more notice of him than they did her daughters. It should have been a comforting sign; if there was any hint of Karan's vileness upon him they would have attacked him without hesitation. She knew this, but her worries persisted.

A sofa officer rode up to her. "Nana, the mansa orders that the mjibwe remain outside the city gates."

"Understood," Sadatina replied.

"Once everything is secure he wishes to hold council with you." The messenger looked into the distance. "The meeting will be held outside the gates so that the mjibwe can participate."

Sadatina smirked. "No doubt Cha's Voice will watch from the ramparts."

The messenger nodded. "Nana is most wise." He bowed and returned to the city. Sadatina waited as the others filed inside before setting out to speak to Rashadu. He waited far away, his arms folded, his face grim.

"More meetings," he grumbled.

"It is our way," she replied.

"Your 'way' will be your death. Karan will not wait for your meeting to end. He will kill you where you sit."

"This is a crucial time for our people," Sadatina explained. "They must be told of what will take place."

Rashadu frowned. "I will wait until the council meets. I don't wish to repeat my words."

Sadatina had other matters to see to before the council meeting. She entered Wangara as if for the first time, her eyes wide with wonder. Nothing had change physically, but spiritually an upheaval had taken. Her absence allowed doubt to spread and she was assaulted by a mix of desperate emotions. Adamubu passed by her, some staring, some glaring but none speaking. Cha's Chosen were losing their faith and their hope.

Her daughters waited before the entrance of the temple, lining the streets with their heads bowed in solemn respect. She entered her home and immediately sensed the neglect. Her sisters sniffed the air and growled their disapproval.

Heewan, the temple matron, met her at the foyer. "Nana! I'm so happy to see you. I prayed for your return."

"As did I. Have the sisters clean the hallways and public chambers immediately. My daughters will clean their own rooms. Replace all the curtains and carpets."

Heewan looked puzzled. "I would think we might concentrate on the condition of our weapons."

"Cha is our greatest weapon," Sadatina replied. "His house must be honored above all else."

Heewan's smile was wide. "Yes, Nana. It will be done immediately!"

Heewan was eager to do Sadatina's bidding. Her real

challenge waited for her in Cha's Chamber bound in gris rope. Adande lay on her back, her arms and legs tied so tight the rope pressed into her skin. She was surrounded by Shosa led by Beyla. The young Shosa glared at Adande with disgust.

"Leave us, daughters," Sadatina commanded. All left immediately except Beyla. She continued to loom over Adande, her hand flexing on the hilt of her saber.

"Beyla, please leave us," Sadatina repeated.

"Karan possesses her," Beyla spat. "You need my protection."

"You know I don't. She is your sister no matter what you feel about her. Do you think I would try to save her if I thought she belonged to Karan?"

Beyla's head jerked toward Sadatina. "She tried to kill you!"

"She was misled. Besides, your feelings have nothing to do with me. When I replaced Adande with you I formed a breach between you. It was my fault. You must forgive me for that, not Adande. Karan thrives on such feelings. He uses these emotions to turn us against each other and eventually to him."

The tension slowly drained from Beyla's face. "Forgive me, mother!"

Beyla let go of her guilt then fell on her knees before Sadatina, who lifted her to her feet.

"Don't cry, daughter. You won your battle against Karan today. Now I need you to be my second again. Go gather the sisters. We must perform purification for Adande."

Shock flashed in Beyla's face. "Yes...yes, Mother. I will summon them."

She sprinted into the hallway and moments later the walls of the sanctuary vibrated to the drumming of summons. The sound reflected the beating of Sadatina's heart. She had never performed purification. Her dealings with Karan's minions were handled with a blade edge. She felt no need or desire to reclaim anyone or anything under Karan's control. Cha was strong inside her, however, and his wisdom was clear. This was a different struggle, more spiritual than physical. It would be won with the soul and the sword.

She knelt beside Adande and ran her hands over her daughter's body. She burned, a spiritual fever manifesting as physical heat. Adande's eyes opened; she stared upward.

"Mother, please help me!" she begged.

"I will try," Sadatina whispered.

"Forgive me, please. I didn't know it was Karan. I was deceived. I wanted Cha's vision so badly that when I heard the voice in my head I was sure it was him. I..."

Sadatina hushed her. "Don't explain. Save your strength. I will not lie to you, Adande. This will be very difficult. I may be able to save your soul but not your life."

Adande's eye glistened. "I will be strong, Nana."

The Shosa filed into the chamber, lining the walls as the lamps were lit. They stood three rows deep, dressed in simple white dresses that brushed their feet, their heads covered by white head wraps. Two sisters lifted Adande's bound body and carried her to the pedestal before Cha's Eye. They placed her gently on the granite slab. Sadatina approached her slowly, more from apprehension than ceremony.

"I will help you." Rashadu's voice boomed inside her head.

"What? How?"

"Place your hand over her chest and empty your mind," he instructed.

"What about my daughters?"

"They do not hear me. Only you."

Sadatina glanced about, searching her daughters' faces. "Why should I trust you?"

There was silence for a moment, and then Rashadu answered. "I have done this before. Place your right hand on her head and your left on her heart."

Sadatina hesitated.

"Do it!"

Her hands snapped into place.

"Clear your mind. Let Cha's will flow through you. He will do the rest."

Sadatina closed her eyes as she strained to remove all thought from her mind. She settled into a calm darkness as she was surrounded by a sensation of love, an endless stream of peace that reached from the beginning of time and extended beyond her into an infinite future. An orb materialized before her; Adande's spirit rested inside it, blocked from Cha's grace by a shell of Karan's hatred. Black hands reached from the serene void, caressing the orb with a wordless song that reverberated around her. As the hands moved gently about the shell, fissures of light appeared, multiplying furiously across the orb's surface. Suddenly it shattered, specks of light spraying into the enveloping darkness. Adande's spirit lay before her curled like a child. The spirit stirred and stretched. Adande's essence sat up and stared into Sadatina's eyes.

"Thank you, Nana," she whispered. "I must go to Cha now."

The black hands cradled Adande's spirit and it faded into their grasp. The darkness ended abruptly and Sadatina stared down on Adande's still body, tears streaming down her face. She heard her daughters sobbing. Even Beyla cried.

Sadatina unleashed her anger on Rashadu.

"You said you would help me!"

"I did," he replied calmly.

"Adande is dead!"

"I said I would help you and I did. Her soul rests with Cha. Her life was unimportant."

"It was important to me!"

"You are a priestess, not a god. Your will pales next to Cha's. It is what he wished and it was done."

Sadatina stood, signaling the ceremony was done. The burial sisters claimed Adande's body to take to the crypt.

"Thank you, Nana," they said. "You saved her soul. She will

be waiting for us when Cha calls us home."

Their words rang true but did nothing to alleviate her despair. How many times had she endured the same scene? Another daughter gone, another soul sent too early to Cha. She wondered when Cha would finally release her from her burden and call her home.

Rashadu's voice reminded her that time had not yet come. "You must rest. Your council will meet soon and you must be prepared to speak for me."

Sadatina did not answer. She trudged to her chamber and collapsed onto her bed.

-19-

The elders sat nervously outside the gates of Wangara despite the sofas surrounding them and Cha's Voice looming over them on the ramparts. Each of their attendants was armed, spiritually and physically, and they were flanked by two units of the Mansa's personal guard. Still the old men and women exuded fear, for they rarely ventured beyond the city walls since becoming elders. They were the foundation of the Adamu, the living repository of knowledge and tradition of their people. Most of them had never seen Karan's minions. Those who had had only seen their carcasses. The coming meeting gave reason for them to fear.

Mansa Toure took a seat before the elders. He wore a simple tobe as was his custom, the only sign of his position the band of braided gold encircling his head. It was a symbol of power older than the Adamu and a talisman of immense power. His gesere stood beside him, the oral historian's outfit a colorful blend of robes, jewelry and gaudy headdress. An outsider would think him the mansa and Toure the servant.

The Mansa's presence was overshadowed by the hulking white-haired mjibwe towering beside Sadatina. Rashadu's face was stoic like mansa Toure's though his lips showed a hint of a frown. Sadatina looked at them both and prayed for a civil exchange.

The gesere stepped before the mansa and raised his staff. "Mansa Toure summoned you to hear the words of the mjibwe Rashadu. The mjibwe claims to have knowledge that will see us to the end of Karan and his hosts."

"Since when do we heed the words of a nyoka?" one elder challenged.

"I have seen Cha enter this being," Sadatina responded. "An Adamu dwells inside him, a priest of long ago who has knowledge of things forgotten. It is he, through Rashadu, who will help us."

"He will lead us to our deaths!" someone shouted.

A murmur of agreement swept the crowd. Sadatina noticed the Voice sofas shifting their weapons toward Rashadu.

"You would be dead by now if I so wished it," Rashadu threatened. "There is nothing here that could stem my wrath, not even those distractions on your ramparts."

He stepped toward them and Sadatina blocked his path.

"Rashadu, don't!" she urged.

The mjibwe pushed her aside like an errant child. "These fools annoy me."

Mansa Toure stepped back and his personal guard shielded him from Rashadu's approach. The elders scrambled to their feet and ran for the gates. Sadatina reached for Rashadu and the battlements exploded in sound and smoke as Cha's Voice spoke in unison. Rashadu fell, the metal projectiles striking him simultaneously. He lay still for a moment, and then slowly came to his feet. Then he was gone, leaping over the fleeing elders and landing on the battlements. He sped down the row of gunmen, striking them as he passed. When he reached the end of the ramparts he leaped and landed with a thunderous grunt before Toure and his guard. The cowered before him; the Mansa's emotionless expression still had not changed.

"If your weapons cannot stop me, they surely will not stop Karan. I am the only being among you who has a chance at killing him. Karan gathers his servants, preparing for a march on this city. He is sick of you. You can wait to be slaughtered in your homes or you can march out and strike before he gathers his full strength."

"If you are so powerful you should not need our help," Toure spoke.

"I am not Cha, but neither is Karan. We both become weaker with every battle we fight. I can defeat him, but I can't fight him and his nyokas at the same time."

Toure's eyes narrowed. "So that's why you are helping us."

"I am not helping you. You are helping me."

The mansa stepped from behind his guards. Sadatina nodded; if Rashadu's words were truth they were useless.

"Why do you wish Karan dead? He created you."

"And I should be thankful for this?"

"So you hate him?"

"I have no feeling toward him. The priest inside me tells me I will know peace when Karan is dead."

Baba Toure looked at Sadatina. "The sofas will be ready to march in a week. Priestess?"

"The Shosa will be ready as well."

Toure smiled at Rashadu. "You have your army."

Rashadu smiled back. "And you have your nyoka."

-20-

The Shosa prepared to fight once again, but this time they were not alone. The nation was going to war, marching to a battle that would determine their right to exist. Toure mobilized his people, calling on every man, woman and child to participate in the army's preparation. Men of fighting age gathered at the villages and marched to the city to receive armor and weapons.

Horses, oxen, sheep and goats were herded from every grassland and pasture to serve as transportation and food. New weapons spiked with gris-gris were forged with nyama fire while chain mail and shields were protected with talismans. The most formidable of weapons emerged from the wooded valleys two days after the mansa's declaration of war. Huge ox-drawn wagons of wood and iron lumbered out of the trees, drawing crowds of Adamubu. Mansa Toura stood on the battlements, a proud smile on his face. Sadatina stood beside him, smirking at another of Baba Toure's war toys. Even Rashadu appeared, though not physically; he reached into Sadatina's mind instead. She found the contact both comforting and disconcerting.

"I call them Cha's chariots," Toure announced. "I intended to use them as mobile fortresses that moved about the land to protect villages from ginanga attacks." He pointed at one of the vehicles. "See the slits? Cha's Voice will speak through them. Bowmen will ride the crest to protect the Voice."

Sadatina gazed down at the vehicles skeptically. "They have limited applications. They're too big for mountain roads and they will be slow."

Toure nodded. "True, they are not very maneuverable,

but slow they are not. The oxen pulling them have been bred for strength and speed. At full speed the wagon can keep pace with a trotting Shosa."

Sadatina shrugged. "We shall see. Please excuse me, Baba. I must tend to my daughters."

"You believe Rashadu, don't you?" Toure's question startled her.

"Yes. Have you changed your mind? What does Cha tell you?"

Toure leaned against the battlement. "Cha is pleased but my heart is troubled. It is difficult to embrace an enemy."

"Rashadu is an enemy before our time."

"You don't understand." Toure look at her intensely. "A mansa's memory includes those who ruled before him."

"Those are the words of your gesere," Sadatina replied.

"No, priestess. It is much more. I will share something with you. At the end of my initiation rites I experienced the Bonding. It is a communion with the ancestors, a time in which I relive their lives and experience their joys and pains. I relived the years of Karan's aggression and experienced the despair and helplessness of my forefathers as Rashadu and the other nyokas decimated our people. So my doubt is real."

"You must trust Cha," Sadatina said, although her trust was as precarious as Sekou's. "It is all I can offer."

"It is all that needs to be said." Toure finally smiled. "Go, comfort your daughters. I must tend to my men."

Sadatina walked away from the ramparts. She was alone, the pad of her soft shoes echoing against the damp stone walls. It always amazed her how a city of so many people could appear so desolate. The Adamubu were not known to be very sociable beyond their family groups. The fear and superstitions planted among them for hundreds of years made them a sullen, distant people. Still, they endured. Now they prepared for a battle that would determine their future and in Adamu fashion they drew close to their own.

Sadatina stopped the temple. Inside her daughters waited to hear words of faith and encouragement. Though Cha's faith burned bright inside her, she needed something more.

She went to the stables instead. The building was empty. She saddled her horse and rode to the gates which were unguarded and unarmed. She road unopposed into the grasslands, following her senses to her destination. It was dusk before she saw Rashadu, the mjibwe resembling an ebony sculpture surrounded by grass and sky. Her mount slowed on its own, shaking its head nervously as it neared the nyoka. Sadatina reined it still and dismounted. She walked up to Rashadu and sat in the grass.

"Why are you here?" Rashadu spoke without turning his head.

"I'm here for the truth."

"You know what Cha tells you."

Sadatina picked a blade of grass and rolled the stem between her fingers. "I know what Cha puts in my heart but my mind struggles with his words."

"It is your way. You believe, yet you don't. You follow, yet you stray. It is why you are easy to defeat."

"So Karan will defeat us?"

Rashadu finally faced her and grinned. "No. He will not defeat you because I won't let him."

Sadatina shook her head. "All my life I have fought to protect the Adamu. Now our savior is the creature that almost destroyed us? It is hard to accept."

"As is the word of Cha."

"It seems so easy for you."

Rashadu turned to look at Sadatina. There was sadness in his eyes, an emotion she had not expected.

"For years I meditated, attempting to discover the terror that struck me the day I stood before Djenna. When I was revived my mind was clear. There is no doubt of the path I must follow."

"Don't you fear you may fail?"

"Karan rules by fear. I no longer answer to him. There is

no fear when one knows his destiny. There is only acceptance." Rashadu tilted his head. "It will be dark soon. You should return to your temple. Your daughters seek your reassurance."

Sadatina lowered her head. "What should I tell them?"

"Tell them what you sought from me. Tell them the truth."

The torchlight of the temple still burned despite the late hour. Sadatina took her horse to the stable and entered through the kitchen quarters. Beyla sat in the dining hall alone, a single candle lit before her, her hands clasped tightly before her face. Sadatina did not try to hide her approach.

"What do you pray for, daughter?" she whispered.

"I pray for many things, Nana. I pray for forgiveness for wishing Adande dead. I pray for Cha's strength when we face Karan and I pray for Cha to keep away my fear."

Sadatina sat beside her young daughter and draped an arm around her shoulders. "Those are good things to pray for. Adande's death was not your fault. She chose the wrong path because ambition blinded her to Karan's treachery. We should be thankful we were able to save her ka if not her life. Cha's strength will be with you as always. As to your fear, use it to fuel your strength. Do not fear death, for Cha waits for us all."

Sadatina lifted Beyla to her feet. "Come, we must gather your sisters. We will pray together."

"Yes," Beyla smiled. "We will pray for victory."

"No, daughter," Sadatina corrected. "We will pray for our souls."

-21-

The Adamubu army lined the rim of the hills that formed the boundary of Karan's lands. They peered down into a natural bowl of gray soil, a desolate landscape stretching from the hill on which they stood to the jagged mountain posing in the distance. A frigid wind climbed from the plains, blowing back the robes of the warriors standing on the edge of the rim. Sadatina peered down into the land, her heart solemn. This desolate ground would be the graveyard for many of her daughters and sons, maybe even for her. It was not the death she had imagined; she grinned at the thought, for she never imagined her death.

Mansa Toure stood beside her, his arms folded across his chest. "Where is Rashadu?"

"I don't know," Sadatina admitted. "He will come."

"I'm sure he will. The question is whose side will he be on?"

Sadatina closed her eyes. Cha's confidence flowed strong in her veins. "You still do not trust him."

"He is a nyoka. How can I?"

"You must trust Cha."

Baba Toure smiled. "You are right. I must trust Cha. We will send the wagons first. They'll form our vanguard. My heavy troops will act as support. The wagons will draw out the ginanga. Once they're engaged I'm sure the washakas will advance."

"That's when the Shosa will strike," Sadatina added.

"The only unknown is the mjibwe and Karan."

"I'll handle the mjibwe," Sadatina assured.

"Are you sure?" Doubt commanded Toure's face once

again. "We don't know how many there will be."

"I'm sure. The others aren't strong enough and Rashadu must save his strength for Karan. My sisters and I will deal with them."

"We will all do what we can," Toure concluded.

Sadatina sensed another meaning behind his statement but was distracted by a powerful and familiar sensation. "Rashadu is here," she said.

The nyoka appeared at the base of the hill, his white hair glowing so brightly it was difficult to look at him directly. He looked up at Sekou and Sadatina, a wicked grin slicing his face. "You cannot kill Karan's minions there. Come! Glory awaits you!"

Toure ordered the wagons down the hills. They crept single file down the steep narrow trails, taking half a day to make the descent. Once on level ground they fanned out. By nightfall the entire army rested at the base of the hills. Morning came too soon; the army broke camp at daylight and marched for Karan's hills. A half a day into the march they encountered the first signs of Karan's resistance. Single ginangas rose from the rocks, striking at the vanguard. As Toure guessed, they were drawn to the wagons. The crossbowmen picked them off easily with their gris-bolts, the enchanted projectiles retrieved by the warriors surrounding the wagons. The warriors were blooded as well, striking down some ginangas before they reached the wagons. Cha's Voice remained silent, holding their fire for the more serious confrontation to come.

That threat arrived at dusk with a piercing screech that forced the warriors to cover their ears in pain. The ginangas hiding in ambush sprang from behind rocks and ran away from the Adamu. A brief moment of hope warmed the faces of the Adamu; their first battle had gone their way. The moment ended quickly as the ginangas formed a dark writhing mass before them, their grunts and hisses dominating the night. The sky was pierced again by their nefarious screech. The ginangas howled in response and surged toward the Adamu.

Toure withdrew to the rear with his generals. The assembly drums rumbled and the foot soldiers retreated as well, clearing the space between the wagons. The wagons dispersed, creating gaps one hundred yards wide between them. Sadatina signaled the Shosa and they also separated, Beyla leading half to the left flank while Nsomi, recently promoted to commander, led the remaining sisters to the right flank. Each unit executed their commands precisely, a product of intense training. As Sadatina watched the ginanga horde draw closer she prayed that the army's bravery would match its precision.

The bowmen held their fire until the ginangas were only few feet away. One deafening blow from the elephant drum summoned a downpour of arrows that split the beasts' ranks, channeling them between the wagons. Cha's Voice sang with thunder and smoke; ginangas fell by the hundreds, slaughtered by the gris bolt deluge. The sofas, positioned to support the wagons, found themselves dragging ginanga bodies from the killing grounds between the wagons.

The first washakas appeared suddenly atop the center wagon, overwhelming the crossbowmen before the Shosa could respond. The shield wall protecting the oxen faltered, rendering the wagons immobile. The gunners continued firing as the ginangas and washakas attempted to engulf them before the Shosa could rescue them. They almost succeeded.

Shosa archers reached the wagons first, their arrows clearing the vehicles of the beasts that managed to climb them. The lancers arrived soon afterward, spearing ginangas and washakas with their double-headed lances and driving them from the wagons. The sisters unleashed their sabers and the real battle commenced as Shosa and washakas hunted each other amid the confusion of sofas and ginangas. The Adamu were clearly winning the struggle though the cost was high. Sadatina held back tears with every daughter she watch fall. She wanted to help them, but she couldn't. This was their fight. Her challenge was soon to come.

Nokofa and Pausa sensed them first. They stood, ears flattened on their heads, deep growls emanating from their throats. Sadatina detected them soon afterward. She spurred her mount and her feline sisters followed, keeping as close to the stallions as they could manage. The mjibwe appeared in the midst of the warring throng. They were heading for the war wagons.

A mjibwe cleared a dozen warriors from the side of a wagon with a swipe of its massive claws. The gunners fired at the beast and it staggered back as the bolts slammed into it. It stood still for a moment and attacked the wagon again, grasping the carriage's bottom. Sadatina snapped her stallion's reins, steering it toward the beleaguered wagon. She drew Judgment then jumped from the horse's back on onto the mjibwe. The creature had barely noticed her presence when she gripped Judgment with both hands and decapitated it with one swift stroke. She jumped from the beast, her feet touching the ground as its body fell. Another mjibwe staggered by, Nokofa's mouth clamped on its neck, her back claws ripping into its spine. Sadatina glimpsed the distance and saw at least two dozen mjibwes; more than she'd ever seen in her life. A sudden jolt of despair was doused by Cha's presence. She would keep killing them until there were none left. Rashadu was nowhere to be seen, but she couldn't worry about the man nyoka anymore. The battle had begun. There was no turning back.

A washaka pack appeared before her. She attacked, slicing the nearest beast in half as she kicked its companion in the chest, shattering its ribs. A third beast managed to rake her back but her armor held. The blow pitched her forward into the fourth beast which managed to bear its fangs before she split its head with Judgment. She crouched low and swung the sword, severing the legs of the beast behind her. The creature attempted to rise but a lance pinned it to the ground. Beyla streaked by, smiling as she snatched the lance up and rode on. Sadatina almost smiled back until she saw what loomed beyond her daughter. The ginangas were in full flight while the washakas grouped together, reluctantly following their skittish brethren. The mjibwes grouped together as well, but they did not flee. Darkness crept into Sadatina's mind, a sharp blackness that tore at Cha's strength and aggravated her fear. Her four-footed sisters came to her; roaring and shaking their heads in agitation. The ground shook under her soles in a steady rhythm. Rashadu appeared at her side.

"Karan is coming," he said.

Sadatina looked up at Rashadu. He was bigger in every way, towering over the waiting mjibwe. He looked down at her and grinned.

"You thought I would not come?"

"I wasn't sure," Sadatina admitted.

Rashadu grin faded. "Come, let's finish this."

He leapt into the midst of the mjibwe. A dozen died before she could move; eight more lay slain as she attacked those closest to her. A nyoka dodged her sword swing and struck her face, sprawling her into the blood-soaked dirt. She stumbled to her feet in time to evade its claws, bringing Judgment down on its back and severing its spine. She held tight to the sword hilt, letting the momentum carry her from the dying beast to another ready to strike. She rolled, pulling the sword from its back then rose to her feet before a huge nyoka holding a boulder over its head. It threw the boulder at her; she ducked and sprinted towards the nyoka, the stone sailing harmlessly over her head and crushing a mjibwe pursuing her from behind. She disemboweled the boulder thrower, covering her face from a spray of blood and entrails. She fought in a battered haze, cutting and killing at random without pain or fatigue until the onslaught stopped. The mjibwe were dead, but the battle was far from over.

Sadatina saw Karan for the first time. The Stone God was a walking mountain, standing twice as tall as Rashadu with a surface as gray and jagged as the peaks in which he dwelled. His eyes burned with molten fire, his mouth barely visible. Acrid smoke seeped from cracks and crevices on his body. Each step he took left a sulfurous pool. He stood before Rashadu and the thin slit that served as his mouth turned upward.

"You've come for me." His voice grated like shifting rock.

"Yes," Rashadu replied.

"You've come in vain. You cannot kill that which created you. I brought you to life. I made you what you are. When the moment comes for you to strike, you will be helpless."

Rashadu grinned. "You made me what I am, but you did not create me. You are no god, Karan. You are a lifted spirit who feeds off the despair and fear of others. You twist dreams to form you own reality. You don't rule your mountains; you hide in them hoping the true gods will continue to ignore your transgressions. But Cha has seen you."

"Cha has seen me before...through your eyes, Ihecha."

Rashadu struck, sparks flying as his knives crisscrossed Karan's chest. Thin lines of magma appeared and Karan grimaced. He backhanded Rashadu and the nyoka-man cartwheeled though the air before crashing into a wall of mjibwes. Karan's minions pounced but their advantage was short-lived. With a deafening roar, Rashadu regained his feet, flinging the mjibwes away like dust. He rushed the Stone God again and they battled with such force the ground trembled like a coming earthquake.

Sadatina stumbled into battle. She and her sisters assaulted the stunned mjibwe. She wielded Judgment like a harvester's scythe, cutting down mjibwes as easily as Karan's lesser beasts. Her sisters were equally efficient in hunting down the beasts, not as a pair but alone. Their ferocity drew the beasts from aiding Karan, but their numbers prevented Sadatina and her sisters from aiding Rashadu. Sadatina no longer felt pain or fatigue; she fought with the rhythm of her heart as cadence.

She hacked a mjibwe to its knees and looked for more. There were none. Behind her the remains of the Adamu army staggered among the dead and dying, oblivious to the terrible battle raging between Rashadu and Karan. She forced her eyes back to the giants. Karan was covered with lava-oozing gouges, his stilted movements betraying his weakness. Rashadu fared much worse. His left arm dangled at his side and he leaned heavily to his right. The behemoths stood like mountains facing each other, both obviously gathering their strength for another clash.

Sadatina trudged towards them, Judgment burning brighter in her charred hands. Her trudge became a trot; her trot evolved into a run. She raised the blade over her head. The stone god's head lifted; with a burst of strength he grabbed Rashadu's shoulders, hoisting him into the air.

"No!" Sadatina shouted.

Karan drew back his left arm and stabbed his hand through Rashadu. His blunted fingers appeared through Rashadu's back again and again until it was nothing more than a mass of torn flesh. Karan tossed Rashadu's limp body aside, a huge child bored with a broken toy.

Sadatina did not hear her own scream. She ran toward Karan, Judgment raised over her head. Karan strode toward her, his wounds healing as he advanced. Sadatina saw the death of everyone she ever loved in the muted malevolent face before her; Mama, Baba, Terte, Teshome and now Rashadu.

The stone nyoka jabbed his right hand at Sadatina's chest. She sidestepped the blow, chopping down with Judgment and severing the appendage at the wrist. Karan's grating cry deafened her as he swung his fist at her head. Sadatina ducked and cut Karan's left arm free at the elbow. It thudded into the ground before her.

Karan stumbled back, its severed limbs flailing and spewing lava. Sadatina jumped through the molten shower and onto Karan's chest. She drove Judgment deep into where his heart should be, and then yanked it free. Gripping the celestial blade with both hands, she cut through his neck and with a final effort kicked Karan's head free. The slain stone god fell backwards; Sadatina managed to back-flip from his chest and crashed to the ground on her knees. The ground quaked when Karan's body met the earth. Sadatina lingered until she was sure the deed was done before crawling to Rashadu's still form. To her surprise he was still alive.

She pushed up to her knees, suppressing the urge to close her eyes and pass out. She placed her hands on him. He was growing cold.

"Are you at peace?" she whispered.

Rashadu opened his eyes and looked at her. "Yes."

Sadatina leaned closer to him. "Who was the man in the temple?"

Rashadu managed to smile. "It was me. I am Rashadu, corruption of Karan, but once I was Ihecha, high priest of Cha in Djenna. I led my warrior priests against Karan and we were defeated. I alone survived. When given the choice to die for Cha or live, I chose life. I lost my faith and was transformed to this. But Cha let me redeem myself. This time I made the right choice."

Rashadu's white crown transformed into a black hue. The glow in his eyes dispersed, revealing brown, intelligent orbs. He touched Sadatina's tear-stained cheek. "Your service is done, sister. Go and live a normal life. Your daughters need your guidance and wisdom. The Mosele will need you, too."

Sadatina stared. "The Mosele?"

"They still live, encased below Karan's mountain. They will emerge now and they will need your help."

"How can I help them?"

"You will find a way." Rashadu shook. "I must rest now. Goodbye, Sadatina." He smiled as he closed his eyes. "Finally."

Sadatina stood, suddenly swallowed by a gust of warmth. She lifted her eyes to the sky.

"Goodbye, Ihecha. Thank you."

-22-

Spring embraced Wangara with gentle winds, spreading its renewal from the mountaintops to the valley. Mountain streams swelled with snow melt, their bounty rushing to fill the expectant rivers. The rivers rose until they breached their banks, their gentle floods seeding the valley with life-giving silt. For decades most of this fertile land lay untouched, for the Adamu were too few and too fearful to take advantage of the bounty. Now the banks teemed with villages. The Mosele settled there, returning at last to their traditional homeland. The transition had been surprisingly peaceful. The Mosele's hatred of the Adamu dissipated upon seeing their lands barely touched; the Adamu were grateful for their presence after suffering a tremendous loss during the battle with Karan. They happily relinquished the land to its former owners. The Adamu were a city folk and welcomed the respite.

Sadatina guided the wagon filled with her exuberant daughters down the muddy road to the valley. The farmers were grateful for the extra help for planting, and her daughters were ecstatic to be working alongside so many unmarried men. They unloaded seed and tools and hurried to their assigned families. Sadatina watched her daughters disperse, all except Beyla. She had been luckier than the others. Sadatina touched Beyla's plump stomach and smiled.

"It will be a girl," she announced. Beyla covered her mouth as she smiled.

"Dapo will be disappointed. He wanted a boy first."

"He'll love her just as much."

Beyla took on a serious look. "Are you sure it will be a girl?"

Sadatina nodded. "Cha has left me with some skills. Your baby will definitely be a girl."

'Then I will name her Adande."

Sadatina opened her arms and gathered Beyla in a gentle hug. "You honor your sister's spirit," Sadatina whispered. "I'm sure she is proud."

A royal messenger interrupted them. "Mother, Mansa Toure wishes that you receive the new group of refugees."

Sadatina was puzzled. "More Mosele? I thought we evacuated the catacombs."

"No, Mother. These are from the east. They say they come from Djenna. They say you visited them with Rashadu."

Sadatina's heart jumped and a broad smile broke across her face. Luanda had not killed them all! "I need your horse," she said to the messenger. He dismounted and handed her the reins. Sadatina rode across the muddy fields to the eastern road. A line of tired and ragged men and women trudged toward her. One person stood out among them, a tall woman covered with a thick cloak. Thick gray-streaked braids tipped with white beads covered her head.

Sadatina rode up to the woman and dismounted. "Tisha!"

Tisha lifted her head and a smile brightened her haggard face. "Priestess," she said warmly.

They embraced like sisters, which in some ways, to Sadatina, they were.

Tisha looked about. "Where is your nyoka?"

"He was never mine and he was not always as you saw him. Before he died, he told me his true name. He was Ihecha."

Tisha gasped and fell to her knees. "He was our high priest!" she cried. "He was a father to me!"

Sadatina went to her knees and hugged Tisha again. "He is at peace now. He has done Cha's will." She helped Tisha to her feet. "You and your people are welcomed. There is land along the river where they can settle."

"We thank you for your generosity," Tisha said as she

wiped her eyes. "Now I have something for you."

Sadatina became curious when Tisha took her hand and led her to the others. The people smiled as they parted, leaving a single woman cradling a baby.

"Her parents were killed by the mjibwes," Tisha said. "We brought her this far because I knew she would be needed."

The young woman extended the baby to Sadatina. She immediately took the baby into her arms, cradling her tight. "Thank you Tisha. Thank you!"

Tisha nodded and led her people away. Nokofa and Pausa joined her, pushing against her legs. Pausa carefully balanced her front paws on Sadatina's back to peer at the baby then hummed.

"See, Pausa?" Sadatina said. "We have a daughter."

Nokofa roared her approval. Together they walked to the walls of Wangara, Cha's blessing cradled in Sadatina's arms.

Sadatina opened her eyes to her family.

"Mama!" Ghe'le shouted.

Sadatina smiled. "Yes, that was your mama. I named her after my mama."

Kiden stopped unbraiding Sadatina's white hair and hugged her around the neck. Sadatina gripped her forearms. "I vowed you would never be out of my sight for as long as I lived."

"And you haven't," Kiden said.

"Time for everyone shorter than me to go to bed!" Kiden announced.

A collective moan rose from the children. They formed a ragged line and trudged from Sadatina's chamber.

Kiden kissed Sadatina's cheek. "Good night, Mama. Thank you for making peace."

She left the room as Nokofa and Pausa strolled into the room. They circled Sadatina, humming and pressing against her.

"We are old, sisters," she said. "Yet Cha still needs us."

She looked above her fireplace. Judgment rested in its baldric and sheath, held high by golden hooks. There it would remain until it was needed again. She stood and shuffled across the room to her candles. "Cha grant me favor to see another day," she whispered. "But if you do not, I will still be content."

She blew out the candles and the room gave way to comforting darkness.

END

GRIOTS

A SWORD AND SOUL ANTHOLOGY

MILTON J. DAVIS & CHARLES R. SAUNDERS

EDITORS